Praise for K.A. Mitchell's *Not Knowing Jack*

"This one goes on my keeper shelf."

~ *The Long and Short of It Reviews*

"I loved the book. I loved the character construction."

~ *Dear Author*

"The talented K.A. Mitchell has created an outstanding tale of heart-wrenchingly realistic predicaments, along with exceptionally sensual lovemaking."

~ *Literary Nymphs*

"*Not Knowing Jack* is yet another example of why I love K.A. Mitchell."

~ *Joyfully Reviewed*

Look for these titles by *K.A. Mitchell*

Now Available:

Custom Ride
Diving in Deep
Regularly Scheduled Life
Collision Course
Chasing Smoke
An Improper Holiday
No Souvenirs
Life, Over Easy
Bad Company

Serving Love
Hot Ticket

Print Anthologies
Midsummer Night's Steam—Temperature's Rising
To All a (Very Sexy) Good Night

Not Knowing Jack

K.A. Mitchell

SAMHAIN
PUBLISHING

Samhain Publishing, Ltd.
11821 Mason Montgomery Road, 4B
Cincinnati, OH 45249
www.samhainpublishing.com

Not Knowing Jack

Print ISBN: 978-1-60928-313-1
Digital ISBN: 978-1-60928-275-2

Editing by Sasha Knight
Cover by Valerie Tibbs

First Samhain Publishing, Ltd. electronic publication: December 2010
First Samhain Publishing, Ltd. print publication: November 2011

Dedication

For Bonnie

Thanks for saving the toddler.

Thank you also to B.F.S. for other saves. Thank you, Jules and Sarah, for sanity saving. Thank you, Sasha, for saving me with your amazing editing skills and your patience.

Chapter One

Tony Gemetti had a rich fantasy life. No, not like that—except when it was like that—but give him an ordinary circumstance, and he could imagine some pretty weird shit behind it. Like now.

He and his boyfriend, Jack, had just walked into Bed, Bath & Beyond to pick up something that Jack needed because Jack always needed something to make the house look more like a picture right out of *Architectural Digest*. Tony couldn't remember what the thing they were getting was, but he knew after they found it, Jack would let Tony drag him through all the kitchen stuff. Jack the chef would explain what some of the freaky-looking equipment was for, and Tony would suggest a much kinkier use for it. Then they'd go home and fuck like something on Animal Planet. Or sometimes they wouldn't make it home. Sometimes they only made it to the car, which was fine with Tony, although they couldn't get up to much today since they'd taken Tony's ancient Rabbit instead of Jack's BMW X3.

But this trip to Bed, Bath & Beyond wasn't going like that. This was Tony standing alone in the seasonal display area near the front—a weird mix of fans for summer and stuff for kids to put in their dorm rooms and seashell string lights. Jack had said something like "I'm going to get the thing," or maybe he went to the can. Tony wasn't paying attention because there had been this tiny little box that looked like it was made out of twisty ties, and he had to touch it. But now Jack wasn't there. And he didn't come back.

Tony checked out all of the fans, poked at the lap desks—which didn't look to be nearly as interesting as a lap dance—and switched on every one of the snake-necked desk lamps, and Jack still didn't come back. The fantasy thing didn't start right away, because there were still the super fuzzy pillows to touch and candles to smell and a bowl of rocks—people paid money for rocks?—to make fun of. When he put the rocks back into the glass bowl, his elbow caught in a rack of shower caddies and by the time he'd picked them up he knew he'd been waiting at least twenty minutes.

Jack had disappeared.

An alien abduction was too easy. It would have to be something really weird. Tony banked on some kind of government conspiracy. Like he'd go up to the checkout and say, "Have you seen that guy I came in with?" and they would say, "Sir, you came in alone" because Jack was really a deep undercover agent, and some guys in black would erase the surveillance tapes of the store.

Tony would go home, but Jack's house wouldn't be Jack's house, and the pictures of them on Tony's phone would be gone, and their friends Sean and Kyle would act like they'd never heard of Jack. So Tony would have to find him, rescue him from some evil military boss, because Tony was the only one who believed that there had ever been a Jack.

"Hey." Jack appeared at his side, and Tony knocked over the caddies again. He wasn't a klutz. Jack had scared the shit out of him, popping up like that when Tony was halfway convinced he was the only person on the planet left with a memory of Jack.

"Did you get the covers for the mop?"

"The what?" Okay. Tony had heard Jack the first time. But

it took a little time to get back from fantasyland, especially when the return destination was a Bed, Bath & Beyond in Canton, Ohio. So, Jack hadn't been erased. He'd still disappeared for a long-ass time.

"I thought you went to get them."

"I told you I wanted to look at a new duvet. I've been all over the store looking for you."

There might have been a few more acres of towels, shower curtains and bedspreads than the entire state of Ohio required in this one store, but it didn't take twenty minutes to do a lap around it. Not even two laps.

"Confess." Tony jerked his thumb at the ladder which provided them both with a view of the better part of a store employee's anatomy as he leaned toward a shelf near the ceiling. "You took bubble butt here into the break room for a little action with the melon ballers."

"Huh?"

Jack's eyes were wide, his mouth hanging open. Tony was so gone on the guy even busted and stupid looked hot. Who wouldn't fall for that wide mouth and those full lips? Tony knew damned well how smooth and hot and tight they were when they slid down a cock.

The expression Jack was sporting right now was kind of guilty, but Tony didn't want to come off as jealous. They hadn't actually talked about whether or not blowing a hot twenty-year-old store clerk would be a problem between them. Because they hadn't talked about much of anything. A year and a couple months ago, Jack had asked Tony to move in. Tony had been packed in ten minutes. Discussion over.

"I mean. If you wanted to suck him off—or anyone else—hey, all I'm asking is you video it on your phone so I can watch it later."

That worked. Jack laughed, ending it in that smile that showed off perfect teeth and made his green eyes sparkle in that way that Tony swore had to have been genetically engineered in some lab to sell shoes to a snake. Jack should have been a model instead of a chef.

"Crazy asshole." Jack's hand landed on the back of Tony's neck for a second.

"That's why you love me."

You do love me, right?

Jack had said it before. In kind of an offhand way, and at least once when he wasn't coming. Tony had said it too, but that had been after the first time Jack had cooked him dinner. Tony had been completely sincere. It had been a hell of a dinner. Jack's restaurant was the best in town.

"C'mon. Let's get the shower-curtain liner."

"The mop covers." Tony's checkered past might have left him with a few crispy neural pathways, but he still had some short-term memory.

"Those too."

On Sunday, Tony found himself in a situation that felt hard to explain even with evil-government-conspiracy fantasies. He dragged his ass downstairs at ten in the morning to find Jack not only showered, shaved and dressed, but dressed up. Not in a tux or anything, which would have stirred up that whole James Bond, secret-agent thing again, but still. Slacks and a collared shirt and a sweater were pretty fancy for a day when they usually didn't get out of bed. Jack hated being dragged out early on Sundays. Sundays were the newspaper and coffee kisses that turned into blow jobs from superheated mouths.

"I'm going into the restaurant." Jack turned away and rinsed out the mug he'd been holding when Tony got into the kitchen.

"Did something happen?" Tony pictured a fire, a flood, a rat infestation and then a power failure that left a hundred cheesecakes thawing in the freezer. The restaurant where Jack worked didn't open until six on Sunday except for their Mother's Day brunch. And Mother's Day wasn't until next weekend. Tony always remembered to take his mom flowers.

Jack didn't turn, just loaded his mug and spoon in the dishwasher, then wiped down the already immaculate granite countertop. "No. Everything's fine. But I need to check some things out for next week. I think I'm going to take the curried chicken off the menu. I keep telling Russ we don't sell enough to make it worth it."

Yeah, Jack had been saying that. But it seemed kind of a weird thing to tackle on a Sunday instead of Monday. Tony was just about to bring that up when Jack straightened and turned around. The smile on his face looked as fake as lipstick on a WNBA coach. If Jack had been some kind of secret agent, Tony could see why they had to erase him. Jack was terrible at undercover shit.

Jack stepped forward and kissed him, something quick that barely landed on the corner of Tony's mouth. "I don't know how long it's going to take."

"No problem." Tony hoped he didn't sound as fake as Jack's lie. "See you when you get home. Bring some of whatever wine you love this week."

"You've got it." Jack scooped his keys from the hook by the door and headed into the garage.

Tony headed over to Sean and Kyle's.

Tony didn't exactly have a lot of models in his life for what a relationship was supposed to look like. Neither his nor his half-sister's dads had stayed around long enough to make much of an impression. And he hadn't been all that thrilled when his best buddy Sean had started talking about Kyle in that whole sappy cue-the-swelling-music-and-run-across-a-field-of-flowers-in-the-sunshine kind of way. It had been enough to turn Tony's stomach. But after seven years, Kyle had kind of grown on Tony. So much so that when Sean and Kyle's happy little love nest exploded last year—reason enough what with Sean taking a bullet during a school shooting—Tony had missed knowing there was a couple out there who got it right.

Then Sean had pulled his head out of his ass and gotten Kyle back, so Tony decided the two of them would be pretty useful at figuring out if he should start packing his stuff up before Jack had to tell him to get out. Besides, they'd introduced him to Jack, so it was their fault if Tony was about to get his heart stomped on.

Tony tried not to let his tongue hang out in desperation when he went into a kitchen full of the smell of coffee and cinnamon and messy with the Sunday papers. Sean fed him at the counter, and Kyle only raised an eyebrow when Tony opted for a beer instead of a cup of coffee. A year ago, Tony would have gotten an eye roll and a sarcastic remark with his beer. Yeah, he and Kyle had grown on each other.

Tony popped the cap and took a swig. There wasn't much point in beating around the bush. His friends weren't so stupid they wouldn't figure out something was going on. "How long have you guys known Jack?"

He couldn't decide who started it, but Sean and Kyle passed this look between them. Back when Kyle first moved in, that was exactly the kind of thing that had twisted Tony's nuts till he could puke. But now that he'd spent all that time wondering if they'd ever patch things up, he didn't mind it so much. He and Jack didn't talk with just a look. Hell, they couldn't even seem to manage it with words. Just bodies. And food.

After the look went on for a few seconds, Kyle answered. "I met him when Russell Brown hired us to design the expansion on the restaurant."

"How long had he been working there?"

Kyle shrugged. "Never came up."

"You going to tell us what's going on? Or are you going to sit there being all cryptic while you mix Michelob with French toast?" Sean's hands landed on the kitchen island, framing Tony's beer.

"You saying it's not the breakfast of champions?"

"C'mon," Sean urged.

The thing was, when it came to it, Tony didn't have much beyond a little weirdness to go on. And who hadn't acted weird once or twice? He'd almost made a career out of it.

"Nothing. Did you guys know that Julia Childs was a spy during World War II?"

For some reason, Kyle was much quicker to follow Tony's bizarre jump of logic. "You think Jack is a spy?"

"No. I mean, it's just weird. He never talks about anything from before we met. Like he didn't have a life before then. He knows everything about me."

"So, he's a good listener," Sean said.

"Or you're a good talker," Kyle added.

"Blow me."

"Get me drunk again and we'll see." Kyle batted his long lashes in Tony's direction.

"Too easy. Dude, your boyfriend's a slut. Hey." Tony lunged after the most nutritious part of his balanced breakfast, but Sean wouldn't give him his beer back.

Sean looked at the bottle in his hand. "I have an experiment in mind. I'm trying to decide which is harder: the gel in your hair or the glass of this bottle."

"Okay, okay." Tony put a precautionary hand over his head. "He's just been a little weird. I wondered if something was bothering him."

"Wow. Here's an idea." Sean put the bottle back on the counter. "Ask him."

"Thanks. Your time on Oprah's couch give you that brilliant psychoanalysis skill, dude? It's not like he's been howling at the moon or anything. Just—forget it." Tony pushed away from the counter and headed for the door.

"Tony, I'm sorry. Wait." Kyle came after him. "No shit this time. What's really going on?"

He tried to think of how to say it. How could you say that after living with a guy for a year, he'd suddenly become a stranger? "You know how you were saying with all the shit that happened this past year that Sean had changed?"

"You're saying Jack's changed?"

"No. I'm saying I wouldn't know if he had because I don't even know who he is." Tony waved a hand in frustration.

"What does that mean?" Kyle spread his hands out.

With them both being Italian, someone could get poked in the eye if they really got a heated conversation going. Tony resolved to keep his hands in his pockets. "I don't know. I'm sorry I brought it up."

"I know what you were saying when all the shit happened this past year: talk to him."

"Yeah, right."

The gate opened in front of him, and Jack drove down the drive of the house up on Marblehead. This end of the Lake Erie peninsula was so high-end he was surprised they hadn't gated the whole block of land. As the drive split at the front of the house, he wondered if Barbara and Phil expected him to go around to the back entrance, the one reserved for "deliveries", the lovely uber-rich euphemism for servants' entrance.

Screw their expectations, he was going in the front door. He knew why he'd been summoned to an audience, knew for the first time since meeting the Howards that he had something they wanted badly enough to leave him holding all the power when they sat down for one of their little *discussions*. Another euphemism, the discussions were negotiations executed with the ruthlessness one would expect from a Harvard MBA and a corporate lawyer. Not that Barbara or Phil needed to work for a living. Their degrees were just extra weapons in the bristling Howard family arsenal.

Barbara herself let Jack in, the big house empty to the point of echoes. They'd probably just come to the Marblehead house for this meeting, down from—what month was it, May?—the family compound out on Mackinaw Island. When Barbara led him to the room that overlooked the lake and Tony saw the big launch sitting at the private marina, he knew he was right. The trip to Marblehead was all about this meeting.

Phil got to his feet as Jack came in. He had to hand it to his former father-in-law. There was only the slightest hint of disgust as Phil shook Jack's hand and waved him toward a seat on the couch. Two heavy legal files dominated the surface of the coffee table. Barbara arranged herself crisply in one of the club chairs across from the couch, and Phil took the other. With his ex in-laws seated, Jack perched on the edge of the cushion and waited.

Phil pushed one of the legal files in front of him. "We've got some things we'd like you to sign. Nothing we haven't talked about before. We just think it's time, don't you?"

From the moment Phil's call had dragged Jack out of Bed, Bath & Beyond and sent him pacing around the parking lot, Jack knew. He locked his back teeth together to prevent any kind of reaction before he flipped open the file. But the words on that blue-backed legal document still wavered and shifted under his gaze. Not unexpected. Just permanent. And more painful than he'd imagined. Locked teeth weren't enough so he bit down on his tongue.

"The financial details are in section four."

Because to the Howards, it was always about money.

"I'm still going to need to run this past my own lawyer."

"Of course." Though Phil's tone suggested he wasn't exactly pleased with that course of action. Not that there was any chance of a fair fight. The Howards had an army of lawyers. Jack had an overworked guy and his two paralegals working out of a Queen Anne on McKinley Street. "Though we'd like to see this all wrapped up by the summer."

"Why the sudden rush?"

"It's not sudden at all," Phil said. "We've discussed this in the past. Is there any reason to think you've changed your mind?"

"No. I haven't changed my mind." Not changed, but still his mind shied away from thinking about it too carefully, about what signing and initialing his way through that file would mean. He'd buried the words and the meanings so deep he could almost forget about the failure of his first life. But there it was in black-and-white legalese. *Constituting an agreement between Phillip Lawrence Howard and John Anderson Noble in the matter of—*

Jack shut the file and thought instead of Tony's grin. Of

what would happen to that grin if he really knew where Jack had gone today. But still... "I want to see them before I sign off on it."

"I'm not sure that's possible." Barbara's thin smile was cold enough to make Jack glad he'd worn a sweater.

"Oh, I'm sure it is." Especially if they were in a hurry. Barbara and Phil might win in a lawyer-to-lawyer slugfest, but the only way to get what they wanted now was for Jack to give it to them. "So you'll call when you've set it up?"

"It would have to be on a Saturday. Provided we can have your signature by next week."

"It will have to be on a Sunday." Jack put his hands on the files. "And on that Sunday, you'll have these. Signed and notarized."

"Fine." Phil stood up, and it was clear his distaste at being in the same room with Jack had finally stripped away the veneer of civility. There was no handshake this time. No showing him to the door. Jack picked up the files that would sever the connection to the last part of the life he'd tried so hard to make real and left the house.

Chapter Two

By the time Tony's bartending shift was over at Hole in the Wall, he'd decided that Kyle was right. It was stupid not to come right out and ask Jack if something was going on. The whole thing was probably just his imagination, or maybe watching Kyle and Sean do their stupid breakup dance last year had given Tony an addiction to drama.

Even if Jack had stayed at the restaurant through the whole Sunday-night shift, he still would already be home and he usually waited up, watching TV and sipping his wine of the week. Tony would pour himself a glass, and then ask Jack in simple, easy-to-understand words what the hell was going on.

Tony had made out pretty good on tips for a Sunday, enough that he was that much closer to getting a sweet little something he'd seen online that would make Jack's eyes bug out when Tony wore it. He was looking forward to that, despite Jack being opposed to Tony's idea of a camera in the bedroom, or at least a few extra mirrors.

Jack wasn't watching TV or in the kitchen, and the silence in the house made Tony's stomach too lurchy with nerves to make him want his usual post-work snack. He went upstairs and found Jack awake, lights on, laptop open as he sat in bed, his reading glasses perched on the end of his sharp nose. Jack thought they made him look old. Tony thought they made him look adorable, but he kept that to himself.

"Hey." Jack glanced up from the screen. "Gimme a second."

"Sure." It wasn't like Tony was all that eager to get the conversation off the ground. He dropped his jeans and his T-shirt over a chair and ducked into the bathroom to brush his teeth. He rehearsed a couple of openers in his mind while his teeth got the kind of brushing that would make a hygienist weep with joy. *You're stalling, buddy.*

Straightening from spitting in the sink, he found Jack standing behind him and almost swallowed the brush. Naked Jack. Very nice. Tony rinsed again and raised his eyebrows at Jack's reflection.

"You're right. We do look hot." Jack slid his arms around Tony's waist.

They were almost the same height, Jack a little broader in the shoulders and narrower at the waist and hips, the bastard, but the contrast of Tony's spiky blond hair and tan skin and Jack's dark longer waves and creamy skin looked better than hot. The heavy press of Jack's cock against Tony's hip meant he wasn't the only one enjoying the view.

Tony dropped his toothbrush in the holder and turned in Jack's arms. "Does this mean you've changed your mind about some mirrors in the bedroom?"

"No." Jack kissed him, and from the first touch of lips, Jack licked into his mouth as if he'd just started the toothpaste diet.

Tony shifted, trying to find space to catch enough breath to say the joke out loud, but Jack didn't let him, hands coming up to hold Tony's head, the kiss going so deep it was like Jack wanted to crawl inside him. It wasn't that Jack wasn't usually enthusiastic about knocking boots, but Tony wondered if Jack was trying to eat him whole. For a second, the generator in his head launched on a zombie, alien, pod-person, werewolf track and then got back with the program when Jack eased up a fraction on jaw-splitting.

Tony rubbed a thumb across the sharp arch of Jack's cheek, and that only made him hold on tighter, kiss harder, hungry noises spilling from his throat. He let go of Tony's head and stroked his dick, but between the tongue in his mouth and the noises from Jack, Little Tony didn't need much encouragement.

Jack spun away, breaths rough and heavy, and slapped his hands on the counter. "Fuck me."

Tony ran a hand over the muscles in Jack's thighs, the hard curve of his ass. It would take a stupider man than Tony's mom had raised to turn down an offer like that. He kissed the top of Jack's spine then let his lips drift lower. "Well, okay."

Jack stopped him when Tony had licked down to Jack's ass, catching Tony's hand and moving it so he could feel how slick Jack's hole already was.

"Hmmm. He comes pre-lubed. How convenient." Tony tugged Jack toward the bedroom. "C'mon."

"No. Here." Jack slapped a condom on the counter and nodded at the mirror.

There was only one answer to that. "Okay." Tony picked up the condom, but he rubbed his bare cock along the slick crease of Jack's ass, the heat and the wet grabbing his skin, making it tighter, harder, until the veins throbbed and ached.

Jack spread his legs farther so that the next rub almost drove the head of Tony's dick inside him.

"You can skip it if you want." Jack's voice was hoarse, full of pleading and so unlike him that the sharp edge of need in Tony's gut dulled, and he stepped back. It wasn't that Jack didn't love a dick in his ass. Or a dildo, or half Tony's hand. The guy liked his ass fucked, and Tony loved doing it. But Jack didn't do sub stuff, didn't get off on begging for it, didn't make sounds like he was going to die if he didn't get it in the next second. And as for the raincoat—yeah, that was something else they needed to talk about first. Other than a split-second you-negative-me-too pause as they ripped off each other's clothes that first time, there hadn't been any discussion, and they'd always used condoms when they fucked.

Tony hadn't wanted to waste time on conversations, just wanted Jack, but now he was starting to think that maybe a little more talking and a little less fucking might be in order. After a quick glance in the mirror to make sure he hadn't turned into a girl, Tony tore the condom wrapper with his teeth and rolled it down.

Jack bent his knees and leaned across the counter, so Tony pushed inside. Tight, Jesus, too tight. As Jack sucked in a pained breath through his teeth, Tony backed off.

"No." Jack reached behind them to keep Tony inside. "Stay."

Tony held still as Jack's muscles pulsed and pulled at his dick. The tension slipped from Jack's back, his ass, and his hand on Tony's thigh all at once, and Tony started to thrust.

"Harder."

Jack arched his back, jamming himself down onto Tony's cock, and that was the Jack he knew, taking what he wanted. But when their eyes met in the mirror, even the flash of heat that made Tony's hips snap hard and fast couldn't completely chase away the chill in his gut from that hungry, desperate look in Jack's eyes.

Jack's gaze was steady as his hips rocked back to meet every thrust. "Wanted you raw. Wanted to feel your come in me. Fucking fill me with it."

Tony shuddered. His balls pulsed and drew up tight. "Jesus Christ, Jack."

Jack didn't smile, his eyes even emptier, and Tony wished he could give Jack whatever the hell it was he needed. Right now, all Tony had to offer was his dick in Jack's body, and Tony was going to use it to chase that look away. Forcing back the orgasm boiling his nuts, he concentrated on hitting Jack right, angling forward until his eyes fluttered closed and he panted. But when Tony reached for Jack's dick to jerk him off, Jack slapped it away.

Tony groaned and clamped down with his stomach muscles until they felt acid-burned. The sweet burst sparkled hot and shivery from his thighs and belly to the tip of his dick, but he ignored its urge to pound the feeling into Jack's ass, just drove deep and then rolled his hips, rubbing Jack inside.

"Fuck." Jack's weight came back against him, head on Tony's shoulder, and Tony caught him with palms flat against Jack's chest.

Tony's eyes opened again, and he leaned around Jack to watch them in the mirror. "Next time, sweetheart," Tony told him. "Gonna feel your ass all hot and wet on my dick. Let you climb on and fuck me stupid."

Jack grabbed his cock. "Don't close your eyes."

Tony bit his lip and hung on while Jack stroked fast, hand a blur in the mirror. Then all Tony saw was Jack's eyes gone dark and wild, lids twitching just like Tony's as they tried to keep watching each other.

A white rope shot from Jack's cock, arcing across the sink to splat on the mirror, right when his ass clamped hard on Tony's cock. He stared as long as he could, focusing on the full circle of Jack's lips as he panted and groaned, eyelids screwed down tight.

Jack slumped forward onto the counter and grabbed at Tony's thigh again. Tony took hold of Jack's shoulders and fucked his own orgasm into him. He'd fought it so long there was no way he could keep his eyes open, but the image of them locked together was burned on his lids, so he still could see it as the hard pulses wrung his balls dry.

Jack didn't complain as Tony fell onto him, hauling air back into his lungs and strength back into his legs. As soon as he could, he shifted to the side, but Jack didn't seem to be in any hurry to move.

"That was really hot," Jack said, voice hollow as it echoed in the brushed copper of the sink.

Hot and a little weird. "We have a bed ten steps away."

"No mirror."

"Whose fault is that?"

"A mirror on the ceiling is way too tacky."

"Who sees our bedroom?"

"Well, I don't know about what you do when I'm not home..."

Tony wasn't going to get a better opening than that, and if they were in bed, and Jack was feeding him a nice little post-fuck snack or drawing patterns on Tony's chest like he did, it would be easy to say something. But here under the glare of the bathroom light, and the mirror leaving no place to hide, all Tony could manage was to stagger to the toilet and flush away the condom. "You don't leave me the energy to get up to anything when you're not here."

"Aw. And here I thought I was the old man in the room."

"You are."

Jack's driver's license said he was going to be thirty-nine in July. But he sure as hell didn't act it. He had stamina like Tony wished he had.

After Jack wiped the come off the sink and mirror and counter, he picked up the condom wrapper. "Did you mean it? About next time?"

"Did you?"

Jack flicked the wrapper into the trash. “I don’t know of a reason why we couldn’t.”

“Me either.”

Jack flipped off the lights, and Tony followed him into the bedroom. For them, it was a pretty deep discussion. When Jack turned off the lights in the bedroom and tucked himself in behind Tony, it seemed like the discussion was over.

Tony woke up with a mission. Screw trust and principles, he was going to look at Jack’s browser history on his laptop. Like Tony had explained to the school psychologist he’d been forced to see back in high school, it wasn’t being paranoid if life kept screwing him over. Once he’d armed himself with some concrete information, he could do better than going fishing with “Is something wrong?” But the laptop wasn’t in the bedroom anymore. He’d have to wait until Jack went to work, since he could hardly ask to borrow Jack’s when he had given Tony his own for Christmas.

Maybe he could just check in the dining room, because if the laptop was open and running, he could always claim laziness as an excuse for using Jack’s, but when Tony came downstairs, Jack was making breakfast. Serious breakfast, a freaking chocolate soufflé and shirred eggs, and God knew what else was still in the oven.

Jack could cook, no doubt about that, but he did it for a living and Tony knew Jack didn’t like to do it much at home. Most of the delicacies Tony got as the bonus of having a five-star chef as a boyfriend were brought home from the restaurant. He figured he was still sitting pretty. How many people had lobster bisque and stuffed quail in their fridge all the time?

So Jack making Tony breakfast was the equivalent of a guy giving his girl flowers for no good reason. He hadn’t tended bar with a ringside seat to constant sinking of relationships without getting wise to the warning signs.

When Jack pulled a fucking quiche Lorraine—topped with crisp prosciutto—out of the oven, Tony swallowed back the drool and blurted, "Is something wrong?"

Jack looked up, but his face was blank as a statue's. "No. Why?"

Tony stared at the three dishes on the breakfast bar.

"I felt like cooking." Jack shrugged.

Jack poured out a coffee, added a generous scoop of turbinado sugar and the flavored creamer he had labeled a disgusting abuse of innocent French roast, and slid it over to Tony.

He eyed the offering suspiciously. "Seriously?"

"What?" Jack turned back to the stove, shoulders solid and unresponsive.

Tony didn't blame him going defensive since neither of them usually spent time on all this analysis shit, but things had officially progressed to beyond weird from Tony's point of view.

"You seem..." Tony searched for a non-accusing word, "...preoccupied with something."

Jack turned back and leaned against the counter, his face set.

Fuck. Why couldn't Tony just have let it go? Eaten chocolate soufflé and quiche and then peeled those jeans from those lean sexy hips and said thank you with a hell of a blow job?

"Yeah." Jack's voice was dry. "I was pretty preoccupied with your dick in my ass last night and with making you breakfast this morning. Is that what you mean?"

Well, when he put it like that, Tony was a total asshole. But they both knew that already. Hell, since he'd already fucked this up he might as well go all in. "If something's going on—at work or—if you need help—" Of course, there was the whole thing Tony wasn't saying. *If you want me to move out—*

Jack's face softened, and Tony's chest got looser. He hadn't known he'd stopped breathing until he started again.

"Nothing's wrong at work." Jack leaned across the bar and put his hand on the back of Tony's neck, thumb rubbing the tattoo below Tony's ear. "Or with you, if that's what you're really asking."

Tony looked down at the soufflé. "It's falling."

"They always do. Once the steam cools."

"Is that the problem?"

Jack wrapped a hand in Tony's T-shirt and dragged him forward. "You really think that's an issue for us?" His words licked across Tony's lips before Jack gave him a kiss that made Tony think about crawling across the dishes because he didn't want to stop to run around the end of the bar to get his hands on Jack.

Jack let him go, but they were both breathing hard.

"I guess not."

"Trust me, Tony. Everything's fine. Have some soufflé before it starts to suck."

"And then I'll sucking thank you."

Chapter Three

A breakfast, a blow job, a shower with a blow job and a quick rinse before the hot water heater ran out later, Tony was telling himself he did trust Jack, at least the Jack he knew. But there were thirty-seven years of Jack Tony had never met, never heard about. That was the Jack he couldn't trust. That and life, which had a tendency to knee you in the balls just when you were thinking it might turn out okay. Reason enough to keep a bag packed.

Tony helped clean up the kitchen, though Jack usually re-cleaned behind him.

"What are you doing today?" Tony winced as soon as he said it. An innocent question any other morning, but now that he'd brought it up, everything seemed layered with suspicion.

"Going in early. I need to finalize the summer menu and put the fear of me into that new sous chef."

"Still a little pissant?" In addition to teaching Tony the difference between champagne and something he could get for six bucks at a liquor store, Jack had a whole new language of insults. Sometimes the age gap between them seemed a lot longer than six years. But then again Tony hadn't studied at—where the fuck *had* Jack gone to cooking school?

"Exactly."

"Guess he should have studied—where did you study?"

There. That was easy.

"Hyde Park."

Tony filed that away for future Googling.

"But he studied at Le Cordon Bleu which he thinks gives him my eighteen years of experience."

"Fucker." Tony went back to an old favorite.

"*Licheux*. Ass-kisser," Jack explained. "It doesn't make you less of one because you do it in French."

"Thought you liked that."

"Well, when it's yours, that's different." Jack ran his lemon-scented hand over Tony's head.

"I'm honored."

"Oh, I think I can make you more than honored." Jack's hand turned from affectionate to arousing, brushing lightly behind Tony's ear, teasing his jaw. "You closing tonight?"

"Probably."

"I'll wait up." Jack gave him a final caress and turned to switch on the dishwasher. "Got any plans for the day?"

"I think I'm going to go over to Akron and see my sister and nephews."

"Okay." Jack went into the dining room for a minute and came back with his checkbook.

Tony shook his head. "Damn it, Jack. That's not what I meant." Darlene and her kids had almost ended up on the street last January until Tony—with a lot of help from Jack—had paid her back rent.

"I know, but it seems silly not to help when I can."

"If she's in trouble, I'll help her. Besides, she's working again."

"Okay, but if she needs help, I don't mind."

That was something Tony knew—but not really. Jack was generous with his money, had a nice house and car, but not anything flashy. Used BMW, not exactly a mansion. Tony had no idea how much was in the bank, but when he'd been trying to figure out how to keep his sister and nephews out of a homeless shelter, Jack had written a check for five grand and handed it off like it was nothing more than bus fare downtown.

Maybe it was a family thing. As far as Tony knew, Jack had a brother in Chicago and a dad in a retirement community in Arizona. Different as they were, they had dead moms in common. "How's your brother?"

"He's fine. My dad too." Jack dropped his checkbook on the counter and pulled Tony into a hug, hands rubbing his back. "You know, not everything turns into a disaster. Sean and Kyle—"

Tony jerked free. "It's not about Sean and Kyle. Or the shooting."

"You didn't used to be this way." Jack sighed.

Fucking sighed.

"*I* didn't used to be this way?"

"Yes. Before Sean got shot you didn't worry everything to death. I know he's your best friend, but he's fine. They're fine. I'm not saying it wasn't a mess, but—" Jack put his hands on Tony's shoulders and pulled him close again.

"Jack, where were you born?"

Jack's body stiffened, but he didn't let go. "Chicago. What the hell does that have to do with this?"

"You've met my sister. My nephews call you Uncle Jack. And I don't even know your brother's name."

"James." Jack snapped the word out but then his voice softened. "Hey." He rubbed the nape of Tony's neck. "Is this about last night? We don't have to go bare if you don't want to.

You don't have to tell me why."

"No. I want to." Jesus, Tony wanted to. Wanted Jack's skin grabbing Tony's dick, wanted Jack bare inside, wanted to feel his come all hot and slick. "I want everything that goes along with that. It's just you, Jack."

"So what's wrong?" The rubbing started again, and Jack pulled Tony's head down to rest on one shoulder.

"Forget it. I think too much." *It's why I miss being stoned.*

Jack kissed him. "Take a class."

"I'm not a fucking housewife, Jack. And I have a job."

Jack let him go. "I know."

"Maybe I can't just write a check for anything that comes up—"

"Neither can I. What the fuck is your problem?"

"I'm sorry." And he was. That was a shitty thing to say.

"You didn't want me to help your sister?"

"I'm sorry I said that, okay?"

"Okay." Jack took a deep breath, and Tony could see the calm settle back onto him like a smooth leather jacket. Bastard.

Tony wished to fuck he could do that. He was still pissed and didn't know what to do with it, but whether he was more pissed at Jack or himself he couldn't say.

"Tell Darlene and the kids I said hi." Jack managed a smile.

It was like the whole conversation never happened. The government wasn't the only one with magical erasing powers.

Chapter Four

Darlene was on the phone in the kitchen when Tony knocked on the screen door. She waved him in. "I told you to kick his ass to the curb three months ago, what did you expect?" she said into the phone.

Tony looked around the corner into the living room. Except for the furniture and a pile of clothes in a basket, it was empty.

"Child support. Take his ass to court," his sister snapped at whoever was getting her advice on the phone.

Tony wished Darlene had been that smart when she first moved out of the house, smart enough not to hook up with the asshole who'd left her with two kids to raise. He wished he'd been able to do more to help her. No time like now. He started folding clothes.

Darlene clicked off the phone and came into the living room. "Men suck."

"They do if you're lucky."

She put her hands on her hips. "Why'd you get all the gay genes?"

"I told you: lucky. Boys in school?" He added another pair of jeans to the pile.

"Nah, shallow graves in Quail Hollow State Park."

"Sounds good. What time do they get back from that?"

“Planning your escape already?”

“No way. I love the little fuckers, you know that. How’s waitressing again?”

“The graveyard shift at Denny’s? Peachy. At least Candy will take the kids overnight.”

“If you ever get back on days, I could take ’em sometime.”

“That’s sweet, but you don’t mean it.” Darlene took off into a bedroom with a pile of clothes.

Tony started folding towels. “How do you know?”

“Because I know you, Tony,” she called back.

“And what does that mean?”

She came back for another pile, but answered him before she went to put them away. “You’re a giant kid yourself.”

“That’s exactly why I have fun with them.”

“Playing with them isn’t the same thing as taking care of them.”

“I can order time-outs with the best of ’em.”

Since they were folding a sheet together, his sister’s laugh huffed in his face.

“I mean it,” Tony said.

“You must really be bored. Why don’t you just go to the gym and work on keeping your ass nice and tight so you don’t lose your sugar daddy?”

“Fuck you. My ass is fine.” Tony cupped it in his hands.

Darlene dropped the sheet onto the pile. “And how’s Jack?”

“Fine.”

“Ohhhkay.”

“What?”

“Usually all I have to do is mention his name and you’re telling me how gorgeous and sweet and amazing he is. What did you do?"

"Why do you think I'm the one who did something?"

Darlene just waited, the next sheet folded over her arm.

"Fuck that. He's the one with all the secrets," Tony burst out.

"Aww, honey." She passed him a sympathetic look along with the end of the sheet. "Men suck. Is he fucking around in general, or should we get a gun and a shovel and take the home-wrecking slut out?"

"I don't know that he is fucking around. If he is, he's sure saving a lot of cream for me."

Darlene looked at him in confusion for a second and then her face screwed up in disgust. "Ew."

"Comes with the gay genes."

She smacked his shoulder. "I think it comes with the guy genes." With a glance at the clock under the TV, she said, "Okay. You've got ten minutes before I pick the boys up at the bus stop. Spill."

He told her about Bed, Bath & Beyond and the trips to work, and even the jumping his bones in the bathroom.

"If you were one of my girlfriends, I'd say he was gay on the side."

"Ha. Right." Jack straight? Pig-for-cock, throw-pillows-in-complementary-colors and matching-table-linens Jack?

Darlene shrugged. "He could pass for straight."

"And I can't?"

She grabbed his hair and pulled him down to face his reflection in the blank TV, twisting his head so they could both see the interlocked double male symbol tattooed just below his ear.

"Okay. Except for that."

He walked with her down the block to meet his nephews' school bus.

As the bus screeched and whined and beeped to a stop, Darlene nodded at it and said, "Mom was right, you know. It's a shame you can't test her theory with Jack."

Tony remembered. *If you want to know how a man really feels about you, tell him you're pregnant.* Mom had only managed to marry Darlene's dad. Tony's sperm donor hadn't stuck around past Mom's six-months-pregnant mark. Darlene's husband had split when their second son Eric was two. She got child support, when the bastard was working and the court could get its hands on his paycheck.

Men didn't stay. If there were any who could make it work like Sean and Kyle, Tony sure as hell didn't know any. Thank God he wasn't likely to get pregnant because he and Jack stopped using condoms.

Still, Jack would make a great dad. Tony could teach the kid how to throw a baseball and a football. There was the whole thing about diapers, but that only lasted a few years. The fantasy took off, and they were hanging stockings and making Christmas cookies, and signing up for swim class and going camping. The kid had Jack's eyes, perfect smile and—

—a ball of energy rolled into Tony's gut and landed him in a pile of crabgrass and dirt.

"Where's Uncle Jack?"

Five-year-old Eric had taken Tony down, now six-year-old Damien piled on.

"He's at work."

A stream of questions assaulted Tony's ears as he peeled off his nephews and they all started back to the house.

"Are you sitting on us tonight? Can we go to your house and play? Mom says Uncle Jack buys you lots of toys."

Tony looked at his sister over the top of her kids' heads. "Does she?"

"Yeah," Eric agreed. "Do you have PlayStation or an Xbox?"

"I don't think Mommy wants you to play with the toys Uncle Jack and I play with."

His sister punched his arm. Hard.

"Are the toys sharp?" Eric asked.

"Are they guns? We can't have toy guns," Damien said.

"Say one word about shooting, and you won't have a reason to go home and play," Darlene threatened in a tight whisper.

Tony pretended to zip his lips.

"Hey, guys. Uncle Tony's going to keep an eye on you for me while I run to the store, okay? He wants to help you make cookies to take to Candy's."

Twenty-five minutes later, Tony was sticky and exhausted in a completely un-fun way. When he and Jack had a kid, they'd get to start from the beginning and train him to have good manners and not throw eggs around the kitchen and not to dump flour on someone's head to see what he would look like as a ghost. Of course, the monsters had waited until after they'd made a giant mess to tell Tony that Mom made cookies from the dough in the fridge door.

The cookies were in the oven and Damien and Eric were currently under orders not to set foot out of the bathroom, though what Tony was going to do to carry out his or-else threat he had no idea. As he cleaned up the kitchen, he wished for a garden hose. Come to think of it, that would be the easiest way to deal with his nephews too.

When the kitchen was clean enough that he was sure his sister wouldn't neuter him and the cookies were cooling on a paper towel, he stalked to the bathroom and yanked open the door. The kids were sitting on the bath mat, Damien drawing designs on the flour on Eric's face. "Strip and get in the shower," he ordered.

Food was easy enough to wash off, though the way Eric kept ducking away turned the stuff in his hair to paste before Tony could get him good and soaked. It would definitely be easier starting from scratch. Like Jack said, you had to control the ingredients if you wanted a quality product. Where would they get the kid from?

What Tony didn't get off them in the tub he scrubbed off when he dried them with one of the freshly washed towels. No wonder his sister did so much laundry. Damien dressed himself, but Eric got into his shirt backward and Tony helped him twist it around.

"Uncle Tony, Mikey Bianci says that living with Uncle Jack makes you a fag," Eric said when his head popped out of the shirt again.

"Is Mikey named for his dad?" Tony asked.

"Yep."

Tony felt Damien's gaze on him from behind, so he moved so both boys could see him and then crouched down. "Well, Mikey's right. I am. But that's not a nice word to say. And you can tell Mikey to ask his dad if he remembers me beating the crap out of him for calling me that when we were in school together."

"Mom says fighting's wrong."

"Well, it is usually. And I'm not saying you should punch Mikey, especially not when what he said is true."

"But not nice," Eric clarified.

"Right." Tony tapped the kid's head. "But when you're a guy, sometimes when someone gives you a lot of sh—crap, you've got to stand up to him."

The look Eric gave his brother suggested that he was

coming up with justification for a sibling smackdown.

"I don't mean your brother. And you never, ever hit a girl. But if you keep getting picked on, sometimes you've got to let the other guy know you're not going to take it. And you always stand up for family, you got it?"

"Even if he snitches?" Eric wanted to know.

"Snitching isn't nice either, unless you do it to keep someone from getting hurt. But yeah. You can count on your brother."

"Even if he's a total dickhead?" Damien's smile made Tony wonder if his sister hadn't made a serious mistake naming him after the kid in *The Omen*.

Better ingredients, that was the way to go. They were definitely using Jack's sperm.

Chapter Five

Jack's meeting with the lawyer went about the way he would have expected. Steve took the files for a couple of days and reported back on Thursday that there were no surprises and that the Howards would be assuming all financial responsibility. There was also some money settled on Jack, though he wanted that section stricken from the agreement. The thought of getting paid for his signature on those papers made him sick.

Steve would handle contacting the Howards' lawyer about that change, and then the final arrangement would be up to them. Just saying the word final made him ache with a full-body nausea. But he didn't see the point to dragging it out. Nothing had changed. It had all been over four—almost five—years ago. They were just pouring water on cold ashes.

As long as Jack didn't fuck up, he could still keep the one thing he'd managed to make work.

When he'd crawled out of bed at seven in the morning, he mumbled an excuse about an appointment to get the X3's tires rotated. Like any other long-practiced skill, lying came almost naturally. Now that he'd left the lawyer's, it was too early to go into work.

All Jack wanted was to go home. Even if he couldn't tell Tony the truth, Jack could forget the whole mess just being with him. Jack had faked happy for so long he'd forgotten what it actually felt like until he met Tony.

No one looked at life like Tony. No one got more joy out of food, or sex, or some stupid commercial on TV than Tony. That much love of life spilled out of him until all you could do was enjoy it along with him.

It would have been easier if Tony was stupid. But although he thought the Cartoon Network was highbrow entertainment, there were only so many trips to the mechanic or going-into-work-early excuses that he would buy. But it would be over soon, before Tony could get wrinkle lines from making that uncharacteristic frown Jack had seen too much of lately.

Neither of them had anywhere to be for hours. Jack could feed him, fuck him and send them both off to work with big smiles. The sight of Tony's hideous car in the driveway had Jack jogging up the walk, calling for him as soon as he hit the door.

"In here."

Tony had his feet on the coffee table and his laptop open, but from the look on his face, he wasn't laughing at YouTube or hunting up porn. He looked surprisingly focused. The hair on Jack's arms prickled.

Tony shut the laptop and shoved it onto the coffee table. Jack took a seat on the other end of the couch.

"I've been thinking."

No shit. The nausea hit him again, had him blinking and swallowing hard. Not against tears, though sometimes Jack wished he could just break down and unload it all, but against a fear that left him sweating and chilled, like an outbreak of malaria in central Ohio.

He couldn't lose this too. Not now, not with everything else piled on top.

What did it take, what was he supposed to do? Sometimes

he swore that the only reason he didn't find a nice quiet way to permanently disappear was that he'd miss the next outrageous thing to come out of Tony's mouth. Every day Jack would find himself headed for the restaurant and see the sign for the interstate and think about driving until the gas was gone. If he left the car in the right place and paid cash at the motel, it could be awhile before they found him. He hadn't made up his mind between pills or a rope. He was sure Phillip Howard would be happy to supply him with a gun.

But he could never leave the man across from him with nothing but a huge *why* to eat at him every minute for the rest of his life, and every day Jack passed the sign for I-77 and drove into work and came back home. To Tony.

Jack folded his arms and leaned back. "I noticed."

"Smoke coming out of my ears?" Tony grinned.

"I think it was that terrible grinding noise. Kept me up all night." Despite the grin, Jack wasn't feeling very reassured.

"Here's the thing."

Jack swallowed again. As much as he loved Tony's unpredictability, he could have done with some certainty right now. Would have traded his best knives to know exactly what was going to come out of Tony's mouth, but Jack didn't have a clue.

Tony leaned forward. "I don't want to take a class. I want to have a kid."

Chapter Six

Tony's words seemed to be coming from the far end of a tunnel. Egg donor, surrogate, adoption. The irony of it all wasn't lost on Jack. The paperwork wasn't finished on his old family and Tony wanted a new one?

"I've got to go outside." Jack was aware of Tony behind him, apologizing, excusing, explaining, but he still went through the French doors and out onto the deck, trying to pull air into a chest that was too full for breath. His ulcer again. That crushing burn spreading up through his body until he couldn't breathe. Tony's surprise was enough to give the ulcer an ulcer.

Tony subsided and sat silently in a deck chair while Jack walked around the yard. The hostas ringing the beech tree would bloom soon. The grass was lush and trimmed. Vinca and mulch decorated the area around the a/c. The roses climbing along the back fence were green, just starting to bud. The lilacs along the side were fading. Everything as perfect as the landscaping service promised.

He came back and straddled the bench on the lounge next to Tony. "What made you think of this?"

"I've thought of it off and on for a while, but seeing my nephews, thinking of how much they miss having a dad, I started thinking again. I want to have a kid with you. You'd make a hell of a dad. You're practically raising me."

"You say Eric and Damien miss their dad. How screwed up would they be if they didn't have a mom? Don't you think a kid needs a mom?" As long as it wasn't Patrice.

"He needs two parents who love him and have time for him. He'd have that. And an aunt. We could do it right."

Do it right? Like Jack had the first time?

"I don't get where this is coming from."

"We've—you've got so much. And we've got time. If you didn't want to do the whole egg-surrogate thing, we could adopt. Even foster a kid."

"Why?"

"Because it would be fun. Don't you ever think about it?"

"Somehow I didn't think it would come up," Jack said, aiming a gesture at their crotches.

"Exactly. That's why we can do it right. We can plan it out. Make sure."

Jack stared ahead. It was only ten o'clock in the morning. How could so much go wrong so fast? Why couldn't life ever stay the way he'd made it? He'd done it better this time, no faking it. Did Tony hate everything Jack loved about the life they had?

"I never thought about it."

"So now you can." Tony walked over and dropped a leg over Jack's deck chair so that they faced each other, knees touching. "I know it's a lot and I just kind of puked it all out there, but like you said, it's not something that's going to come up on its own." Tony looked down and then back up. "It's not a deal breaker or anything."

A laugh got trapped in Jack's throat, fluttering like he'd swallowed a moth, a choking, frantic tickle. "Glad to hear it."

"I'm down with the doing it bare, and I don't want to be

with anyone else. I just wanted to put it out there. I think we'd make a good family."

It escaped. A cough, a reflexive gasp, but there still wasn't any room in his burning chest.

Tony swung off the chair. "Okay then. Let's forget about it. You want to fuck before work?"

"Tony." Jack pulled him back down. "It is a lot. So you can't just puke it and expect me not to blink."

"If you'd blink, I'd feel better. I feel like I'm talking to a statue."

"Are you saying I look like a god?" Jack dredged up a smile.

Tony looked away and shrugged.

"Okay." Jack put his hands on Tony's thighs. "Answer this. Is something else going on? Something that's making you feel like you need this?"

"You mean the fact that you've been disappearing a lot lately? A feeling that you're not telling me something?"

Ouch. Sometimes Tony's hedonism made him easy to take for granted. "Yes. Something like that. And you think having a kid is the answer to it?"

Tony held his gaze steadily. "It started me thinking about it. But no. If things aren't okay between us, I don't think it's a good idea to have a kid."

Jack got a deep breath, the flare in his stomach settling down to a glow. So this was just an elaborate way of Tony asking if Jack was planning to dump him. Tony was really fucking smart.

Jack leaned in and kissed him. "I want you here. As for a kid—I don't know."

Tony didn't move, like he was checking each of Jack's words for truth. "Okay."

Chapter Seven

Tony hadn't realized how attached he'd gotten to the idea of having a little human being to raise until Jack shot him down. When he'd thought of it, it had only been an idea, a test, one of the million versions of reality that flickered through Tony's brain. But doing his research and seeing smiling pictures of two-dad families, it had felt real. Like they could have this, be something more than the two of them just rolling through life having a good time. Which, given the strain of Tony wondering where Jack kept disappearing to and then the whole awkward discussion yesterday, they weren't having. As in fun or sex. When Tony had reached for Jack last night, Jack had pulled Tony close like a blanket and dropped back into sleep.

This morning, Tony woke up with a hard dick and an empty bed. After waiting two minutes in the hope that Jack's guilt might lead to breakfast—or a blow job in bed—Tony got up. Since he did most of the laundry, he was rubbing this one out in the shower.

He teased himself a little as he washed, keeping the edge without hitting the point of desperation. Just when he was about to get down to business, he heard Jack moving around in their room, but was still surprised when Jack yanked open the curtain and stepped in.

"Let me give you a hand with that."

Tony wanted to hang on to his bad mood, but he couldn't.

He'd never managed to hold a grudge, and he couldn't blame Jack for being honest about not wanting a kid. Even if none of that were true, it was impossible to be pissed at the guy when he was turning a cucumber-conditioner-slick hand job into a fucking work of art.

Jack's grip wasn't tight, but he knew all the right spots. When he got a second hand involved to work the shaft while he rubbed the head, the pressure was more than enough to make Tony stagger and slap a hand against the tiled wall. The tug reached inside, tingling low and sweet on Tony's balls, twisting in that spot his orgasms seemed to explode from, the place where his dick and ass and belly and balls dumped all the fun feelings. But he wasn't close. Not a hard enough grip to make him come. Just a good and dirty buzz along every nerve.

It went a long way toward making up for being a secretive bastard, and the look on Jack's face said he damn well knew it. Tony wouldn't be the first or last guy to get led around by his dick. Any guy who hadn't wasn't playing for the right team.

Jack pressed a fingernail into the slit, and Tony was going to have to spend tomorrow re-grouting where he was digging at the tiles. Goddamn, the guy knew his way around a cock, knew just the way to tease, when to speed up and slow down. Tony's breath whistled through his teeth.

Jack grinned. "Something wrong?"

Tony shook the water off his face. "Nah. I'm good." He tried to match Jack's grin.

Jack moved fast, spinning Tony so his back was against Jack's chest. With one arm around Tony to pin him close, Jack shoved his cock under Tony's ass until the head pushed up on his balls. Tony squeezed his thighs together, and Jack's groan vibrated between them. Taking a tighter grip, Jack pumped Tony's dick fast and sure, but the pressure of Jack's cock on the spot behind his balls, the way the thick root dragged the skin near his hole, made Tony want more.

"Fuck me." He panted the words out. "You want to go bare? Do it."

Jack took Tony's ear between his teeth then whispered, "Not like this. Make it special."

"Don't need that shit." Want shivered down his back, his legs, want hotter than the water splashing on them, hotter than the come he wanted to feel Jack shoot inside him.

Tony felt Jack shake his head. "Trust me. We'll do it right."

With that on the table he was asking for trust? Frustration was enough to push Tony back from the edge.

Jack didn't seem to notice. He grunted, hips bucking as his cock drove hard into Tony's nut sac, and that hurt enough to dial him back another few notches. He rode the feeling, the back and forth between the sharp jab of Jack's cock and the good friction of his hand on Tony's dick. The arm Jack had wrapped around Tony clamped down on his shoulder as Jack thrust a few more times then stilled as he coated Tony's thighs and balls with come.

"Love you." Jack muttered the words into Tony's throat then lapped at the water there before picking up the rhythm again.

Of course he'd say it now. Never in one of those moments when Tony could be sure. Always in some offhand kind of way. Looking for better proof of it, Tony wrapped an arm around the back of Jack's neck and twisted them into a kiss.

Jack's fingers closed tight, palm polishing the head while the fingers squeezed underneath like he'd pinch the orgasm out. The feeling rushed back, faster now, a need to push into Jack's hand until everything shook loose in a blur of pleasure. Jack's other hand dragged over Tony's hip and between his legs from the back, gently pushing his balls forward, and that was it.

Pulling off Jack's mouth before teeth got involved, Tony let his head drop back against Jack's as a long come snapped out, bursts of it echoing through Tony's dick even after he'd stopped shooting.

Jack kept Tony on his feet, tipping them forward until the shower rinsed them clean. After they stepped out, Jack toweled Tony off, rubbing the thick maroon terry over his head like he was a kid. Tony pushed away and stepped in front of the foggy mirror to fix his hair.

Jack put his arms around Tony's waist. "Leave the gel off for now. I like it when it's soft."

Even if Jack hadn't just made Tony come until his legs felt as stable as a soap bubble, there was no way Tony could resist the look in Jack's eyes. The distracted, anxious look was gone, leaving nothing but a happy shine.

"Okay."

Tony combed it with his fingers and let it flop. It parted in the middle, and he tried to get it to stop. Jack reached for his head, but Tony ducked away. Jack caught him and turned him away from the sink. The happy look was still there.

"Sorry. I had some things I had to take care of, but none of it was about you."

Tony waited.

Jack's gaze didn't waver. "And it might take a little longer, but then I'm all yours again."

"Can I help? I'm not much of a sous chef, but I've worked in a kitchen before."

"It's not work."

"Okay." What else was there? There was work and there was personal. If personal didn't involve Tony, then where were they?

"It's my stuff. There's nothing you can do."

Between Jack toweling him dry and then that brush-off, Tony felt younger than his nephews.

Of course, if Tony hadn't spent the last sixteen years acting like he was still a teenager, Jack—and the rest of the people who knew him—might take Tony a little more seriously. But it still pissed him off.

"Any other grooming suggestions? Do I need to shave?"

Jack's thumb scraped the stubble along Tony's jaw. "No. I like it. Did you have anything planned before work?"

"Besides laundry?"

"Let's go for a drive."

They used to go for drives all the time. Jack had taken Tony on a lot of day trips when they were first fucking, and even after Tony moved in, Jack would suggest a trip up to the beach or to Cleveland or Columbus. One memorable Camembert and apricot picnic had led to semipublic sex just off the trail in a state park. Far enough to be out of sight, but not so far they couldn't hear the people walking by. Tony had almost bitten through his tongue trying to be quiet.

Executive chefs worked holidays, and a whole day off was rare, but the day trips were nice and more than Tony could have managed on his own with a twenty-year-old car. They hadn't gone anywhere since the fall.

"Will there be food?"

"I think we can manage something."

Chapter Eight

Tony liked Jack's trips, even though he was usually suspicious enough of surprises to always stick his finger through the bottom of a donut to check what kind of the filling was in there. It wasn't that he didn't like pretty much every donut ever invented, he just didn't like not knowing what to expect. He wasn't sure Jack thought the end destination of their drive could possibly be a surprise when they turned down the driveway and the sign out front made it obvious. *Farley Breeders: Goldendoodles, Labradoodles.* Had he thought Jack made him feel five? Tony was dropping the age down to three. He couldn't have one toy, so Jack was giving him another.

Jack shut off the car in front of the house and glanced over. "I know what you're thinking and I know it's not the same thing. But we could just look."

If Jack wasn't so fucking reasonable, it would be easier to be pissed, but there he was, reading Tony like he came with pop-up messages. Just move the cursor on the screen and the little box explained everything.

After his first five minutes of looking in the pen, Tony knew it had been a mistake to get out of the car. He'd never wanted a dog, but the puppies, the litter of Golden Retriever/Poodle mixes, were heartbreakingly adorable. They wriggled and sniffed and licked until Tony wanted to take every one of them home. The breeder lifted one out, and it happily nuzzled Tony's hands and climbed up into his lap. He turned to look for Jack.

“He said he had to take a call,” the breeder said.

The puppy tried to tunnel through Tony’s arms to get closer, staring up with a wide-eyed appeal that cut right through to Tony’s spine, snapping all his frustration loose. He dropped a kiss on the puppy’s nose and handed it off to the breeder before the whole cute thing calmed him down again. With a smile and a “We’ll let you know” for the woman holding the soft ball of curls, Tony went out to find Jack.

He was still on the phone, pacing next to the car. Whatever call he’d had to take wasn’t making him happy. Good. That made two of them. And made for a better fight. Because they were definitely having a fight. Watching Kyle and Sean go through that slow breakup drama last year had been painful enough. Tony wasn’t going through it with Jack. As much as having to walk away from the best year of his life would kill him, he’d rather do it cleanly.

He knew Jack saw him because he stopped mid lap and turned and walked in the other direction. He slid the phone closed and put it back on his belt. At least Jack didn’t treat him like he was stupid. Didn’t ask about the puppies.

“What’s. Going. On?” Tony bit off each word.

“I told you. I have some stuff I have to take care of. I also told you it didn’t have anything to do with you.” Jack’s voice was icy. Tony had heard him use that tone once or twice in the kitchen when Tony sat in the restaurant bar before it opened. But Jack had never used it on him.

“Yeah, I remember. But if we’re going to dump a load in each other’s ass, it might be time for a little more sharing of *stuff.*”

Jack’s right shoulder dipped, like some impulse of motion got swallowed back. “Can we do this in the car?”

"It's hot."

"I'll turn on the air."

Tony yanked open the door and slumped in his seat, remembered he was trying to act a little more like an adult and straightened up.

Jack cranked the ignition and warm air blasted from the vents.

It didn't take long for the a/c to kick in, but even German-engineered dual climate control wasn't helping cool Tony off.

"Either tell me, or tell me why you can't, because this-is-my-stuff shit is pissing me off. I thought we were working on a together kind of thing."

Jack shifted in the leather seat, and Tony met his look.

It wasn't a good look. It was hurt and scared and angry. Whatever was coming was big and ugly. But at least Tony was going to get the truth. With that look on Jack's face, Tony's fantasy of secret agents and government conspiracies sounded pretty fucking cozy.

"I was married before."

The words didn't seem to make sense. "Before what?"

"Before I came to Canton. Before I met you."

"Married? Like in Massachusetts?"

Jack shut his eyes, shut Tony out until Jack was a complete stranger. "No. To a woman."

That made less sense. Tony knew it happened. Guys faked it or denied it or didn't let themselves know for a long time, but those guys weren't Jack. When those guys came out, they were weird, freaked. They didn't steal a kiss and a grope in front of the spatulas at Bed, Bath & Beyond. They sure as hell didn't go out in public in pressed khaki shorts and mandals.

Jack's eyes weren't closed, but he wasn't looking at Tony

anymore.

"How long ago?"

"We separated four years ago last November."

Okay. That explained it. Jack had lots of time to get out of the closet and on with life. So what was the big hairy deal?

"So?"

"So, her family has a lot of money and there's still some legal stuff that needs to be worked out."

"I don't get what the problem is. Why didn't you just say that? You've been acting like you were doing black ops."

Jack's mouth moved, like he wanted to laugh. It really wasn't that big of a deal. Tony was only freaked because it was unexpected, but it wasn't like someone was dead.

He put his hand on Jack's knee. "You know, I always suspected you weren't a virgin. How much was she worth? I could still be your mistress."

Jack swallowed hard. Any chance of a laugh was gone. Whatever the big, ugly thing was it wasn't this simple, but he put the X3 in gear and turned around.

All right. As a sign of the fact that Tony was trying to grow up some, he'd wait until they got home before digging again. It wouldn't be any different from how he usually got information from Jack. One word at a time.

Jack knew everything about Tony. Except that fantasy he had sometimes of getting Kyle drunk and fucking the shit out of him, though maybe Jack had Tony figured enough to know that too.

His brain chewed on the whole married thing as they drove back into Canton. Jack in a tux was easy—and damned sexy—but kissing some Barbie in a big white gown? It did not compute. He snuck a look over and tried to picture it.

"I can feel that," Jack said. "This is why I didn't want to tell you."

"Because I'm trying to picture you nailing a girl?"

"Are you?"

"Actually I was just thinking of you doing the whole wedding-album trip and then the two point five—holy fucking shit."

Jack didn't have to look at him. He couldn't hide the grimace.

"You did—you do? Jesus Christ, Jack. How many kids do you have?"

Jack's whole body went rigid. This was it. This was the thing he couldn't say. And for a damned good reason. He fucking knew how Tony felt about disappearing dads.

"I have two. They're fine. They go away to school, but I see them."

This was why the fucker had wanted to have this conversation in the car. Tony wanted to scream and yell and stomp around, and Jack had a perfect excuse to not look at him. But they were five minutes from the house.

"You work holidays. When's the last time you saw them?"

Jack's face twisted again. "February. When I went to Chicago."

"You mean when you said it was for work? That Russ wanted you to look at a restaurant there?"

Jack didn't have an answer for that. Exactly how many lies had Tony swallowed?

They turned down the road to the development of upscale houses, past Breton Court, Northwinds, and finally the snootiest of the bunch, Bridgeway Terrace, where Jack lived.

Tony started piling up his ammunition. If Jack didn't have

a good enough defense, he'd be living in Bridgeway Terrace alone again.

Jack didn't stop in the drive but pulled around Tony's Rabbit and hit the garage door opener. No chance of a scene for the neighbors.

Tony hopped out as soon as the car stopped moving and beat Jack to the side door. He went on through the kitchen and the dining room, and Jack damned well better be following him.

"Tony?" Jack's voice was so urgent Tony came back toward the kitchen.

He waited.

"Are you leaving?" Jack asked.

"I was just going into the living room. You want me to go farther than that?"

It almost felt good to know he wasn't the only one who worried about when this was going to crash and burn. Almost, but mostly Tony just felt like shit for putting that look on Jack's face.

"Okay. I need some wine. Do you want a beer?"

Tony folded his arms. "You need wine to talk to me?"

"If you really think that, maybe you should leave."

Tony would have done it too, if Jack's voice didn't sound so hollow. "No beer."

Tony went on into the living room and dropped onto the couch. It wasn't like they never had serious conversations. Sometimes Tony forgot to start the dishwasher or lied about getting the laundry done, but he'd never left his kids behind like they were trash.

Jack took a chair and poured himself a glass of wine. God forbid he should drink out of the bottle. He swirled the dark red liquid around in his glass before taking a sip.

"All right. What do you need to know?"

"Try everything."

Jack's shoulders made a tiny shrug. "I met Patrice when I was working at the Grand Hotel on Mackinaw Island. Her family summers—"

"Sorry, but I don't really give a shit about your ex-wife. What about the kids?"

"Like their ages?"

"Like how the fuck do you not see them more? Why don't you have joint custody? How could you listen to me bitch about deadbeat dads and not say a fucking word? Not a word, Jack."

What had Jack thought when Tony complained? Had he thought writing the check for Darlene made up for the fact that he'd been ignoring his own kids?

"Brandon is fourteen and Sarah is twelve. They were ten and seven when we split. At first we did the joint-custody thing. I got them a few days a week, but she came to get them when I worked."

"And then what?"

"I tried."

"What the hell does that mean?"

"Jesus. Do I need a lawyer?" Jack drank some more of the wine. "It means I tried to be a part-time dad. I was only ever part-time with my work schedule anyway. It turned out they were better off without me."

"What happened?"

"It didn't work. They weren't happy." Jack buried the words in the bell of the wineglass.

"They have an issue with you being gay?"

"There was that." Jack held the bottle up to the light and then poured another glass.

"They'd get used to it."

"Some things you don't get used to."

Tony wished he'd taken the beer. He could stand having something to do with his hands. He kept wanting to fold his arms across his chest, but every time he did, he remembered Mom or Darlene in that stance, listening to the lies some guy was selling them. "You know, I hate my father for running out on my mom. She had to work so much it put her in the ground at fifty. But if I got the chance to meet him, after I punched him in the face, I'd still want to know him."

"Why?"

"Because he's my dad."

"Yeah, well, maybe if you'd had a dad you wouldn't say that." Jack's voice wasn't hollow, or icy or angry. It was so thin and flat it scared Tony.

He got up and moved to sit closer. "Tell me."

"You want to know why I don't talk about my family? Because I hated them. My dad's the reason I got into that whole fucked-up mess with Patrice anyway. There wasn't much he liked, but there was a hell of a lot he hated."

Jack knocked the wine back like it was whiskey. The hair on the back of Tony's neck prickled a sharp warning. Jack didn't do that. Not with—he glanced at the bottle—a Mark West pinot noir.

"Dad hated everyone, blacks, Hispanics, Jews, but especially fags. I never let myself think it, but somehow he could see it. He was sure he could beat the queer out of me. He beat my brother too, but when James got older it stopped. Not with me. And the weirdest things would set him off. Like me helping my mom with the groceries."

Tony had asked, and now he felt sick. Jack poured his third glass and shoved the bottle out of reach.

"You think your dad put your mom in the ground? I know mine did. She tried to keep him off me sometimes, but usually just ended up crying. One day when I was almost sixteen she wouldn't back down, not when he was aiming a belt buckle at my back. Again. She wrestled with him and then she just hit the floor. I'd thought he hit her and I was going to punch him back, no matter what it cost me, but he was just as shocked as I was. She stroked out. Right there in the kitchen."

"Jack. God. I..." Tony wanted to hold the wineglass to Jack's mouth himself, stop this from spilling out.

"You wanted to hear it, right?" The smile Jack gave him would have made Tony run if he thought his legs would work. "At least he never hit me after mom died. But he still hated me. And I hated him. I knew I could prove him wrong. But finally all that lying was worse than getting beat every day because I did it to myself."

Tony tugged the wineglass out of Jack's hand and put it on the coffee table. Then he pulled Jack up and onto the couch with him. Jack came willingly, but he didn't respond to Tony kissing his neck or wrapping his arms around him.

"All that doesn't mean you'd be a shitty dad."

"But I was."

"You didn't hit them?"

"God, no."

"So. It's not too late. Whatever this legal stuff is it means there's still some connection. Your kids probably miss you. Why don't you have them stay with you for awhile when they get out of school? I don't have to be around, I could stay with Sean and Kyle."

Jack shook his head.

"I could meet them." Tony offered it hesitantly.

"No."

"I'm not saying all that shit with your dad doesn't suck. And hey, if therapy can work to get Sean to be less of a pain in the ass, maybe it wouldn't be a bad thing for you, but that happened a long time before your kids came along. They shouldn't have to pay for it."

"Well, they already did." Jack pushed free and walked across the room.

"How?"

Jack shook his head, lips pressed tight enough to pale.

"How?" Tony asked again.

"They should never have been born."

This wasn't Jack. It wasn't happening. Tony had fallen through some wormhole into an alternate reality where everything looked the same but wasn't. And if he could just figure out why, he could get back to his life. To his Jack. The guy who might be a bit constipated when it came to discussing the future or the past, but he made Tony feel like there was a reason for things. A reason to laugh and a reason to keep trying to remember to take the laundry out of the washing machine before it got moldy. Not someone who wished his kids had never been born. Maybe the wormhole was in the wine.

He picked up the bottle and looked in it like he expected a genie to wave back up at him.

"Get thirsty all of a sudden?" Jack said from where he leaned on a bookcase.

"No." Tony looked back up. His eyes were slow to focus, so he blinked. It was probably a wormhole effect. "I'm just trying to figure out who the hell you are."

"I thought I was the guy who got you out of your shitty apartment. The guy who offered to buy you a new car."

Tony was on his feet now. "Fuck you." He repeated it more softly, and then started to walk away, but came back. "This was never about your fucking money, Jack. As soon as I can find another shitty apartment, me and my shitty car can stop cluttering up your perfect little kid-free existence."

Chapter Nine

"Tony, wait."

The words got stuck and didn't make it past Jack's lips until Tony was already out of the room. And he wanted to follow him, took a few steps in that direction, but then he heard Tony's car cough to life and he stopped. Because it wasn't anything he didn't deserve. He'd practically shoved Tony right out the door. Given him every reason to go and not one reason to stay.

It wasn't just what he'd said about Tony and the money. It was what Tony had made him say about Brandon and Sarah being better off never having been born. He'd never said that, even to himself. But he couldn't help but wonder if it wasn't true. If maybe Brandon and Sarah wouldn't come to hate him for the same thing. They were probably too young to really understand it now, but later, when they knew how Jack had taken everything from them, every chance of having the kind of family a kid deserved—yeah, they'd have more reason to hate him than they already did. The sooner he signed over his parental rights, the better. Phil and Barbara weren't exactly the Cleavers, but they were better than nothing, and Brandon would always look out for Sarah—he had been since the accident. Like when he'd looked up at Jack in the hospital, Sarah's hand tight in his, and said, "Don't you have to be at work, Dad?"

The wine burned in his stomach, working steadily with the ulcer to carve away new pieces of flesh to fester in. He was going to have to go back to the doctor, unless he decided to let himself bleed to death internally. Like Tony walking out on him, it might not be any less than he deserved.

He capped the bottle and carried it and the glass back to the kitchen. Tony was only supposed to work three to ten tonight. When Jack got home from work, he'd know if Tony was gone, one way or the other.

One of the best things about running a kitchen was that even when there were no disasters, the constant stream of mini crises left no time to think about whether or not your boyfriend had left you. Better yet, there was almost always some kind of disaster, so if your brain did start to drift toward the kind of panic that would pump more acid over your ulcer, a fire or sliced-open tendons or third-degree burns would drag you back.

The kitchen had kept Jack sane all those years of forcing a happy marriage and fatherhood on himself. It was the one place where he knew he could keep control over the outcome, even if he had to do everything himself. Still, at the moment he held a server's steam-burned hand under cold water while yelling for the maitre d', he kept thinking of how Tony had looked at him when he said he was getting out of Jack's perfect kid-free existence.

If Tony wasn't home, Jack would track him down at Darlene's or Sean and Kyle's or in the bar storeroom and tell him everything. Maybe it would be worse if he told Tony why Jack had no business being anyone's father, but Jack would rather lose Tony with the whole truth instead of with the half-story he had now.

Tony's car wasn't in the driveway. He only put it in the garage if it was going to snow because he liked irritating the neighbors with his junker on display. Jack pretended to ignore it, but the horrified disgust on the pinched faces of the Carraways still amused him. Jack punched the garage opener and pulled the X3 into the empty garage.

He'd known, but he'd let himself hope. And hope was a fucking bitch.

Hope made him look for a cereal bowl in the sink and then the dishwasher, made him look for a milk splatter on the counter or a TV left on.

Okay. Hope was a cunt.

Jack went upstairs. It was almost midnight. He'd shower off the kitchen smells and check the bar first.

As he flicked on the bathroom light, his breath came quick and deep and finally steady for the first time all night. Tony lay sprawled across their bed, the sheet tangled around his hips, broad back and narrow waist on such artful display, Jack would have thought Tony had posed, but Tony never posed for anything but a laugh. The light from the hall made marble out of his muscles and spine, picked out the lines of the tattoo between his shoulder blades, his mother's name with angels' wings. Strength and vulnerability stretched out and waiting.

In that moment, the need to protect Tony from those ugly secrets was stronger than the urge to bury those sins inside him.

Tony shifted and looked around.

"You're here." Jack's mouth was dry.

"Yeah."

"Your car—"

"I had a few after my shift—during it too." Tony ran a hand across his face and then scratched his jaw. "Too many roadblocks. Took a cab. I'll get it tomorrow."

But you're here. Jack wanted to say it again, make it more real. He crossed to the bed and grabbed Tony's head, breath tight at the familiar crunch of gel under his palms as Jack held Tony for a kiss. He tasted sour with whatever he'd been drinking, but Jack didn't care. Tony was here. Jack kissed the taste away until it was only them, breathing steady and together. And despite feeling how pissed off Tony was, it was still there, that crackle between them, the sensation like a tongue on his skin just from being near him.

Tony's hand came up between them to fist in Jack's shirt and drag him the rest of the way onto the bed. "Don't think this means we're all right, because we're not."

"Okay." Jack could live with that. The fact that Tony was here meant that he wanted them to be all right again.

Releasing Jack, Tony propped his head on his elbow. "You were a total asshole to me today."

"I know. I'm sorry."

Tony grunted. "I'm still pissed."

"Want me to make it up to you?" Jack ran his hand over Tony's belly, thumb dipping below his navel.

Tony flopped back. "You know, if I really wanted a sugar daddy, I bet I could do way better than you."

"Sure. You could probably find someone with a live-in maid so you wouldn't have to do the laundry."

"Damned right."

As Jack leaned over him, his hand slid on slick paper. Picking himself back up, he looked at the pictures stuck to his hand.

The Howards always sent the school pictures, five by sevens, and a copy of their report card. Jack put them between the pages of an antique herbology he'd found at an estate sale.

"I went snooping," Tony said.

"Must have taken awhile." Jack sat on the edge of the bed, back to him.

"Not really. You're really neat, which made it easy." Tony sat next to him, holding the pictures. "They look sad." He put them into Jack's hands.

Jack tried to remember if it was cool to smile for the school picture when you were fourteen. Brandon looked serious. Despite her full smile, Sarah looked the way she had when she was in the hospital—like nothing was ever going to chase the fear from her eyes.

He stood and let the pictures fall to the floor. In three strides he had the bathroom door locked behind him. One more breath to turn on the water to cover the sounds and he spit up blood and bile into the toilet. There wasn't anything else to come up. He hadn't eaten since breakfast.

Tony banged on the door. Jack rinsed his mouth, wiped off some of the sweat from his face and neck. *How many lives are you going to ruin?* he asked the fuckup in the mirror. He should go out there and make some more digs about Tony just being with him for the money, find the one that hurt enough to make him leave for good.

Tony stopped slamming his hand on the wood. Jack's stomach tried to reverse its lining a few more times and then it gave up too. He washed his face again, and Tony yanked open the door, holding a butter knife.

Jack leaned over and flushed the toilet, then dropped the lid and sat on it.

"Now you're really scaring me." Tony flew through the door like he'd been shoved.

"You're the one holding the knife. Did you break the lock?"

"I just popped it. Wish I'd known about these when I was a kid." He looked down at the appropriated flatware. "Much easier to get the angle." Tony tossed the knife into the sink. "God. Don't distract me. You're too fucking good at that."

Jack could almost smile. Tony could almost always make him smile.

Tony looked around the bathroom, the shower, even the garden tub before he sat on the floor in front of Jack.

"What did you break in here to find? A manly suppression of tears or a suicide victim?"

"I don't know. I just had to get in here."

"So now what?" Jack leaned back against the tank, cool ceramic against the sweat on his skin.

"I wish to Christ I knew." Tony leaned against the wall, legs bracketing Jack's feet, and looked up. "You say you couldn't do it. Couldn't be a dad. I still think you're wrong, but I'll back off."

Jack looked down at Tony's comic-strip boxers. Superman charged right out of the fly.

"Jack?"

"You aren't telling me anything I didn't think of myself. I wanted to be there for them."

"You still can."

"No. They deserve a fresh start." He'd call Phil, tell him to forget about the meeting, and waive his rights. The kids would be better off without a reminder.

Chapter Ten

After a while Tony started to drift off. Ace made a hell of a kamikaze—easy on the lime juice, heavy on the liquor. The vodka made for a nice floating sensation until Jack nudged him with his toe.

"Hey. Last I checked there was a bed in the other room."

"Yeah. I'm beat." Feeling like he'd been through a war—and come out on the losing end—could do that. Christ, when Jack had shot up from the bed like that, face gone still and flat and cold, Tony had thought he'd lost more than the argument, he'd lost Jack. His imagination kicked into full gear and sent him sprinting for anything that would get that door open, brain showing him Jack with a razor to his wrist. The last time Tony had seen that expression on someone's face, the guy had downed two shots and gone out and drove into a tree doing seventy-five. The tree didn't make it either.

A glance at Jack's face showed a reassuring softness around his eyes and in the curve on his lips. Tony levered himself off the tiled floor with a hand on Jack's thigh. The warm hard muscle made Tony's breath come easier. They'd been sitting so long without Jack moving, Tony had convinced himself that Jack had turned to marble like some guy in one of those pre-CGI, stop-animation mythology movies.

Tony was on his feet, but Jack didn't move. The panic that had Tony digging for the butter knife prickled his skin again, lifting his hair better than Bed Head gel.

"You comin'?" Tony tried to keep his voice even, but it sounded hoarse.

"In a minute." When Tony still hesitated, Jack added, "I won't lock the door."

Tony believed him, he did, but he still took the knife and listened to make sure the lock didn't click. The kids' pictures stared up at him from the floor next to the bed. He picked up the boy first. The kid probably had his mom's coloring—the eyes and hair were much lighter than Jack's, not as blond as Tony's, but still blond. But the tilt to the kid's jaw and the eyes full of confident charm, that was Jack.

The girl had Jack's green eyes and dark wavy hair but she looked...breakable, like if the wind blew the wrong way she'd shatter. The tight-lipped smile didn't come anywhere near the wide, wary eyes. Her face looked so thin it seemed like her hair would pull her over with its weight.

He heard the water running again and put the pictures up on Jack's dresser—face down.

In bed, Jack didn't move much and Tony was careful with him, unwilling to touch and get a cold shoulder in return. In the morning, it was as if nothing had happened. Tony stumbled into the kitchen to find Jack shaved and dressed and sipping coffee while he scanned the screen of his laptop.

"Hey." Jack put his coffee down and ruffled Tony's hair before pulling him into a hug. "You look like shit."

"Yeah. Slept like shit, thanks for asking."

"You were snoring pretty good when I got up this morning."

Tony snorted and went off to pour out a bowl of cereal. He was glad Jack hadn't made him breakfast.

Jack delivered a news-and-weather report from the internet

as Tony slurped on his fruity sugar bombs.

"It's going to thunder later."

"Oh my, and the wash is on the line," Tony said.

"Yeah. That might be a little more believable if you didn't just throw a pack of new shorts in my drawer."

"New underwear is sexy."

"I need help with that now?"

"Same old thing in bed gets boring now that it's almost forty."

"That same old thing like the fact that a change in air pressure's enough to get you horny?"

"According to the weather report, you're in luck." Tony grinned and let the milk drip off his chin.

"I think I've lost interest."

"I can fix that." Tony started toward him when the doorbell rang. "I'll get it."

"You're not dressed."

Tony looked down at his Superman boxers. "All the more easy to get rid of whoever it is. Our garbage can probably rolled over the property line or something."

"Do not invite the Jehovah's Witnesses in and then stick your tongue down my throat again."

Tony was still laughing at the memory when he pulled open the door.

It wasn't a pissy neighbor or a Jehovah's Witness. It was a woman, blonde and pretty, tight trousers short enough to show tiny ankles above towering heels and a pale green sweater unbuttoned to show a bit of lace above her breasts.

She smiled with shining pink lips. "Hi. I'm looking for Jack Noble."

Tony barely had time to blink, to take a guess at her

identity, when she said, "Oh, you must be the boyfriend. Hello. I'm Patrice, the ex-wife."

Tony'd been in enough pissing contests to know what was going on. She probably figured Tony had no idea who she was—and if she'd stopped by yesterday, she'd have been right. Thank God he'd dragged the story out of Jack so he was able to smile right back.

"Oh, yeah. Jack's told me all about you."

"Really?" She looked put out, then smiled again. "Everything? He must have changed a lot."

"Guess so." Tony fixed his eyes on the tits she was trying so hard to show off. He stepped aside to let her in, then turned his head to yell, "Hey, babe, your ex-wife's here."

While they waited for Jack, Tony glanced past her to the Mercedes in the drive. It looked like it had just rolled off the lot. He thought about asking about the kids, but then remembered Jack said they were away at school. He sure as hell didn't want this woman figuring out Tony didn't know their names.

"Not even close to funny, Tony." Jack stepped into the foyer, and Tony actually got to see it for real. See a man turn to stone so fast the edges almost crumbled.

Saying *You look like you've seen a ghost* wouldn't have covered it. And Jack hadn't said that Patrice was dead.

"Hello, Jack. I'll bet you're surprised to see me."

"Patrice, what are you doing here?" Jack's voice was as brittle as it had been when he was talking about his dad. So maybe there were a lot more issues about this divorce than Jack had said. No surprise there.

"I just got home. It wasn't that hard to find you. I can't wait for the kids to come back from school. I've thought of going out to Massachusetts to see them."

A tight breath escaped through Jack's clenched jaw. "What

did your parents say?"

"They think I need to wait. They didn't want me to talk to you."

"I'll bet."

Tony might as well have not been in the room. "Do you guys want to sit down in the living room?"

"I don't think so," Jack said with another audible breath. Between the glare and the breathing, he reminded Tony of the Big Bad Wolf. One more huff and the house would blow down.

Maybe things wouldn't be as hard on Jack and his kids if he had a better relationship with his ex.

"You know. We were just heading out. But maybe you could stop by again another time," Tony offered.

Patrice's polite smile never wavered. Now she lowered her eyes to take in Tony's boxers. "Where were you going?"

Tony could always lie. "Water heater broke. Need a new one."

Patrice looked confused. "Why don't you just call someone?"

"We like to do it ourselves." The idea of either of them messing around with plumbing was funny—and horrifying. It would be a bad sitcom episode, probably one with giant soapsuds spilling out everywhere. He was about to add something about laying pipe when he remembered he wanted things to get better between Jack and his ex.

Patrice seemed to give up on understanding Tony and turned to Jack. "We have so much we need to talk about. Maybe your boyfriend could go get the water-heater thing, and then we could talk."

Tony wasn't about to be sent to his room by Soccer Mom Barbie. "His boyfriend—"

Jack cut in. “Patrice, I really don’t think there’s anything for us to talk about.”

Patrice’s gaze flicked to Tony and then slid away like he was something she’d found underneath her shoe. “But, Jack, things—everything is much better now. I understand about...you and—”

“Where are you staying?” Despite her soft pleading tone, Jack’s voice was harder than Tony had ever heard it. He hoped he never heard it turned on him.

“With my parents, of course.” Patrice’s smile was back. “Why don’t you fly out to Boston with me. We’ll surprise Brandon and Sarah with a visit from us both.”

“Go home, Patrice. And tell Barbara and Phil to expect my call.”

Her lashes dropped over her blue eyes. She’d shifted from competition to an object of pity.

“Patrice.” The unfamiliar name slipped out easily—the rest of it followed too quickly for Tony to think about what he was saying. “We’d be happy to have the kids stay here, anytime. Even if you just wanted to bring them over for a quick visit that would be fine.”

“Tony. Shut up.” Jack’s voice was harsh but not cold.

Patrice laughed. “It’s good to know you haven’t changed at all. You have my sympathy—Tony, is it? I’m sure Jack’s unused to introductions. After all, when we were married, he didn’t bother to get names, right, honey?”

Tony hadn’t thought much about Jack’s marriage—not that he’d had much time to think about it. He probably had cheated. Tony knew if he’d been forced to marry a woman for whatever reason, he’d have been desperate for some dick on the side, but he hated that Jack’s silence, all these fucking secrets, made Tony feel sorry for Patrice. And after what Jack had said about his dad, the fucker, Tony should be more worried about his boyfriend than this life-sized piece of plastic.

Jack jerked open the door. "Patrice." He nodded at her car.

"I suppose I shouldn't be surprised. But you'll see. Things will be better. It was nice meeting you, Tony." Patrice flashed a blindingly white smile.

Jack held onto the door after she went through, leaving it open, but blocking the space with his body.

Tony knew better than to try to talk to him, but he couldn't help himself. "Jack."

Jack kept staring through the door as the lights of the Mercedes flashed once before the car backed out of their driveway. When the car had disappeared down Vander Drive, he said, "I've got to go."

Tony put a hand on Jack's arm. "Okay. Where?"

Jack flung him off and turned around. "You said you were going to back off. So back off."

If Jack's voice had been as tight and thin as it had been when he spoke to Patrice, Tony would have just cursed him out and not waited to pack before hitting the door. The heat in Jack's voice, the empty desperation in his eyes, made Tony calm enough to take a step away and say, "Fine. How far back do you want me to go?"

The Jack Tony had been half in love with since the minute Jack pressed him up against the sink in the upstairs bathroom at Sean and Kyle's, disappeared into statue-Jack again, though this time Tony could have sworn he was an ice sculpture for a really fancy party.

An ice sculpture that had been to Walt Disney's workshop and could move. It was like seeing something in a comic book spring to life. Every motion precise and rigid, Jack picked his keys from the bowl near the door.

Before he went out, he gave Tony the answer he'd been dreading since he found himself alone in the seasonal display at Bed, Bath & Beyond.

"Unless you're dumber than you pretend to be, you'll back pretty fucking far away from this house."

Chapter Eleven

No matter how active Tony's fantasy life might be, there was only one way to take Jack's words. At least there wasn't much to pack. His vintage concert T-shirts, some CDs and DVDs, a few comic books, his Christmas-gift computer—which he was not too proud to keep, thank you—and the rest of his clothes. Big surprise. The house and everything in it was all Jack.

Tony had never had a reason to own luggage, so he was carrying two recyclable grocery bags out the front door when he realized his Rabbit was still parked downtown.

"Motherfuck!" He dropped the bags in the driveway and then kicked one. It wasn't all that satisfying. They were full of dirty clothes and didn't do anything but roll and spill. He was scooping up the laundry when a familiar blue Durango pulled into the drive. As soon as he heard the locks click open, he yanked open the back door and threw his stuff in.

"This is all your fault, fuck you very much," he said into Kyle's shocked face then turned and stomped into the house.

Sean and Kyle followed him all the way into the kitchen and exchanged another one of those looks that had Tony thinking about smashing something—of Jack's—over their heads.

Sean leaned against the center island. "That conversation

didn't go well, huh?"

With the amount of steam making Tony's skull a ramekin for a brain soufflé, it took him a minute to backtrack. Conversation, Sean and Kyle's advice, oh yeah. Back when all this was still fixable. "You think? What the fuck are you doing here anyway? Don't you have jobs?"

"It's Saturday. You came over last Sunday on some kind of freak out. We wanted to check up on you."

"Maybe you could try the phone." Tony had never needed friends more, and since he'd planned to schmooze a place to stay until he found another apartment, he should really dial it back, but they'd interrupted him mid tantrum and someone needed to hear it. Besides, it really was all their fault, for introducing them, and for making him think that two guys really could get that whole happy-ever-after shit. He'd known better. And they'd had to go and set this stupid example.

He fucking wished he could afford a hotel.

Sean plucked Tony's phone from the counter where Tony had dropped it this morning, when he and Jack were pretending nothing weird was going on. Sean waved the phone in his face to show two voice mails and a text. "Maybe you could try turning your phone on."

"Sorry. I was busy packing my life up."

"What happened?" Kyle looked up at Tony through those long dark lashes. No wonder Sean was so fucked.

"What didn't?" Tony folded his forearms on the counter and then let his head thud against them. "My life is a fucking Spanish soap opera. Seriously. Because I still don't understand what's going on. Want to maybe translate for me, man?" He lifted his head.

Kyle hitched his cute ass up onto a barstool, and Sean leaned over from the other side. Tony let out a deep breath.

Yeah. He did need his friends. Sean ran his hand through Tony's hair once, then smacked him.

"Diva moment over. Talk."

It wasn't really Tony's story to tell, but tossing him out had punched Jack's ticket to Gossipville. Tony gave them both the play-by-play and the color commentary right up to Jack telling him to back the hell out of the house—no, wait—the fuck out of the house.

"So you're leaving?" Kyle asked.

"I'm packing."

"But are you leaving?" Sean said.

Fucking double teamed. Maybe he liked them better when they weren't speaking to each other. Of course if there was a better way to be double teamed... The fantasy evaporated when Tony realized he and Sean would be arguing over who was going to drive.

Tony shook his head to clear it. "I don't want to. He may be a secretive fucking asshole, but..." Tony couldn't finish it. He didn't have to. They knew.

"Yeah," Sean said, giving Kyle another one of those looks.

"There's more to this than what I've been able to drag out of him."

"Have you snooped around? Checked his email and stuff?" Kyle asked.

Sean gaped at his boyfriend. "You sneaky bastard."

"Just so you know, you should be careful. Your passwords are way too easy to figure out." Kyle grinned.

"Excuse me." Tony flung his arms across the counter. "Your window of opportunity for drama has closed. This is about my shit now, thank you."

"Yes, your highness." Sean bowed. "We'll figure it out."

Chapter Twelve

When Jack called the lawyer and told him it was an emergency, Steve agreed to see him at home. His home office looked like the one in the Queen Anne, a fort made up of thick legal-sized folders. He flipped through the papers Jack had handed him. Jack was impressed at the lawyer's game face. No outward display of shock as Jack filled him in.

"The case should be open and shut, your sexuality notwithstanding. These funds show that you have been financially involved in child support throughout the time you were separated from your children. With the mother unfit, I don't think the grandparents' case will be particularly strong. There was never a court order; you never waived your parental rights. A private arrangement of temporary guardianship should be no trouble to reverse."

"You've only had to deal with them when they're getting what they want."

"What they want and what they're legally entitled to are two different things. Don't worry about it, Jack. Your kids should be home with you in a few weeks."

Weeks. Five weeks until they left school. Enough time to make sure they didn't have to see Patrice?

"Put as much of a rush into it as you can."

Steve might think that the Howards wouldn't put up a

fight, but Jack knew better. In family court, records were sealed and names were protected. Jack needed backup—a nuclear arsenal full of backup. Someone with a finger on the button to be sure the Howards couldn't fight back.

He flipped his phone open as soon as he left the lawyer's office. Just when he thought it would go to voice mail, Sean answered with a curt, "Yeah."

"I need the number of the guy who did your PR after the shooting. Brandt someone."

"And?"

Sean didn't sound very helpful. Acid got busy burning through Jack's stomach again. He reached into his pocket for the over-the-counter stuff he'd picked up on the way to the lawyer's. "Can I have it?"

"No." Sean hung up.

Tony hadn't wasted much time. Not that Jack had given him reason to. And it's not like Tony had any other place to go.

Jack dry-swallowed the pill capsule and punched his speed dial to call Tony.

"What?"

Who knew one word could carry so much hurt? "I need you to get the number for that PR guy from Sean. Remember? The one who was at the Super Bowl party."

"Out shopping for something pretty already?" Tony had a nasty sneer in his voice.

"C'mon, Tony, you know that's not it."

"Well, I'm busy backing the fuck away. Try 411."

"I need that number."

"Really? Because you know what I need? A fucking explanation."

The burn knifed through his chest, stealing his breath. If

hadn't lived through the whole ulcer mess six years ago, he'd e sworn he was having a heart attack. He spread his hand out across his abdomen, like that would stop it. "It's for my kids. I need it for my kids."

"The kids you haven't seen since February?"

He hated the idea of telling him, wanted Tony far away when all the shit hit the fan, but if the truth was what it took, Jack could do it. He'd swallow his pride—swallow acid—if it would keep Patrice from getting near his kids again.

"Meet me at the house. I'll tell you what's going on."

"Honestly, I don't think I'll believe anything you say."

"Will you be there?"

"Three o'clock." Tony hung up.

Three hours. He could drive out to Marblehead—if the Howards were there—but he'd rather wait to see them until he had his finger on the button, an assurance of orchestrated public exposure should be enough to get them to back off. Steve might think the court system would prefer a gay dad to a psychotic mom, but Jack lived in the real world.

A flare of heat tore at his chest again and he pressed his palm hard against his sternum. Maybe he had time to get a better prescription from the doctor. The most obvious cure "Cut back on your stress" wasn't an option. Jack's stomach had been functioning as an advance-warning alarm since he could remember. He killed the three hours driving aimlessly around.

Tony's car was in the driveway, but Jack couldn't find him. The house was silent, clean, perfect. Jack had half expected Tony to leave like a tornado, but that wasn't him. Passive aggressive wasn't Tony's style. He was more of a "fuck you" to your face kind of guy.

Jack was about to start looking upstairs when he saw the note on the counter. *In shed.*

The only shed was a four-by-eight storage shed near the back fence, though why Tony would be in it Jack couldn't imagine. When he pulled on the door latch the sweet smell poured out the reason. Tony sat in a lawn chair wedged next to an extra fence section, flicking a lighter.

"Are you high?"

Tony flicked the lighter again and stared at the flame for a few seconds. "Not nearly enough."

"For Christ's sake, Tony."

"See, if I really was high, I couldn't read this." Tony pulled a folded paper out of his pocket. "Woman Drives Self, Kids, Into Lake—Patrice Noble, 31, drove a vehicle down a boat launch into Lake Erie at 1 p.m. yesterday."

It had been January twelfth. So cold that Sarah had been unconscious from the minute they went in. If Brandon hadn't pulled his sister out, it would have been too late. Jack hadn't been there, but his subconscious had no trouble providing him with the details. For the last four and a half years, Jack never went more than a week without the dream. Frightened faces against the back window, hands beating against the glass, screaming for him to save them while the freezing water swallowed the car. And he just watched. Ice water pumping from his heart to lock his feet to the ground, skin frosting as he reached for them.

Tony read on. "The driver of a car witnessed the event and alerted authorities. Two bystanders risked hypothermia to aid in the rescue. Harrison Manfield, one of the bystanders, reported that Noble appeared calm and rational as she unlatched her seat belt. The two children, ages 10 and 7, were treated and released at the hospital. According to police reports, Noble is under a physician's care and medication may have affected her judgment. Charges are pending." Tony looked up. "Wow. You'd think they could have spent at least two sentences on your kids."

The Howards, with the PR resources to make the Exxon Valdez look like a leaky gas tank, had managed to keep it buried to the local section of the Sandusky and Toledo papers. Neither Chicago or Cleveland or the wire service had picked it up.

"Of course, you didn't waste much time on your kids either. Tell me you didn't just leave them with her while you went off to—"

"To what? Fuck tons of guys? You heard Patrice. I was already doing that." Tony was almost making this too easy, asking all the wrong questions.

"Where the hell are your kids, Jack?"

"In school. Like I told you. Their grandparents—Patrice's parents—asked for custody and I gave it to them. They go to school in Massachusetts and summer camp in Pennsylvania."

"And visit their mom in jail. Oh, wait. She's out now. What do you get for attempted murder these days? Seven years with time off for good behavior?"

"They didn't see her. And she didn't go to jail. Last I heard she was in a secure treatment facility."

"Facility—oh, nice. Crazy plus therapy gets you off. Who the hell are these grandparents? Politicians?"

"Howards." A laser cut deep behind Jack's chest. Pot was good for pain. What would Tony do if Jack unfolded another chair and asked Tony to help him blow the whole thing away in a cloud of sweet smoke? "What's on your cereal box?" Jack asked instead.

"Fruity Jewels? A treasure box and a parrot wearing an eyepatch." Tony looked confused. "Which of us is stoned here?"

"No, the company name."

Tony squinted as if he was looking at the box in front of

him. "The fat little bakery guy? Howard?" However much he'd smoked slowed him down enough that Jack could watch the understanding break across his face in a stunned wave. "The cereal company Howard? Your in-laws?"

"Former."

"Holy shit." Tony chewed on that with about the same grace he used to slurp up Fruity Jewels. "Holy fucking shit. So what, they bought the kids from you?"

Guilt slammed Jack so hard his knees buckled, and he leaned against the pile of fencing. "No."

"Then what? How the fuck could you leave them after that? They needed you. They needed their dad."

"They didn't want me. In the hospital after or any time I tried to see them. It was all my fault, and they knew it."

"How? Did you drive them into the lake?"

Jack turned his head until he couldn't see Tony anymore and watched a spider swing between two of the roughened slats that made up the shed walls. Free from the transparent disgust all over Tony's face, Jack told him the whole story.

"I didn't tell Patrice I was gay when I asked for the separation. I just told her that the marriage wasn't working for me. I knew she saw a therapist, all her friends and cousins did. I didn't know why." The spider swung back, leaving a thread behind him. Neat. Precise. Perfect on the first try. "I worked eighty-hour weeks at the restaurant I ran then. I was gone more than I was home, so I didn't think moving out would matter that much."

The lawn chair clacked as Tony moved. Jack willed Tony to stay away. If he touched him, if he looked at Jack with those blue eyes full of the same pity they'd held when Jack told him about his father, Jack didn't know if he'd deck him or let himself drown in undeserved comfort. Either way, Jack would stop talking, and he had to get this out.

Funny. He'd have sworn a day ago that he'd never tell this to anyone and now the words came faster and faster.

"I did the weekend-dad thing, the few hours in the morning on weekends I could spare from work, managed to make an appearance at a few school things. The kids didn't seem much different, but I was never around them all that much anyway."

Tony's sneaker scraped against the concrete floor. Jack pulled himself closer to the wall. "Don't." He took a breath. "A few months after I moved out, I had the kids. Patrice was early picking them up. She said she needed to talk to me. While the kids were engrossed in some video game, she pulled me into my bedroom. I didn't think anything of it until she started to kiss me. She said she understood and that things would be better now, that she could be what I needed. And then she pulled off her clothes and she was in some lacy gartered set. I should have felt something. I mean, I managed to for ten years. But there was nothing. And she knew it. She got this look on her face—"

"I think I know how she felt."

"No you don't." Jack turned and found himself exactly where he couldn't be, staring into Tony's face. No grin there now. Narrowed eyes and tight lips when he should be bursting with giggles and the profoundly inane pronouncements of the stoned. Jack had never meant for this to spill into his life with Tony.

Fighting the need to cup Tony's head and kiss away the guarded look in his eyes, Jack said, "I know I've been..." he swallowed, "...lying to you, but it's never been like that. Never." He had to finish this now. "She was crying and I wanted her to know she hadn't done something wrong so I told her. She calmed down and said it explained a lot. She left with the kids and the next thing I know the cops are at the restaurant, and my kids are in the hospital.

"I saw her once after. I asked her why. 'You didn't need us anymore, Jack. I told Brandon and Sarah that too, so they'd understand.' I may not have driven the car, but I pushed it." His legs didn't work anymore, so he slid down to the floor.

Tony squatted next to him. "Why didn't you tell me all this before?"

Jack hated every word full of soft sympathy. "And interrupt your endless party?" He waved a hand like there was still smoke in the air.

That knocked Tony back a little, but the stubborn shit kept going. "You didn't have to give up your kids."

Anger put the strength back in Jack's legs. He shot to his feet. "You don't know shit about it. You have no idea what it's like to fail that way. To know what your decision cost them." Their hands, little fists against the window, Sarah's no bigger than Jack's thumb. Brandon, only ten and already more of a parent than Jack would ever be. His own father may have been a sadistic monster, but at least he'd been there.

"Don't take this out on me, asshole." Tony stood and faced him.

"Not so understanding now? Good. I got all the understanding shit I could take from her. You really want to know why I never told you? Because you couldn't understand. You live your whole life around zero expectations. No career, no responsibilities, no decisions. Just Tony out for a good time. How the fuck could you possibly know anything about what I've had to do?"

"You could have given me a chance."

"I did. Sorry for interrupting your perpetual adolescence. I told you when you moved in not to smoke in the house or in my car."

"Yes, Da—" The word cut off as Tony's mouth shut with an audible click. "It's not the house." But his words didn't have much force and neither did his argument.

Jack turned so that he could rub a fist into his chest where Tony wouldn't see. "Tell yourself whatever story you need to, but move out."

Chapter Thirteen

Tony flicked his lighter again and squinted through the flame. Jack hadn't latched the door, so there was a good bit of daylight peeking through. It had to be close to a record breaker. How many guys got tossed out twice on the same day by the same boyfriend? Tony figured he'd go all out for one more. He'd never been able to stop himself from picking scabs no matter how many times his mom smacked his hand.

But when he made it into the house, Jack was already gone—off to work to take control of his little kingdom. Tony flipped open his phone. The tinny echo of the X3's Bluetooth couldn't hide the exasperation in Jack's "Yes?"

"What are you going to do about your kids now? You're not going to let her raise them?"

A funny gasped breath whooshed over the airwaves. "No. That's where I went this morning. I've got a lawyer petitioning for custody right now."

"Good."

"So you can see why I don't have room for a pot-smoking boyfriend."

"I'm sorry about that." But it was true. Child Services freaked about little things like illegal drugs and big things like gay lovers. Maybe if Tony were more like Sean or Kyle, tie-wearing and with a real job, it would be different, but a tattooed bartender wasn't likely to make much of an impression on a social worker.

"Yeah. So I guess that's why you needed PR guy's number. Gonna launch a counterattack."

"Something like that."

"Sean gave me the info but said you'd better be willing to pay the guy."

"I know." The quieter voice, the absence of background noise, meant Jack was parked at the restaurant.

"I'll call back, but don't pick up. I'll leave it on your voice mail."

"Thank you." Jack's didn't sound all that grateful. And Tony sure as fuck knew what gratitude sounded like in Jack's voice.

But he still didn't want to hang up the phone. "I'll be at Sean and Kyle's until I find a place. If you need anything—for the kids I mean—"

"Okay." Jack sounded impatient now, like Tony was something that needed to be crossed off his to-do list.

Fuck him. "Bye, Jack."

"Bye, Tony."

Jack switched the phone to vibrate as soon as it clicked off. He couldn't handle the blast of Warrant's "Cherry Pie" when Tony called back, didn't need the extra reminder of what he'd just thrown away. The phone buzzed in Jack's palm, and he wrapped his fingers around it, squeezing until he felt the plastic shift and grate.

There must have been more smoke left in the shed than he'd thought because he had the strangest idea that if he could swallow the phone with Tony's message, it would plug the hole acid was tearing in his gut. He put them both in his pocket and went to work.

He called Brandt first thing Monday morning, and by Tuesday afternoon Jack was spending more time on the phone than he did overseeing the prep work in the kitchen. Several shots had been fired back and forth between the enemy camps. Brandt had a couple of interviews lined up if they had to go with the nuclear option, and Steve was a lot less laid-back when it came to filing briefs. Sitting on the sidelines as his future played out in a volley of phone calls, emails and legal notices, Jack could see that Brandt and Steve enjoyed the fight. Easy for them. It wasn't their life—their kids' lives—on the line.

Brandon and Sarah got even less say in things. As far as Jack knew, they hadn't been told anything. Not about their mother's release or their father's petition. The thought of seeing them, of facing down that too-adult look in his son's eyes, scared Jack more than all his nightmares combined, but there was no way he was leaving them where Patrice could get at them. The doctors might think she was better, but Jack had seen her. Now that he knew what she was capable of, he could see right through her delusions. Somehow she thought that this would end with them settling down in Marblehead again, one big miserable family.

Just before the restaurant opened on Wednesday, Jack's phone buzzed against his hip. After asking Brandt to hold on a second, Jack went out the back door and glared at a busboy until he tapped his cigarette out against his shoe and went back inside.

Brandt might be good at his job, but he didn't do direct. It took all of Jack's patience to wade through Brandt's self-congratulatory pleasantries before getting to the point. "I got a nice package from the Howards today. Pictures of you. Do you make a habit of making out with feathered drag queens?"

"Shit. Call it a lost Pride weekend."

"We can call it whatever you want, but it's not good for the case."

Had the Howards been following him or was it just his luck to end up in some article somewhere? "It was five years ago."

"I know. And I think we can counter it easily. You're settled now, in a committed relationship."

Or not. "I thought with the laws in Ohio it would be better if—"

"The boyfriend's not trying to adopt the kids, and it's not a marriage thing. This is about a stable home life with two responsible adults."

Jack wanted to laugh but he couldn't. Not with the acid oozing up from his stomach. "Did you talk to Steve about this?"

"That's my next call. Look, they're going to know about your boyfriend anyway. We should manage it as an asset. Clean him up some. It'll work. And don't pose for any more pictures."

Jack checked his pockets, but he was out of pills. A doctor visit was more than he could manage right now. He could always swallow baking soda.

"Jack, trust me. You're going to win this. If not on the first round, after I get through with them, they'll beg to hand the kids over. Piece of cake. All you need to do is buy your boyfriend a suit."

Jack flipped the phone shut. Nope. No problem. Should he start out on his knees or crawl on his belly right away? Maybe he could hire a boyfriend instead. Someone who came without tattoos and piercings and read *The Wall Street Journal* instead of *People*. Someone who didn't make it impossible to eat a filled donut that didn't have a thumb hole in it to check the filling. Someone who was all grown up and boring as hell.

Chapter Fourteen

Tony clicked through a page of online apartment listings, counted the number where the deposit wasn't more than he had in his checking account and came up with zero. Facebook was a lot more fun. Maybe he could design an apartment game for Facebook and rake in the bucks. Of course, that would require more computer skills than knowing how to type out the dashes and symbols to make an image of a monkey swinging from a branch.

He hadn't exactly been planning on being homeless. Jack was always so quiet, so hard to piss off that Tony had figured even if things cooled off between them, Jack would give him time to find someplace to live. He couldn't stay here for long. Sean and Kyle's codependent lovefest drove him nuts.

When the doorbell rang, Tony considered the Terminator movie, hot evangelists and crazy ex-wives before settling on package delivery. It wasn't that hot out, but maybe the delivery guy was in shorts anyway. His brain was just settling on a little scripted porn where he admired the delivery guy's package when he remembered the door automatically locked and he had to screw with the knob for a second.

Standing on the front step with his hands in his back pockets, Jack looked way too good for a heartless, lying bastard. Tony walked away from the door and heard Jack shut it behind them. Tony could spin a lot of fantasies, but he couldn't buy one where Jack came begging less than a week after he'd kicked him out.

He turned into the living room and shut the laptop before dropping onto the couch. The TV he left blaring on Cartoon Network. Jack looked around for a minute, found the remote and clicked the TV off.

"What?" In the sudden quiet, Tony's voice sounded shaky. This was fucked. Friends with benefits was totally the way to go from now on. No mess. No thinking you'd found someone who mattered—or someone you mattered to.

Jack moved closer, hands flying free in some kind of aborted motion, and then he tucked them back at his sides and sat on the recliner, leaning forward.

Tony leaned back.

"My lawyer thinks he can get us on the docket by the end of the month."

The custody thing. Good. But why would Jack be telling Tony any of it? He didn't want to be friends. Couldn't look at the guy without thinking of how good it felt inside him, how hard Jack shook when he came, hearing the soft, deep huff of an I-love-you against sweaty skin.

It didn't add up for Jack to be here looking sexy as hell and catching Tony up on life like they were old buddies.

"And the PR guy says he can squeeze the Howards so they won't fight me on it," Jack went on.

"Great. Good for you." Tony crossed his legs, ankle to knee, and began swinging a bare foot.

Jack watched his foot and then stared at Tony until he met his gaze straight on. "The thing is, Brandt thinks it looks better if I'm in a committed relationship. So I want you to move back in."

Tony came up off the couch. "You've got to be fucking

kidding me."

"You said if I needed something for the kids—"

"I know what I said. I meant it. I got you that fucking number, but you can't— Jesus, I'm not a fucking Ken doll."

"I know."

"Do you? Do you actually feel anything? You want to use me as a garnish on some perfect family plate you're serving to the judge."

"No."

"Yes. Tell me you didn't just say you want me to move back because the PR guy thinks it would look good."

"I did. I know this is all screwed up—"

Tony couldn't stop the snort of laughter. This was screwed up. Not *I* screwed up, but *this*. How fucking convenient.

Jack glared. "That's why I don't talk to you. You don't take anything seriously."

"Then maybe you should find a boyfriend on Craigslist or something. Hire someone to be picture perfect."

"Believe me, I thought about it." As soon as the words left his mouth, Jack looked so surprised Tony had to fight off another laugh. Jack didn't say stuff he didn't think out first—except maybe when he had a dick up his ass.

Tony dropped back onto the couch. "I get why you were freaked about the pot. Sean ripped me a new one when I told him. Said he wouldn't give me time to pack if I did it here, just throw my shit on the street. He could lose his teaching license. So with the custody thing, I get it."

Jack sat next to him, just far enough away that they couldn't touch unless someone did something deliberate. "It's not just that. This whole thing could get ugly, no matter what the Howards decide to do. You might like the shed better."

"I could get a sweet setup in there. Hang a hammock, run cable out."

"Gee, it would be like a tree house. You could have a no-girls-allowed club."

Tony pushed off the couch again. "You brought it up. Since I'm so fucking immature, let me know how that hiring someone works out for you."

Jack hunched, head falling into his hands, and he squeezed his head like he was afraid it was going to burst open. Tony didn't blame him. His head felt a little loose too, and he hadn't had anything since Jack tossed him, not even one of Sean's Xanax.

"I can't think of a single fucking reason why you would come home with me." Jack lifted his head and met Tony's gaze. His voice dropped to a whisper. "But I don't know if I can do this alone."

That hoarse whisper wrapped around Tony's spine, took control of his nervous system until he was walking to the couch. Jack didn't ask for help. Ever. Tony couldn't resist the plea or the hollow look in Jack's eyes. Straddling Jack's lap, Tony rested his hands on those solid shoulders, rubbed the tense muscles.

"Not one reason?"

Jack put his hands over Tony's but wouldn't meet his gaze. "Not even that one. Not with kids in the house."

That wasn't what Tony had meant. Not that sex wasn't really fucking important. And enough to distract him again. "Wait. You're saying you're not going to have sex anymore because the kids are moving in with you?"

"While they're there, yeah. But if I had to, I would. They already almost died once because of it."

"Because of sex?" Tony pulled his hands away and rested

them on his thighs.

"Because of me being gay."

"No. They almost died because your ex-wife is a fucking fruitcake."

Jack smiled, but this Jack, new Jack, was one seriously fucked-up man. Tony wasn't sure he could be the levelheaded one, the one who made rational adult decisions and kept Jack from turning into Robodad. Who was he kidding? Tony knew damned well he couldn't do it. Jack would be better off hiring someone, or going it alone. He should do the easy thing, the sane thing. Bail.

He shut his eyes and tried to find a non-asshole way to say it. *I'm not sure I can handle this*—too wimpy. *This is too fucked up for me, Jack*—too blunt.

Jack's thumb pressed against the knob at the base of Tony's neck, rubbing tingling warmth down his spine. He did it so often Tony wasn't sure Jack always knew he was doing it, like the bump there was a worry bead for Jack to rub when he got stressed. It made Tony want to purr like a cat. Nothing sexual about it, just a touch they both needed.

The first time Jack had done it was after blowing Tony in the bathroom upstairs at Sean and Kyle's barbeque. Jack had jerked himself off at the same time, and when he stood up he'd put his salty thumb in Tony's mouth. Keeping Tony pressed up against the sink, Jack had replaced his thumb with his tongue, filling Tony with the taste of them together as that wet thumb rubbed the back of his neck.

"You want to go back upstairs? Start over?"

Tony had given up trying to figure out how Jack read his mind, but doing that neck thing didn't mean everything was peachy keen again. "And this time after we'd hooked up a few times you'd tell me you were married once. And then after you ask me to move in you might let something slide like 'By the way, I don't have custody of my kids because their mom tried to kill them because I'm gay and I blame myself.'"

Jack's lips pressed together and his hand slipped down Tony's back. "I can't fix it. And I can't say I would have done anything differently. Maybe if you didn't turn everything into a joke, I might try to have a serious conversation with you."

"Well, maybe if you weren't such a tight-assed control freak, I wouldn't have to."

When Sean and Kyle had said talk to him, was this what they meant? Dump all the shit you'd been saving for a nice pity party one day? It didn't seem to be working.

They just looked at each other.

"Fine," Jack said.

"Fine?"

"I'm a prick and you're an asshole. Perfect match," Jack said without inflection, but Tony was pretty sure he saw the smile hiding in Jack's eyes.

Tony didn't know when his escape hatch had sealed up on him, but all the pods had left the ship. He was going down with it now. "Well, I'm glad we got that taken care of. So what, we're just going to stay together for the kids?"

"Tony." Jack shoved him off.

"I was serious."

"I don't know. If that's what you want—I just want them safe. If I'd thought there was a chance Patrice would get to them, I'd never have agreed to the custody arrangement. The Howards were rushing me to sign over my parental rights because they knew Patrice would be coming home. They knew I'd fight them then."

"Do they ever get a say? Has anyone asked them about this?"

"Being with their grandparents was what they wanted. Brandon couldn't stand to be in the same room with me."

Brandon. Tony attached that name to the blond boy with Jack's chin. "And your daughter?"

"Sarah had nightmares. But her grandmother told me she got over them."

The idea that all Jack knew of his kids was a third-hand account from some psycho's mom—who'd raised the psycho in the first place— "Jesus."

"So after things are settled, I'm not expecting anything from you. I don't think this is what you had in mind when you talked about having a kid."

"Fuck that." Tony dug his knee into Jack's thigh. "I'm not pulling a disappearing act. If you want my help, I'm in all the way."

Jack's brows came together. For a gorgeous guy, it wasn't a good look. "What do you mean?"

"I mean, this isn't going to be for show. We do it together. Which means you actually have to tell me what the fuck is going on before I read it in a newspaper archive."

Jack shook his head. "And I thought you'd be easier than hiring someone."

Chapter Fifteen

Jack started the fresh batch of pesto whirring in the processor. He hoped it was enough to last them until delivery on Tuesday. The gallon of it oozing down the drain in the sink next to him had enough sand in it to qualify as Pesto Beach. As he sent the olive oil streaming in, someone tapped his shoulder. He looked up, ready to tear that someone's head off, but the sous chef who'd decided to skip washing the basil for the last batch still skulked at the other end of the kitchen.

Carlos, the maitre d', stepped back two paces. Jack wondered what his face looked like to get that reaction.

"There's a lady who insists on speaking with the chef. Says she has specific dietary requirements."

In other words, she was a picky eater. Jack couldn't send Ted, the sous chef who'd fucked up the pesto. He'd get an allergy wrong and they'd get sued.

Jack yanked Wendy away from her vegetable prep station and told her to finish the pesto. After washing his hands he went out front with Carlos. He hoped it wasn't some overindulgent parent with a kid who would only eat beige food.

But it wasn't. It was Barbara Howard, alone at a table with only her martini for company.

"Phil isn't here," she said before he could ask. "I needed to speak with you alone."

"We could meet—"

"Without lawyers. It won't take more than ten minutes."

Jack controlled a wince at the thought of how much disaster could be created in his kitchen in ten minutes, then nodded. He glanced at Carlos, who headed for the kitchen. Ted was enough of a dick to everyone that Carlos would know to keep an eye on him.

Barbara picked up her martini and swept through the lounge exit. She didn't stop until she reached her Mercedes and climbed in. Feeling like he was in a spy movie, Jack slid into the passenger seat. It wasn't muggy like it would be in June and the warm smell of leather filled the car.

She didn't say anything immediately, just sipped her martini. "Your bartender does an excellent job. Is it your...companion?"

Tony at The Royal Mile? Not in this lifetime. Belatedly, Jack realized it was Barbara's attempt at geniality. Not award-worthy, but she probably didn't get much practice.

"No. But I'll pass on the compliment."

She took a longer sip.

"You're an intelligent man, Jack. I'm sure you know why I'm here."

He had a feeling her words were intended to make him feel the exact opposite. "Not to discount your assessment, but I have no idea what you're talking about."

Barbara looked straight through the windshield. "Patrice has her father wrapped around her finger. He honestly thinks she can...function in this environment. It was he who pressed for her release and for your parental rights."

"Unless you're going to just give me custody that's not a lot of help."

"Whatever you may think of me, I want the children to be

safe."

"And you know they're not as long as your daughter is around."

She offered a shrug of concession so small it was almost subliminal and sipped more of her drink. "I think these may prove useful to you." With her free hand, she flipped open a compartment in the dashboard, took out a bunch of envelopes and handed them over, her eyes never leaving the windshield.

There was enough light in the parking lot to read the childish script on the first one, addressed to him at the Marblehead house, postmarked four years ago.

Tension shot through his fingers until the thick paper started to crumple in his hand. This was a violation of their agreement. In addition to permitting unlimited visitation, the Howards were required to forward any communication from the kids. He forced his fingers to relax and lowered the letters to his lap.

"Why?"

"At the time, I thought it might complicate things for the children. And it's not as if you expressed a great deal of interest in them."

Jack looked back down at the envelopes. One didn't have his name, just Dad above where someone else had printed the address. Acid raced from his stomach to his sinuses, burning behind his nose and eyes, choking off what he wanted to say.

"You thought it was for the best too, Jack. Or you wouldn't have signed the custody papers."

The kids wouldn't stay in the same room with him. Sarah screamed when he tried to take her home. He hadn't seen that he had much choice. An ingrained thank you died on his lips. *Thank you for keeping them from me? For making them think I've been ignoring their letters?*

Barbara finished her martini with a healthy swallow and handed him the glass. In this light, her blue eyes looked icy enough to power The Mile's walk-in freezer. "Good luck, Jack."

He kept a tight grip on the envelopes as he climbed out of the Mercedes then shuffled through them as he walked to the kitchen door with the martini glass tucked under his arm. Eight letters. One from Sarah, two from Brandon postmarked May and June of the first year. Another from Sarah the next June. Brandon's childish cursive matured into a tight, forceful print on the next two envelopes, November and December of the following years. Sarah again, the postmark matching her brother's and then January of this past year, three weeks before he'd seen them, silent and hard-eyed in Chicago at their grandparents' condo.

None of the envelopes had been opened.

He opened the November one from Brandon. *Dad,*—at least he was still Dad. *Grandma and Gramps say they are traveling and that me and Sarah*—a cross out—*Sarah and I need to stay at school for Christmas break. Can we*—crossed out—*Sarah wants to stay with you instead. We get out on December 21. Your son, Brandon. P.S. Do you have email? Gramps said he mailed you the other letters but that you might have moved.*

A thick crunch sounded under his arm as the stem of the martini glass cracked. He threw the cup as far as he could into the parking lot. The thin crinkle of glass didn't help, so he ground the stem to powder under his heel. But he still saw them, beating on the back window, screaming for him, heard Sarah's bone-numbing shriek as she suffered through a nightmare. And he'd left them again.

It hit without a warning this time, the burn, the spasm of muscles so strong it sent him to his knees to spit out the blood-tinged bile. His eyes watered as his stomach twisted again and again. If he could actually manage to start spitting out chunks of his guts, maybe he wouldn't be around long enough to fail them again.

And leave them with Patrice? Or the grandparents who were too busy to take them home at Christmas?

He stuffed the letters into the pocket of the shirt he wore under his whites and climbed to his feet. Christ, what was he going to tell Tony? Tony already thought he was a heartless asshole for leaving them with the Howards in the first place. Jack leaned against the dumpster to catch his breath and wiped his face with his sleeve.

Warm nights meant the dumpster gave off the steady smell of rot, but Jack stood there until the smell faded out of his awareness, heart pounding, head aching and throat burning. From the minute the dirt had hit his mother's coffin, he'd had a plan to be richer, better, more successful than his bastard father. Patrice and the kids, they'd been part of the plan, but even without them, he hadn't failed completely. He had a career, awards, the write-up in *Bon Appétit*, and then Tony.

Tony hadn't been part of any plan. But like rum sauce on bread pudding, once you had it, you couldn't imagine it any other way. For now, Tony was back in his house, in his bed, in his life. And no matter if the children hated the man who'd failed to be their father when then needed one, Jack would still see them safe, with a place to go other than school and summer camp. He'd bury the ulcer in pills, the kids would be safe, Tony would stay and The Royal Mile would make it into a Zagat's with thirty points. Yeah. Nice dream.

A burst of shouting was followed by the unmistakable sound of a fire extinguisher blasting chemical smoke, and he ran back into the kitchen.

Chapter Sixteen

Although Jack spent less than a hundredth of his time there, he had made sure his own kitchen was as far from the bright stainless steel of the restaurant's as it could get. He'd had the lighting done so it only focused on work stations and could be individually controlled. He usually left the one over the island on for Tony's three a.m. cereal fix, but at the moment it shone on Jack's fifth glass of Argentinean Malbec. With the rest of the kitchen in darkness, the wine looked like a giant garnet in a museum display case. It had taken four glasses before he could bring himself to read the rest of those letters, but a whole case of wine wouldn't dull the acid-etched image of Sarah's first letter: *Happy Father's Day. Sorry I cryd alot.* A shower of blue teardrops completed the letter.

Jack wanted to snap the base of the glass and drive the stem through Phillip Howard's black heart. He would have gone to get them, would have found a way to keep them together, wouldn't he? The idea of kids in his life during that first year of freedom was ludicrous. He'd been working ninety-hour weeks at Luc-Michel's in Chicago and when he wasn't at the restaurant, he'd had a dick up his ass, fucking away all those years of denial and lying—trying to fuck away the shame of being a worse father than Richard Noble could have dreamed of being.

Brandon's last letter forced a twisted smile to Jack's face. It was something his own fourteen-year-old self would have written, beginning with *I bet your stupid ass doesn't even read these letters.* Anger and hatred clear in every tightly printed letter, the pen cutting in so deep the back of the paper could be read by touch—if a blind person was interested in Brandon's graphic descriptions of the ways in which he hoped his father would die. That was good. Hate was good. Jack sure as hell knew hate could get you pretty far in life.

The front door opened, keys clattered onto a table. A pause as Tony listened for the TV, for a sign that Jack was still up. Sneakers thunked into the basket in the foyer and then socks whispered across the floor. In the heavy silence the sounds were familiar, warm in a way the bottle of Malbec hadn't been.

Exactly how long was he going to be able to hang on when this new life had become as much of a fake as the old one? Tony was here because he thought he had to be. No matter how much work Jack put into anything, nothing could stop it from going to shit. Tony's determination to help him through this would last about as long as it took to hear the truth from Brandon and Sarah or worse, see it printed in their faces. Jack was a failure. As a father. As a partner. As a man.

"Hey." Tony's greeting held a breath of surprise.

"Hey."

Tony lifted the wine out of the spotlight, took a swallow and put it back. "I'd ask why you were up, but I can see you're supporting Argentina's export economy again." He raised the bottle, checking the weight. "Whoa. What happened?"

"Barbara Howard came to see me."

"Your mother-in-law?"

"Ex." The word came out with more force than Jack had intended. For an instant, he wished he'd had a chance to meet Tony's mom. Except that she'd probably have seen through Jack right to the empty core of him. She'd have warned Tony away.

"And?" Tony prompted.

"She was surprisingly helpful. It turns out they've been violating our arrangement. We were supposed to have unlimited communication. They never passed on some letters the kids tried to mail me."

"See. You're their dad. They still want a dad. It's going to be fine." Tony opened the fridge, stared for a long time and then closed it. "But why'd she tell you that? Why not just drop the case?"

"As much as she might be aware of her daughter's faults, I don't think she's willing to rock the boat that much."

"The yacht, you mean." Tony flashed his grin.

"I'm sure Barbara is not without her own resources."

"You use really big words when you're drunk."

"I'm not drunk." He wouldn't have let himself drive anywhere, but he wasn't about to fall down either. He'd been able to type awhile ago. "I booked a flight to Boston."

"To see them, the kids?"

Jack nodded. The world nodded with him and his fingers tightened on the edge of the counter. Perhaps he was a little drunk.

"Two tickets, right?" Tony's chin tilted, showing the tattoo on his neck, the light catching the glint of the piercings lining the edge of his ear. At some point, Jack would have to ask him why he'd stopped at five.

The hallowed halls of the Academy at Lexington might never recover from a visit from Tony Gemetti. Jack took a perverse delight at picturing robed professors recoiling in horror. But for all he knew, tattoos and piercings were part of the kids' uniforms. He'd never bothered to visit the school before.

"Jack?" Despite the folded arms and tilted head, there was

an uncertainty in Tony's voice.

"Two tickets. We leave on Tuesday."

The smile Tony gave him wasn't anything like his usual grin. It was a shy kind of thing that Jack almost never saw. Maybe Tony was just as big a liar as he was.

"Did she give you the letters?"

Jack started to nod, but considering the last trip on the Fermented Grape Carousel, he decided to stick with words. "Yes."

"And what did they say?"

Jack had hidden them in his car. No way was he letting Tony get his hands on those.

"They wanted to see me."

Tony's smile vanished. Telling the truth sucked.

"Shit. What a bitch."

"If you're referring to their grandmother, she's the one who gave me the letters."

"Son of a bitch then. Jesus. Jack, I don't know what to say."

"I don't either. I don't know what I'm going to say when I see them either."

"Those people are seriously fucked up. No wonder they raised Miss Bat Shit Crazy. And—" Tony's jaw clicked shut.

Jack finished it for him. "And I left my son and daughter with them."

"I didn't—" Tony tried to lie, but he spun away and then came back, standing square in front of Jack, gaze level and steady. "What can I do?"

Since Tony moved back, they hadn't so much as slid a hand over each other as they passed in the bathroom doorway. Jack shouldn't have been surprised at how easy that was, should have known two people could share a bed and a house with a space as wide as the Grand Canyon between them. He'd been a master of it in his marriage. But he and Tony hadn't been able to keep their hands off each other since they met. Jack wondered if Tony was punishing him for being such a jerk.

The light made strange shadows on Tony's face. Jack wasn't sure what kind of an answer he'd get, but he was asking anyway. "You could fuck me."

The angry look faded as Tony reached for Jack's head. "I can do that."

Jack waited as Tony pulled them together, waited until Tony kissed him before letting out a breath and holding on tight. Tony slid his lips along Jack's, teased with the warm, wet tip of his tongue while his fingers went deep into Jack's hair. This time the breath came out of Jack on a sigh that loosened everything up in his chest.

Tony scraped his teeth along the edge of Jack's jaw, then kissed and licked down his neck and back up to his ear while Jack just stood there.

"You are such an idiot." Tony's breath was as warm as the laugh in his voice. "You honestly thought we weren't going to keep doing this?"

Jack hadn't really thought it all out, but he didn't know how everything fit together now.

"I always want to fuck you, Jack. Love the sounds you make. The face you make when I get in you. The way you squeeze my cock so tight."

As much as Jack liked Tony's filthy whispers in bed, he'd never quite managed to respond without feeling like an idiot, and all those fermented grapes weren't helping. "Yeah" was the best he could come up with. It was good enough for Tony because he shoved until the counter pressed into Jack's lower back. Tony's tongue slipped between his lips at the same time his hand slid into Jack's pants.

The wet thrust of his tongue kept matching the action of his hands. His fingers drifted down to lift Jack's balls as he licked around Jack's mouth. When Tony stepped back, Jack would have followed him, even if he didn't have his hand around the base of Jack's dick.

"Upstairs, c'mon." Tony grinned and tugged him forward.

They stopped to make out on the stairs. Tony a step above, hauling Jack up to meet his mouth while Jack squeezed the hard muscles in the arms around him, slipped his hand inside Tony's loose jeans to squeeze his ass. They were at a slow simmer, both of them just half hard. Sometimes it was better like this, blood thudding, arousal building so gradually Jack could feel each pulse lift his cock and balls.

Tony didn't seem inclined to wait much longer, though. As soon as Jack's pants hit the floor Tony was licking the tip of Jack's dick, wet and hot, soaking him before his lips eased down the shaft and back up. Another bob and lick and Jack had gone from turned on to diamond hard. His skin prickled everywhere, every inch aching for Tony's skin on him, mouth and hands and cock.

Tony lifted his head and pushed Jack onto the bed. Yanking his shirt over his head, Jack watched Tony drop his clothes. Tony was more lean than big, but still solid, abs tightening and shifting with his breathing. A dark red flush around his neck veed onto his chest like an ascot against his pale skin. Beautiful. Hot.

And his cock...

Tony had a wicked—if inappropriate—wit and a determined loyalty Jack never felt worthy of, but the first thing Jack had fallen for was that cock. He'd been in love with it from the minute he'd gone down on Tony in Sean and Kyle's bathroom. In love with every thick red inch as it slid across his tongue and into his throat like his mouth had been made for it. He dove for it now, lips gliding over the crown while his tongue lapped up Tony's smoky taste.

A hoarse grunt and Tony's hand came down heavy on Jack's head. No need to urge him, Jack could spend hours worshipping Tony's cock. The twisting vein, the spot under the head that made Tony buck his hips, the feel of his pulse against Jack's tongue. Letting the head slide on the back of his throat, he tightened his lips at the spot where the skin shifted color, right where he'd been cut, and Tony's thigh muscles shook under Jack's hands.

But Tony knew Jack too. Slipping a hand between them, Tony squeezed Jack's nipple, tugged and pinched until Jack was groaning around Tony's dick.

"God. Stop." Tony yanked on Jack's hair to get him to pull off.

With hands on Jack's shoulders, Tony flattened him on the bed and knelt between Jack's legs. That spit-wet cock was aimed right at his ass. No lube. No rubber. A rush of fear and want had Jack's legs tensing even as he opened them. He was fine with it. He'd already told Tony that. And however much going with only spit for lube would hurt, it could only distract him from some of the pain in his gut.

Tony rubbed his dick under Jack's balls, between them, then over his cock, spit and precome slick. Jack arched up as Tony worked the shafts together, skin dragging sweet and good, Tony's dick pulsing right next to his. When Jack locked his hand on Tony's hip, he got the look.

It wasn't a completely serious look, because that would have been strange on Tony's face. But the eyes were full of intent and focus above an open-mouthed grin that said *I'm gonna fuck the shit out of you and you're going to love it.* It hit Jack the same way every time he saw it. A hot rush of blood flooding from his ass to concentrate at the tip of his cock, setting a moan to burn in the back of his throat.

"C'mere." Jack grabbed the back of Tony's neck and pulled him down.

Tony grinned through the kiss and pressed the tip of his cock into Jack's balls again before driving it up along the shaft of his dick and sliding the rims together. Heat and hard, slick pressure. Jack had been insane to think he'd ever fit in that other life. That he could be happy with softness when he needed this, the shift and press of a cock against his, the smell of their sweat and come together. What had all that faking earned him? Two ruined lives—three because he had to count Patrice. And now he'd dragged Tony into it.

Tony brushed his mouth across Jack's neck before fixing on his nipple. The first tight suck, the first hint of teeth, shot electricity from nerves that had a direct line to Jack's dick. His balls tightened and he flung his head back.

"You like that, sweetheart?"

Like the look, *sweetheart* only happened in bed. Tony could use a pile of annoying substitutions for people's names—a litany ranging from dude to son—but somehow when it was just the two of them, Tony's hoarse whisper of *sweetheart* sent a good deep buzz in Jack's balls.

"You know I do."

Tony moved his mouth to the other nipple, his cock still gliding along Jack's as their hips worked together.

"Yeah, I do," Tony whispered against the wet skin and sucked again.

He was going to take his time and that was fine with Jack. The longer it lasted the farther away Tuesday was. If Tony would keep fucking him, he never had to find out what a shitty job Jack had done, how much he'd failed his kids. Every minute they stayed locked together he wouldn't have to think about that.

Tony eased back until his dick was riding the crease of Jack's ass and then he moved his mouth lower, tongue making a wet trail until he lapped at the head of Jack's cock. God, he hoped that was something Tony only did with Jack, because he couldn't imagine that the guys weren't lining up around the block for a guy who could manage to fuck them and give head at the same time.

Tony lapped around the head softly while the thick rim on his dick pulled and stretched Jack's hole.

"Shit." The word whistled out between his teeth.

Tony made a sound that might have been a growl or a laugh and drove his hips forward again and again, until Jack grunted, "Fuck me. C'mon."

Tony laughed then, scooting his hips back and diving for the nightstand.

Lube yes, but when Jack saw the package between Tony's teeth he said, "I told you, you don't need to."

"Yeah, I do." Tony tore open the condom and lubed his dick before rolling it down.

It was punishment for all the shit Jack had put him through. "I wouldn't lie about it."

Tony's eyes closed, his face gone tight and drawn. "We can talk about it later." He opened his eyes again and gave him the look. "When I'm not an inch from your ass. I'm not thinking too straight right now."

That was how Jack wanted them both, not thinking, but he knew Tony was being a dick about the condom as payback. When Tony touched him with a lubed finger, Jack rolled onto his stomach. Tony liked to watch his face, Jack wanted them bare.

"Okay." There was a little hurt laugh in Tony's voice that said he knew exactly what Jack was thinking.

But as much as Jack might have wanted him to, Tony didn't take it out on Jack's ass. His finger just rubbed the lube around and gently stretched the skin, pressing and retreating, until Jack lifted his hips and slammed back against Tony's hand.

"Okay." Tony's voice got more determined, and Jack felt the broad head of Tony's dick stretch his ass.

Tony eased past the stinging resistance, swiveled his hips and backed off. Jack didn't want it slow anymore; he wanted it hard and fast. Wanted it to hurt. Tony had a tight grip on Jack's hips, though, and they were going at his pace.

Tony pressed in again, shifted and then shoved into the balls, making the same sweet sound he made when he tucked into Jack at night looking for warmth. The sensation and the sound flooded Jack with a need that had him reaching back between their legs, gripping Tony's thigh to keep him tight and deep.

"Not going anywhere, sweetheart."

Maybe not now. But when Tony saw how much Jack had failed his kids, he'd be lucky if he could get him to stick around long enough for the hearing.

Tony started the quick hard slams Jack loved, the ones that made them both pant loud enough to be heard over the slap and thud of flesh together, the ones that shuddered through Jack, building a pressure that made him think he could come from nothing more than Tony's dick jerking in him like that. Tony put a hand on Jack's spine and pressed him down so that his hips tipped up higher. The cock inside him stabbed deeper, the thrusts a push and pull inside that made Jack's thighs shake. Tony did everything he knew Jack loved, lifting him so that he could play with his nipples, holding Jack up and fucking him with rolling hips that kept Tony deep but moving.

Tony reached for Jack's dick, and Jack slapped his hand away.

"Okay." Tony slowed and eased out. "Gonna turn over for me now?"

Jack flipped onto his back, feeling like an even-bigger idiot for having made a point out of it. The shame burned his gut as Tony slid back into him, because Tony had been right. It was better like this. Better with the way Jack's body opened for him, with the way Tony's fat cock rubbed all the right places inside, with Tony looking down at him, mouth slack but eyes focused.

Jack'd had sex with guys while he was married, and a lot of sex with a lot of guys afterward, but it was always better with Tony. Jack knew Tony too, knew how much he liked his neck and back rubbed. Jack used his thumbs from the base of his spine to the top and Tony arched up, driving so deep inside Jack felt him under his ribs, ass so perfectly full he thought it would make the pleasure explode from his cock.

"So good inside you."

"Yeah." Jack tightened his muscles around Tony's cock, a fast pulse, and Tony's eyes narrowed. "Feels good from here."

"Oh yeah." Tony dropped down for an open-mouthed kiss, tongue filling Jack's mouth with Tony's taste and texture, that combination that wasn't like anything else but was everything he loved.

As Tony started to move them together, Jack stroked him everywhere he could reach. The rigid muscles of Tony's arms supporting his weight, the sensitive edge of fuzzy hair at the nape of his neck, the big muscles of his back and his flexible spine as it moved in a wave to drive his hips and cock into Jack. And it would never be this good again. Couldn't be. So Jack had to make it last forever. He tightened his ass until Tony gasped and stopped.

"Okay?"

"Yeah."

Tony dropped down again, licking and sucking at Jack's nipples while fucking deep, slamming up so their bodies made that thick sound again. Jack felt his voice growing hoarse as he panted.

"Fuck me. Fuck me." He grabbed Tony's ass and urged him faster.

Tony started those quick thrusts again, and the rush of pleasure built in Jack's balls. Lifting his head from another long kiss, Tony said, "Love making you look like that."

Jack loved Tony making him feel like that, but he couldn't answer him with anything but the pulse of his muscles and the squeeze of his hands.

Tony fucked faster, his head dropping onto Jack's shoulder and groaning so loud Jack thought Tony had come, but he just caught his breath and pushed up again, grabbing Jack's shoulders and holding him against the force of his thrusts.

"You close?" Tony asked.

Jack didn't want to be, but he would if Tony kept that up. In answer, he dragged Tony down for another kiss, another rub of his neck and spine before tracing the tattooed wings on his shoulder blades from memory.

Tony's weight shifted, and Jack hiked his legs up higher. Tony ran his hands down Jack's chest, got a good squeeze on his pecs, rubbing the nipples over his palms as he moved the muscles and skin back and forth.

A sharp spike of heat in Jack's balls and he threw out his hand to stop Tony's motion. "Stop."

"Okay." Tony gave him that open-mouthed grin. "I can go longer. I'll fuck you stupid, sweetheart." He started that slow undulation of his spine, fingers lightly flicking Jack's nipples. "Why don't you get a tit pierced?"

"Because it would hurt." Jack spit the words out between gasps. "They work fine."

"Yeah, they do." Tony bent to lick him again.

Tony suddenly lifted Jack's hips and sat back, hauling him onto solid thighs, fucking quick and tight and hard. As Jack tried to keep his eyes from rolling all the way back into his head, Tony's fingers lifted Jack's balls, teased them and rolled them around.

"Fuck." He didn't want him to stop. Not now. It felt too good. They could do it again later. And again. He'd get a few more times with him before Tuesday. He had to.

Tony put him back down on the mattress and went for his nipples. Jack cradled his neck, rubbing it with a thumb. He knew what was coming, and he wasn't going to stop him this time.

Tony's mouth dipped lower, spine bending impossibly as he managed to lick just the tip of Jack's cock. He ran his lips over the edge and Jack's body spasmed. It was almost too much sensation, so full and fucked with that sweet hot wetness on his dick. Tony's tongue curled around the head and Jack jerked, everything winding tight. Tony's hips started to move.

And then everything stopped. "Shit." Tony froze.

"What?"

"The condom broke. Jesus. It feels...God. I'm so close."

Jack pulsed his muscles. "So. I don't care." He grabbed Tony's hips and held him as tight as he could. "Just go."

Tony wrenched himself away. "Fuck you. You don't get to decide that alone. Do you even know what I did when you threw me out?"

Jack had never told Tony he couldn't fuck around, but the

words still hurt as much as the hard scrape of muscles when Tony yanked his dick out. Jack propped himself up on his elbows. "I think you went to Sean and Kyle's and got drunk and slept in their spare bedroom."

"Maybe you don't know everything about me."

So this really was payback. "I wouldn't risk it if I wasn't sure and neither would you."

"That's why I'm getting this." Tony reached back into the drawer. "We finishing this or not?"

Jack wanted to beg, to climb into Tony's lap and put that look back on his face. Instead, he put every effort into trying to sound like he didn't give a shit either way. "Whatever you want."

Tony rolled down the condom and slicked it with lube. "Fucking bastard." He bent and sucked Jack's dick, firm pressure, almost too much on skin gone hyper-sensitive, and then straightened up and shoved inside. Jack's ass was a lot less ready after that rough exit, and he winced. Tony sighed and slowed his strokes, whispering, "Bastard."

Tony might be pissed as hell, but their bodies were too close to care. They fell back into that rhythm, Tony holding Jack's hips or his shoulders and fucking fast and deep until Jack was gasping. Tony's head dropped again and Jack cradled him against his shoulder, licked and kissed the ink on his neck, scraping their cheeks together. Despite the gel in the rest of it, the feathery hair at the back of Tony's neck was soft under his fingers. Tony gave him a quick kiss and bent down again, offering one or two teasing licks on Jack's dick before just fucking him, strong and steady, eyes shut.

"I'm gonna come, so you might want to—" Tony's words cut off as he started to groan. "Fuck." He shuddered, but his hips kept his dick moving. The red at his throat spread over his face and his chest, and Jack started jerking off to follow him over.

Tony groaned again and shook, hips moving in twitches, but it was all Jack needed. A few sharp tugs on his cock and he was shooting onto Tony's chest, his own chest, thick ribbons of it as his body gasped out the sweet release. Tony rocked gently against him until Jack stopped shaking and his breathing started to slow.

Tony rolled off the bed and didn't come back from the bathroom until Jack was half-asleep.

"Tony?"

"I don't feel like talking about it now." Tony tossed him a towel, but Jack had already cleaned up with some tissues.

Tony climbed in and turned his back, but before Jack drifted off, he felt Tony watching him.

Chapter Seventeen

Tony didn't know what to expect when he got off the plane in Boston. But then, he hadn't known what to expect getting on the plane. He'd never been on one before. He'd seen the security lines and heard the jokes, but he really didn't realize how much of a pain in the ass the whole thing was. Too many people, not enough space and lines and rules all over the place. He wondered how much more expensive it was to fly first class than to be crammed into seats made for toddlers. He could ask Jack. It wasn't like they weren't speaking. But they weren't exactly chatty.

Sex the other night had reset factory defaults. No fighting. No awkward silences, but not a lot of unnecessary conversation. When Tony had first moved back in, he'd figured Jack needed time to deal with all the shit from his past being raked up, and the whole knowing that he was going to have two kids moving in soon. Tony had a lot to think about too. And it wasn't that Tony didn't want to fuck, because that was pretty much default mode for him, but they needed to have a conversation before fucking again, and Tony was still too pissed about Jack trying to make the decision for them. They used really thin condoms anyway, but the feeling of Jack's skin on the part of Tony's dick the condom had split from had been amazing. Stopping had been one of the hardest things Tony'd ever done. He wasn't exactly a poster boy for responsibility and self-control, but he'd always been careful. If he didn't ever try it bare, he didn't know what he was missing, right?

Jack didn't get to just change all that, especially not when the only reason Tony wasn't looking for another place to live was that Jack's lawyer and that prick Brandt had decided Jack looked more like Dad material in a "committed" relationship. Tony raised his eyebrows as he thought the air quotes.

Not only was the airport an alien planet and Jack acting even less Jack than usual, Tony's clothes were bugging the hell out of him. He'd borrowed a pair of non-ripped jeans from Sean and a shirt from Kyle and endured an entire round of jokes about being the evil stepmother. He thought he looked like he worked at Best Buy. The shirt was the right shade of blue for it. Give him a name tag and he'd be set to go.

The shuttle to the rental car place seemed to take forever, though they never left the airport. One thing Tony knew was there were a whole hell of a lot more cars at airports than planes and he hoped the rental car had GPS because he had no idea how anyone could find their way around this maze of roads.

He waited by a fake plant covered in enough dust, dirt and cobwebs to qualify as its own ecosystem as Jack filled out the paperwork. Somehow when Jack told him they were flying out to see the kids who were in some ritzy boarding school, Tony had gotten this whole England vibe. Like they'd have tea in a silver set on the plane and there'd be a driver waiting for them with white gloves saying "Very good, sir" with a snooty British accent. Instead it was traffic hell.

There was a GPS in the Chevy, but that didn't stop Jack from a lot of cursing and muttering as they tried to make it out of the city, though there really wasn't an out of the city the way Tony understood it. There was only a really big city and then smaller buildings and regular city.

Some guy in an SUV whipped around them as they tried to merge with about ten yards of ramp. Tony felt like he was on a school trip to Cedar Point, only none of the roller-coasters' brakes were working. He just managed to keep from grabbing the oh-shit handle above the passenger door.

"Fuck. I thought the drivers in Chicago were bad." Jack let out a breath.

"I'm glad to hear there isn't something worse."

According to the GPS, they would be at their destination in twelve minutes. Tony thought he was more likely to see the morgue before that.

"The kids don't know I'm coming. I thought they might refuse to see me."

Maybe it was impending death that put Jack in a sharing mood. "Uh-huh," Tony said.

"In one point five miles, exit right," the voice on the GPS said. At least that was British. And kind of snooty. But female.

Jack started to move right, but someone flew up in the lane next to him. Jack floored it and Tony eyed the oh-shit handle again.

After a few more near-death experiences, they sat at a light at the end of the ramp. "Turn left," prompted the GPS for the third time. Definitely snooty.

"They probably won't be really happy about seeing me. And I don't know if they'll believe that I didn't get the letters."

"Jack, I've met kids. I've been a kid. They're going to be seriously pissed and probably act like shitheads. You've met my nephews. Hell, you've heard stories about Kyle's nephews."

"I just didn't want you to be surprised."

"Yeah, well, I think as far as surprises go, you've already shot your load. Unless you're a secret agent or something too."

"No. But, um, saying 'shot your load'—"

"I'm not a fucking moron. I know not to say that in front of your kids."

"Okay."

"All right." They turned left on Academy Road and drove toward what looked like a scene from a movie. It was all white houses and black shutters, with trees and paths, and a big old brick building looming in the back. If there was ever a place in America where he was going to see a silver tea set, this had to be it. And if he didn't see one, he'd never trust a movie director again.

The parking lot was about ten spaces, between the historical-looking houses and the still more historical-looking brick building. Tony was expecting to see those brass *History Happened Here* plaques all over the place. Then he saw the big one, *The Academy at Lexington. Founded 1896.*

He looked down at where his brightly painted Converse stuck out from under Sean's slacks. He hadn't been able to borrow any shoes. He glanced over at Jack as they climbed out of the car. Jack fit perfectly into the clipped green lawns and shining movie-set New England houses. He had special wrinkle-repelling legs, because despite being on the plane for two hours and then driving here, there were no wrinkles in his brown slacks. He didn't have on a tie, but he was wearing a buttoned, tucked-in shirt that made Tony think of country clubs.

Tony's pulse kicked up more than he could blame on their quick pace toward the buildings. Usually he didn't give a shit about fitting in, but this was about Jack's kids. "Was your family rich—when you were growing up, I mean?"

"Not like this, no. But we weren't starving or anything."

Not like this didn't come close to how Tony grew up. For the first time since he'd gotten it, he wished he could cover his double-male-symbol tattoo. Not that he was ashamed to be gay, but just wearing visible ink seemed so out of place here. He thought about flipping his collar, but it wasn't the fifties or the eighties. The Academy at Lexington was just going to have to deal.

"Not a lot of spaces. Where do the teachers park?"

"I think most of them live here." Jack nodded at a sign that pointed to the left for Faculty Housing.

Tony thought of Sean. The guy loved his job, but not twenty-four/seven of it. "Man. That would suck. How do they get laid?"

"Tony."

"What? There's no one else here."

But a guy was coming toward them in a short-sleeved brown janitor's outfit complete with Stu in gold cursive stitched over his breast pocket.

"Can I help you gentlemen?"

"My name is Jack Noble. I'm here to see my son and daughter. There's a family emergency."

"Do you have some ID?"

After everything that happened with Sean's school, Tony was kind of relieved that the guy asked, though he wasn't exactly sure how he felt about trying to explain why he was here. Telling a guy who looked old enough to have kicked it with his great-grandmother that he was the boyfriend didn't feel right.

Jack handed Stu his driver's license, but Stu was looking at Tony instead.

When Stu handed it back, Jack said, "He's with me."

Stu made a sound in his throat that could have been acknowledgement, disapproval or just a phlegm problem. "Go on into the main building there, office on the left as you go in."

Stu pointed.

"Thank you."

Tony tried to smile but Stu's wizened gaze and the Academy's looming five-story brick edifice swallowed it before it hit his lips. He hurried after Jack.

"Was this always a school? It looks kind of like a factory or maybe a hospital."

"I never read the brochure." Jack pulled open a reassuringly normal-looking glass door set in the middle of the building.

The inside didn't feel much like a school though. Dark paneling and oil paintings and an Oriental rug in blue and gold made it look more like the courthouse in downtown Canton. The only thing missing was the marble stairs, but when he looked down the hall, he found them. And for a school it was really quiet. A secretary sat behind a high counter ringed with plants.

"Can I help you?" She sounded a lot less friendly than Stu.

Jack went through the verbal and proof-of-ID thing again and they got passed on up to the principal, or the Head as they called him here. Tony managed to control his snicker. When he was in school, he would have loved to be able to refer to being called to the principal's office as a trip to the Head.

Apparently the Head had done some looking stuff up while Tony and Jack were left to stare at the pinched faces in the oil paintings. The men and women all looked like they'd gotten some bad clam chowder.

"I am sorry, Mr. Noble, but I don't find you on the visitor's list for Brandon and Sarah Noble."

Jack had his cell phone out and was dialing before the Head got past the *I'm-sorry* part of his speech. The ex-mother-in-law or his lawyer, probably the mother-in-law. Tony could feel the anger coming off Jack in a fiery wave, but the Head had to be aware of how clipped his voice was, how tight he was holding the piece of plastic in his hands, as if he'd reach through and strangle whoever he was talking to.

Tony gave the Head credit. He didn't seem at all impressed by the drama acted out on his Oriental rug and only gave Tony's tattoo a brief glance before resuming a polite, bland look.

Jack slid the phone closed. "Mrs. Phillip Howard III will be calling to correct the misunderstanding. I hope that will be sufficient."

The name worked like mojo. The Head's expression changed to one of interest, and the secretary looked down at the phone on her desk which obligingly lit up forty-five seconds later.

Correcting the misunderstanding took all of five seconds and then the Head was walking them toward the marble staircase. "Brandon is at lunch right now, Mr. Noble. If you require, we can set aside a room for you to discuss your emergency. Will the children be finishing out the term?"

Tony wondered that too. Going from this place to McKinley High would be a hell of a shock, even without all the other shit that was about to land in the kids' lives. He hoped Jack could see that. Again, they hadn't talked about it.

"I hope they will."

As they went down the marble stairs, the quiet was really starting to get on Tony's nerves. It was a school. Kids talked. Or did rich parents have their voice boxes removed like creepy people did to their dogs? Normal school sounds started to reach their ears, muted conversation and the sound of people shifting. At the foot of the stairs, two large wood-paneled doors opened into a cafeteria with round wooden tables. But it only held about twenty students, and they were hunched over books and papers, probably trying to get their homework done before an afternoon class. Looking through large multi-paned glass windows that lined one wall of the cafeteria, Tony found the rest of the school. It was a beautiful May day and the kids were out on a big green stretch of grass. Some at tables and chairs close to the windows, the rest stretched out on the lawns or engaged in the Frisbee game going on at the center.

Would they open those doors and find more of a soundless world, like the kids were all in some kind of vow-of-silence monastery? Maybe it was a school for the deaf. Jack hadn't said the kids were deaf. Would he have? Did he think Tony would have made fun of that too? Tony looked again at the kids out on the lawn. Other than uniforms, there didn't seem to be anything Tony hadn't seen at a school before. No one—wait, two kids under a maple tree were having a rapidly signed conversation.

The Head opened the door and noise blasted in to meet them, laughter and talking and someone yelling about a missed catch in the Frisbee game. "Sarah is at dance class. The Performing Arts Center is that building." The head pointed to a building with an odd angular shape off to the right. "When you're ready, just come to the office and I'll show you to the small conference room."

The Head evidently assumed that Jack could pick his son out of a shifting crowd of kids in uniform. Tony wasn't too sure, but Jack took a deep breath and started off across the grass.

Chapter Eighteen

Brandon saw a perfect opportunity to cut in front of a defender and grab the Frisbee. He signaled to Hank, but the pass caught a little air and floated, and Brandon had to change his course. He launched himself into the air, and his fingers closed on the ridged edge a nanosecond before he crashed into Chance, who had decided for some freakish reason that only made sense in his thick skull to stop playing and stare off into space.

"What the fuck, Random, I'm on your team." Chance elbowed Brandon in the ribs as they rolled apart.

"What the fuck are you doing just standing there?"

Waite, one of the defenders, marked Brandon and started to count. The whole drive was screwed up now and Brandon was going to have to make a backward underhand pass before he got timed out.

Chance shrugged as he jogged backward to take the pass. "Visitors. Never seen 'em before. But the one guy looks like a punk taking a prep vacation."

Waite got to five and Brandon snuck a look back over his shoulder. The blond guy did look like the singer from the Dropkick Murphys trying to fit into prep school. Brandon was pretty sure that in addition to the ink on his neck there was something at the edge of his sleeve. The other guy looked just like—shit.

Brandon almost ended up back on his ass in the middle of the quad. Dad. Dad here. Now. Were Gramps and Grandma dead? The punk-prep guy followed right behind Dad. Shit on a cracker. He must be Dad's—boyfriend? Brandon was going to throw up. He could run. He knew Lexington really well. He had a T-pass. He could get a train to the city. Get a bus anywhere. Except his feet were nailed to the grass and he couldn't leave Sarah.

"Ten." Waite grabbed for the Frisbee. "C'mon, Random. Time. Gimme it."

"Random, what's up?" Chance came back over.

"Shit." Brandon finally said it out loud. "It's my dad."

Waite's head snapped around to watch the men walking toward them. "Your dad? I thought your folks were dead in an accident and that's why your sister is—"

Brandon shoved the taller kid so hard he flew back five feet. "Finish that and I will break your fucking face."

"Jesus, Brandon, chill," Chance whispered. "You did say your dad was dead."

"He is to me." Brandon's hand was still curled in a fist. He'd just as soon put it through his dad's face as Waite's.

Waite raised his hands and walked away, no doubt to tell everyone that dead parents was just another "Random" Noble story. Screw him.

"So who's the other guy? An uncle?" Chance was Brandon's best friend, but seriously dense sometimes.

"I have no fucking idea." At least it wasn't a total lie. "Do me a favor?"

"Sure."

"Get lost."

Chance stood there for a second, then it penetrated through his thick red hair. "Oh. Yeah." He jogged away.

Brandon walked at an angle to his dad, off of where the Ultimate field was marked by traffic cones, but not exactly toward him. The path got them farther away from the other guys in case his dad said anything embarrassing, like introduced the other guy as his husband or something. At least neither of them looked really gay. Until the punk-prep guy got close enough to show the tattoo on his neck.

Brandon tried to unclench his fist while he waited, but his fingers wouldn't uncurl any more than his stomach would stop heaving around inside him. Though he told himself things weren't all that freaky. He'd been waiting for his dad to show up most of his life.

"What's up, Dad?" he said like he saw him every day.

His father stopped abruptly. Brandon would have high-fived himself, but that would have been...gay.

"I need to talk to you and your sister."

"Are Grandma and Gramps all right?"

"They're fine. Don't worry."

Yeah. What was there to worry about? Except the whole school finding out his father was gay and his mom was psycho. It wasn't cool like Honey's two moms who owned the biggest B&B in town, or Liam whose dad was gay, but a writer and way cool and went to dinner parties with that famous gay guy on TV. This was Jerry Springer shit.

They stood there looking at each other. Which was what they always did. Whenever his dad bothered to remember he had kids, he stared at Brandon like he was inspecting him or something. Brandon figured whatever Dad was looking for he didn't see since each time all they did was stare at each other. Brandon knew he looked kind of like his mom. He just hoped to

God he didn't get her psycho genes, though Grandma and Gramps seemed okay so far.

The guy with the tats and piercings didn't seem to know where to settle his eyes. He glanced from Brandon to the game behind them and then back at Dad.

"This is Tony. He's..."

"Yeah, I figured." Brandon swallowed.

"Hi." Tony held out a hand, and Brandon just blinked at it. There was a cool red-eyed skull ring on his middle finger. Tony dropped his hand.

In addition to the ring and the queer Jeez-advertise-it-why-don't-you tat on his neck, Tony had a bunch of piercings in his ear. Brandon wanted to get his tongue and his lip done more than his ears, but his grandparents would have a cow and he looked too young to BS his way at the tattoo and piercing places in town. Jenny offered to do his ear, but she wouldn't mess with his tongue or lip.

"I wasn't sure you knew," Dad said.

Brandon rolled his eyes. "Only forever." He'd heard stuff and then guessed, even before they came out here to school. And then when he'd asked Gramps why Dad didn't answer the letters, Gramps had said, "He's a fag who doesn't have time for you. You're better off without him."

Brandon looked back at the guy's piercings. "You have your tongue done?"

Tony stuck it out to show him. "Nope."

"Why not?"

"Can't afford to get a tooth fixed if I break one."

"Gauges?"

"Nope. I'm going to have enough sagging on me when I'm old. I don't need droopy earlobes."

That was kind of funny but mostly gross.

"So what did you have to tell me?" Brandon looked his dad in the eye. It seemed to bother him, because his gaze drifted off somewhere to Brandon's left.

"Why don't we wait until we go meet your sister?"

"No. Just tell me. I can tell her."

"I'd rather you both hear it at the same time."

"Please, Dad. I'll tell her." Fear made his voice shake as much as the shame of having to ask his useless father for anything. Even if Grandma and Gramps weren't dead, it had to be something pretty big for his father to bother coming here to tell him. It would be so much better if he told Sarah. She didn't know Dad at all. Sometimes Brandon wondered if she remembered anything from before. Sometimes it was hard for Brandon to remember that time himself.

A light touch tickled his arm and then a soft hand slid into his, and Brandon knew what his dad had been looking at. Jenny. Brandon was so screwed.

"Hello. I'm Jack Noble." Dad broke out with a big smile. Fake, but Jenny fell for it. She giggled when she shook Dad's hand.

"Are you Brandon's uncle?"

Dad didn't correct her, but he raised his eyebrows at Brandon.

It would be all over the quad in two minutes anyway. "No. It's my dad. This is Jenny."

"It's nice to meet you, Jenny."

She squeezed Brandon's hand. At least she didn't ask why Dad wasn't dead, but she didn't seem to be going anywhere either.

"And this is Tony." If Brandon introduced them, the whole

boyfriend part didn't have to get said.

"Cool kicks." Jenny nodded at Tony. "Ed Hardy Converse?"

"Yeah."

"Where are you from, Jenny?" Dad asked, like this was some kind of normal thing. Like he gave a shit about anything in Brandon's life.

"Well, my dad lives in Boca, but my mom is in Larchmont."

They went on about school and then the theater program until Brandon thought he would explode.

"Jenny, my dad came out because he has to give me some news."

"Oh." Her hand tightened on his again and he could feel the sweat there. How could she stand it? It was seriously gross.

The thing with the Academy was that if you lived here, and even for most of the day kids, there weren't any secrets. Sooner or later, everyone knew your business. But the rest of the kids at the Academy didn't have business like Brandon and his sister. They had divorces and steps and halves and gay parents and then there was Terre's dad who was living in the Caymans because if he came to the US he'd be arrested for some stock-market stuff, but no one else had a mom who'd tried to kill them.

Finally, Brandon managed to pull her a couple of steps away.

"Oh my God, Random, your dad is seriously hot. And the other guy is cute. Are they like a couple? Is that why you said he was dead? Because that's totally lame and homophobic. And I can't go out with you if you're like that. It's not like you're special or something. I mean Liam doesn't—"

She didn't seem like she was ever going to take a breath so he cut her off. "No. I don't care about that. And there really was an accident. But I don't see him a lot so—"

"Oh my God, it must be really serious. I can come with you. Like if it's a funeral or something. Did someone die? Do you want me to get Sarah?"

"No. I just need to talk to my dad alone."

"Okay. Fine." She flung away his hand.

"Jenny, if you want to do something, make sure no one says anything to Sarah."

She nodded and walked off.

Brandon went back to where his dad was waiting.

"Maybe we should go someplace private," Dad said.

"Maybe you should stop freaking me out and tell me."

"Let's walk." Dad started off across the back of the quad. "What do you know about your mother?"

Brandon shot a look at Tony. If Dad had brought him, the guy probably knew already. "Besides that she's in a psych ward because she's psycho? Wait. Is she dead? Did she..." *finally do it?* He couldn't say it. There wasn't anything in the world Brandon hated more than his mother, but he wasn't sure what it would be like if she were really dead.

"No. Your mother is fine. She's...home."

Brandon froze. Every sound—the leaves, the guys on the quad, Dad's voice—it all turned into a rush of noise pounding against his ears, like the water closing over his head as it filled the car, fast. So much faster than he thought it could. And his hands were so numb he couldn't make the seat belt work.

"Home?" He knew he said it, but he couldn't really hear his own voice.

"With your grandparents."

"How could—how—why would they let her? Why isn't she—no. She should—she has to be—"

Dad's hand was hot and it weighed a ton when it landed on

his shoulder. “Son—”

“Don’t you ever fucking call me that. Never.” Brandon wrenched away and ran off the walkway, just ran until he hit the river and the jogging path and kept going.

Chapter Nineteen

Damn, Jack's kid could run. They'd covered almost half a mile before Tony managed to get close, but before he could try and stop Brandon, the kid turned on another jet. Tony could barely keep him in sight, legs and lungs burning as he hoped the emotional burst would tire the kid out before Tony lost him.

The trail turned away from the river up a hill, and that's where Tony's longer legs finally let him catch up. He ran next to the kid for a few seconds and then at the top of the hill, Brandon stopped and looked at Tony with a pissed-off respect. Tony got that look a lot.

"Dude. You can book," Tony gasped out.

"You still caught me."

"But I have to throw up now. You gonna take off again?"

"What for?"

"Good choice." Tony flopped onto the grass.

"Where's Dad?"

Tony sat up and pointed. Jack had cleared the trees, but he was still a couple minutes back. He waved and Jack waved back.

"How come he couldn't catch me? It's not like he's fat."

Tony tapped the kid's foot with his own sneaker. "They're not just cool looking. Your dad's in business-guy shoes.

Besides, running like hell is a skill I learned when I was younger than you."

"What for?"

"So I didn't get caught."

Brandon dropped down onto the grass. Five feet away, but at least he didn't seem about to start running again. "You're supposed to walk for awhile so you don't get cramps." He did something like a yoga stretch over his legs.

"Be my guest." Tony rolled back onto his elbows, keeping his head up enough to see Jack still jogging toward them. Puking didn't seem to be on the menu anymore and he sat up again. "Thank God I quit smoking."

"Smoking what?" Brandon watched him closely.

"What do you think?"

Brandon turned away.

"Listen, dude, you should know that your dad never got those letters you and your sister sent. Your grandfather never passed them on."

Brandon looked back, the yeah-right expression on his face so like the one Jack pulled that Tony had to fight off a smile.

"You can think I'm full of—crap—if you want, but it's true."

"Yeah? So what? It's not like Dad couldn't see us if he wanted to. He didn't give a *crap*." The way the kid loaded that last word said Tony'd lost about a million points for word substitution.

"Can't argue. But I thought you should know that."

"Like it matters now."

Tony thought about telling him it did, or that maybe it would someday or that a dad this late was better than no dad at all, but figured under the circumstances Jack's kid was entitled to the last word and shut his mouth. Jack was climbing the hill at his steady jog. Jack may not have speed, but Tony knew if Jack wanted something, he'd get there eventually. Hell, maybe Tony ought to warn the kid.

As soon as his dad came into view, Brandon stopped his stretching and jumped to his feet. Tony probably should have done the same, but his legs were still on the rubbery side of things.

"So now what?" Brandon faced his dad in a fighting stance, like he was going toe-to-toe in a cage match with the best mixed martial arts had to offer.

Jack was winded, but not gasping as he said, "Now we tell your sister and then we talk."

"About what?" Brandon's sneer would have done any sullen teenager proud.

"About what the two of you want."

That was a move even Cain Velasquez couldn't have seen coming.

Chapter Twenty

Floor-to-ceiling windows lined the Academy's dance studio, flooding the wooden floors with a golden light, but Jack would still have sworn his daughter had a certain glow around her. Smaller than the rest of her classmates, she moved with a grace that belied her age. When the students lined up for a leap, Jack held his breath, certain that her tiny bones couldn't support a landing from the height she achieved. She landed with no more impact than a butterfly and finished the move across the floor.

"She's good," Tony murmured in his ear.

A flush of pride warmed Jack's chest and faded just as quickly. Sarah's grace and beauty had nothing to do with him.

The three of them watched from the windowed door to the studio. No one was allowed to interrupt class for anything less than a fire or flood of Biblical proportions.

"Are you going to let me tell her?" Brandon persisted as he had the entire length of the walk back to the Performing Arts Center.

Jack thought back to the parenting books he'd tried to read years ago. Giving in was bad, he knew, but none of the books had really covered maternal attempted murder. Brandon knew Sarah better than Jack could ever hope to, and if Jack was going to have any kind of chance at a relationship with his son, respect and trust were a good place to start.

“We’ll do it together,” Jack said. Brandon opened his mouth. “But you can do the talking.”

Brandon shut his mouth, but his eyes were still narrowed, lips tight.

After a critique from the instructor the girls dispersed, grabbing towels and sweatpants and jackets as they headed toward the door.

Stepping farther back into the hallway, Jack waited, jaw clenched to keep his promise to Brandon. A murmur of sound burst into a stream of high-pitched chatter as the class came into the hall. The girls looked older than twelve, and so much taller than the one drifting along behind them.

Sarah stopped, and Jack got his first good look at her face. Her hair was scraped back into a tight bun, but wispy curls had escaped around her sweaty temples and forehead. Her eyes, his own eyes, stared back at him, dark green and wide with shock.

Without a word, she flew at him. Her tiny body held surprising force as it collided with his. Her head punched up into his diaphragm as she latched on, arms clinging to his waist.

“God, Sarah.” Brandon’s voice was full of irritation. “He didn’t come to get us. He’s just here because—” His voice faltered.

Sarah’s head turned, digging in deeper, but she didn’t let go.

“He came to tell us something,” Brandon finished.

Sarah tipped her head back to look up at Jack. He swallowed. “Your principal set up a room for us to talk in. Let’s go.”

Sarah stepped back slowly, arms sliding off, but Jack could still feel them, like the imprint of a small band wrapped around him. Should her arms be that thin? Jack was astonished that something so delicate could hold a strength that had driven the air from his lungs.

Sarah looked down at her sweats and then at Brandon.

"She has to change into her uniform," Brandon explained.

Jack wanted to growl with impatience but he forced a smile and said, "Okay. We'll wait here. I'm sure the principal will let your other teachers know where you are."

"Yeah. I almost wish I was in Global History." Brandon slumped against the wall as Sarah trailed off in the direction of the other girls.

"She's—does she eat enough?"

"What, you care all of a sudden?" Brandon aimed a kick backward at the wall.

"I've always cared."

"Yeah, right."

Tony cut in. "Look, dude. I was straight with you about those letters."

"Like you could be." Brandon rolled his eyes.

"Funny kid." Tony grinned at Jack.

"You told him?" Jack rounded on Tony.

Tony didn't flinch. "Didn't figure you would."

"I would have. What made you think—?" But Jack had dragged Tony along. Had promised him he was a part of this, that they'd do it together. But it was hard enough trying to talk to the kids without worrying about what Tony was saying when he wasn't around. "Next time talk to me first." He tried to pitch his voice low, but he was sure Brandon still heard him because his son smirked.

"So, was it bullshit?" Brandon challenged. "About the letters?"

"No. It wasn't." God, they'd have to tackle appropriate

language another day. “I never got any letters from either of you. I would have come, Brandon. If I’d known, if you’d said something when I visited, I would have come to get you.”

“So you could ignore us for work again?”

Jack bit his tongue. Restaurant work did mean a lot of hours, but back then he’d needed that time away from his fake-perfect life, from the expectations that left him bewildered and ashamed. “If you need me, I always have time for you.”

“That is such bullshit.”

“Watch your language.”

“Or what?”

Brandon had him there. Jack was nothing to his son and they both knew it. He had no more control than a stranger in a crowd.

“Is that the way you want your sister talking?” Tony asked.

Brandon kicked the wall again, jaw tight as he swallowed rapidly, and Jack could see the boy’s eyes fill as he turned his head away.

“What?” Jack said. “What’s wrong with Sarah?”

“She doesn’t talk.” Brandon spoke his whisper to the wall.

“Still?”

“Whoa. What the fu—hel—what do you mean, still?” Tony grabbed Jack’s arm.

This was it. Tony would see the real failure now. A man who’d left behind a defenseless, damaged child for his own selfish reasons. Left her to the indifferent care of people who had failed her. He looked into Tony’s eyes and tried. “I didn’t know. She said—” He turned to Brandon. “Your grandmother told me she was better. She’s been getting good grades and—”

“Oh, yeah. Good grades. Terrific,” Tony said.

Jack could see why Brandon thought kicking the wall was

a good idea. "Brandon, why did your grandmother say she was better?"

"She stopped screaming. At night. I don't think she does it here. Jenny's in her house. She'd tell me if something happened." The words came out as slowly as someone with arthritis counting change.

"Has she seen anyone?" Christ, he was asking his fourteen-year-old son for information about his daughter's psychiatric care. He was the worst father in history.

"Grandma said the doctor says she'll talk when she's ready."

"Would that be the same doctor their mom saw?" Tony asked.

Jack couldn't take anymore. "Shut up or go wait in the car."

Brandon had his head tilted, watching them, no longer on the verge of tears.

Jack was spared breaking down and kicking the wall like a petulant teenager when Sarah came back into the lobby in her navy and gold plaid skirt and white blouse, ponytail braid instead of a bun. She blinked at him a few times and stepped closer, putting a hand on his arm. When Jack would have touched her, she shied away, hiding behind her brother.

"Hi, Sarah," Tony said.

She looked around her brother and then lowered her eyes.

"That's Tony. He's Dad's friend. Ready?"

Sarah nodded and slung her backpack over her frail shoulders.

"Here, honey. Let me carry that for you." Tony reached out and slipped a hand under a strap. Sarah twisted so that his hand didn't touch her, but she let him take the pack.

"Wow, kid. You must have some serious muscles. This thing weighs a ton. What you got in here, bricks?"

She looked up at Tony but didn't smile. Why hadn't Jack thought to do that? Because even someone trapped in adolescence like Tony could be a better father.

"So where are we going?"

And Brandon was clearly the one in charge.

If that made Brandon feel better, maybe Jack could use it. "Your principal said something about a small conference room. Do you know where it is?"

"Yeah, but he's not a principal. He's Head of School." Brandon led the way out of the Performing Arts Center.

With a few leather-upholstered chairs and a sofa, dark paneling and low tables, the small conference room looked more like a lounge. The dark brown leather swallowed up his daughter as she slid into a chair in the corner, legs looking no larger or stronger than celery sticks as they stood out from her plaid skirt.

Brandon gave the spot on the sofa next to Tony and the chair next to Jack dismissive glances as he stood next to his sister's chair. Sarah's feet swung from her ankles, tapping out a rhythm in ankle socks and white canvas sneakers. When she saw her father looking, her motion stilled, and Jack couldn't think of anything to say to reassure her.

Tony grinned at her and then glanced around the room. "When does Jeeves bring the tea?"

She looked back at him and something flashed behind her eyes, something a little less frightened, so Jack didn't tell him to shut up again. He was ready to honor his promise to Brandon and let him speak first, but a glance at Brandon's tightly shut mouth showed Jack he was on his own. Sarah smoothed her skirt over her legs, but it wouldn't quite cover her knees. She kept tugging it down and pressing it flat, but her eyes peeked up at him.

Honey. Tony had said that so easily, but Jack had surrendered that right.

"Sarah, I came to tell you and your brother that I am very sorry. I didn't know you wanted to come to stay with me."

Brandon snorted with disgust. Sarah darted a quick look at her brother and then her eyes were completely focused on her skirt.

"I would like you to come and stay with me. Live with me."

"What do you mean?" Brandon said. "Like today?"

"Not today. Because your grandparents have temporary physical custody of you both. But as soon as I can make it all official, I want you to live with me."

"Where would we go to school?"

"Well, it will probably be summertime when you move in, but we can talk about what will happen in the fall."

"I like school here," Brandon said in a tone that would have done Chef Luc-Michel proud.

"Sarah?" Jack said. "What do you think of that?"

She looked up at her brother.

"Tell her why, Dad," Brandon challenged.

Jack was aware of Tony shifting on the sofa, of the sound of his daughter's hands as they smoothed down the wool of her skirt, a soft purring scrape, but he looked at his son, at the boy he'd help to make.

He remembered chubby fingers helping him weed his herb garden, round blue eyes always so focused on everything Jack did. Turning to find Brandon toddling after him everywhere, standing next to him as he dressed, pretending to comb his hair or tie a tie.

The slip and slide of the silk of Brandon's first real tie as Jack showed him, kneeling behind him in the mirror, both of them in sober gray suits as they dressed for Patrice's grandfather's funeral. "What's going to happen, Dad? Will I get to wear a flower too?"

Jack had taken a few petals from the pallbearer's carnation in his lapel and tucked them into Brandon's vest pocket. "You'll grow into it."

There were no memories of the four of them. As the lie tightened and chafed like a noose, Jack spent more and more time at the restaurant. The herb garden filled in with weeds.

Brandon's words, the way he'd always looked to his father for answers, cut deep under Jack's skin. He'd figure out how to do this. Be the right kind of man in front of Brandon and Tony both.

Jack knelt in front of Sarah's feet, wishing he could offer her something more. He'd never been more than a shadow in her life, a stranger who came and went. "What do you know about your mother?"

Sarah's lips paled as she pressed them together, gray against her already blue-white skin.

Brandon sighed and shouldered Jack aside as he crouched next to her.

"You know how Mom was sick so she was in a hospital?"

Sarah nodded.

"The doctors think she's better, so she's not there anymore. She's living with Grandma and Gramps now."

At the first mention of her mother, Sarah fixed dry but frightened eyes on Jack. As Brandon spoke, she began to tremble, the shaking increasing until she vibrated with the speed of a hummingbird's wings. Brandon reached for her, a hand on her shoulder, but Jack held out his arms and she came into them, landed like a starfish across his chest and clung. She wasn't crying, no sounds, none of those heartrending shrieks that had left Jack paralyzed with the fear of making things worse.

He settled a hand on her back and cradled her head with the other, stroking her hair. "Sarah, I swear, I won't let anything happen to you again. You and Brandon can come live with me and you don't ever have to—"

"How long?" Brandon demanded.

"What?" Jack turned to face him. Sarah weighed less than the bags of rice that came to the restaurant. She couldn't be more than sixty pounds. He didn't think it was possible to hate anyone more than he hated his father, but at that moment Jack could have easily killed Phillip Howard.

"How long until you get tired of us again?" Brandon gripped the back of the chair where Sarah had been sitting, knuckles white against the dark leather.

Was he asking for a time limit, planning his escape the way Jack had counted down the days until his own high-school graduation and freedom? Brandon was fourteen. That was four years plus college, of course.

"You'll stay as long as you need," Tony said.

"Yes." The answer was that simple. As much as Jack had regretted bringing Tony along five minutes ago, now he was glad he was here. Tony did seem to know his way around kids. Given his behavior, it shouldn't have been a surprise. Jack met Brandon's challenging stare. "I'm not walking away this time. I know you don't believe me, and I don't blame you, but, Brandon, I never would have stayed away if I thought you wanted to see me."

Brandon looked away first and swallowed. "Yeah. Because why would we have wanted to see you? Why the hell would we need a dad?"

Tony couldn't have missed the sarcasm in Brandon's tone, but he answered literally. "You seem to have been doing pretty good. But it can't hurt to try one on for awhile, right?"

Brandon's look said he couldn't believe Tony was that stupid, and then he got the look Jack saw a lot around Tony, the one where someone realized he was going to have to readjust his thinking about what kind of man he was up against.

Tony went on. "I'll bet Sarah missed lunch. There's got to be a McDonald's somewhere in this town, and I'll bet you know where it is, dude."

Brandon's expression shifted to one of anticipation. Apparently the craving for high-fat, crappy food gave Jack a temporary stay in his adolescent murder fantasies. "Yeah."

"I bet it's all tasteful and sh-stuff too, right? Got no big sign and tries to look like it's not a Mickey D's?"

Brandon nodded. Well, it took one teenager to appeal to another.

"So, I'll bet we could sneak off long enough to stuff our faces and keep you out of whatever boring stuff you had planned this afternoon."

Tony was a fucking genius with Brandon, but Jack couldn't work up any resentment with his daughter still clinging to him like she was afraid he'd evaporate if she let go. There was no resentment in that either. He couldn't believe how good it felt to be needed like that, as if she believed in his ability to keep her safe. Tony was right. A normal meal at a fast-food restaurant, however disgusting, would go a long way to chasing away the horror of the news he'd brought them.

Exactly when had their grandparents planned on telling them? When they came down to breakfast and found the woman who'd tried to drown them sitting at the table?

He held more tightly to Sarah and went out to the receptionist.

Apparently the receptionist had been suitably impressed with Mrs. Phillip Howard III—and the Howard history of donations to The Academy—to grant them safe passage out to lunch. The difficulty arose when Jack tried to put Sarah in the backseat. No amount of reassurance that he was only going to be as far away as the driver's seat could calm her repeated attempts to hang on to him again.

Finally, Jack slid her across the backseat and sat next to her while Brandon took the passenger seat and Tony drove. Jack tried not to think about the fact that he hadn't put Tony down as a driver on the rental car, of how screwed they were if Tony got into an accident or got a ticket, but Sarah gripped his hand as the car slowly backed out of the slot in the visitor's lot and Jack knew he'd made the right decision.

Tony met Jack's eyes in the rearview mirror. "I'll drive like a sinner on his way to confession, I swear."

"What's that supposed to mean?" Brandon asked.

Jack winked at Tony.

"Well, if you d—" Tony abandoned that path. "You want to be free of sin in case something happens."

"Are you Catholic? Have you been in those booth things like on TV?"

Tony was the one squirming for once. "Yes. You talk to the priest and then all your sins are gone until you sin again."

"So all you have to do is say you're sorry and that's it?" Brandon looked at Tony, but his words hit Jack right between the eyes.

"Well, you've got to do some penance. The priest tells you what to do to make up for it," Tony said.

"What if it's really bad? Like killing someone or something?

You can't just make up for something like that."

"The priest would probably tell you to go to the police. But he can't turn you in."

"That's true? I thought that was just for TV."

"Nope. No matter what."

"Do you still go to confession?"

Tony's laugh got swallowed by a cough. "No. The priests and I don't see the same things as sins."

"Like you and Dad?"

"That's one thing, yeah."

Jack had never been happier to see a McDonald's in his life, though the golden arches as Tony had predicted were low to the ground and the siding was tastefully weathered so as to not intrude on the quaintness to which Lexington aspired.

Jack was curious about how Sarah would order food, but she pointed and Brandon gave her order and his before Tony put in a request for an item with so much doubling it sounded like he stuttered. The cashier looked expectantly at Jack, and he was about to put in a request for a flash-frozen mound of flavorless iceberg when Tony lightly kicked his instep. He amended his order to the first combo on the menu.

Since he had his arms full with Sarah, Tony produced the twenties necessary to cover their artery-hardening feast. Jack's ulcer would be engaging in a firefight after the first bite. Maybe he could dislodge Sarah long enough to run to the bathroom for an antacid break.

As they ate, Brandon unbent enough to tell them he had to be back by one thirty for a review class in biology. Sarah made a reassuringly steady progress through her fries and chicken bits, though she ate almost robotically, hand reaching out for the next item as she swallowed the last, a dunk in sauce or ketchup and then onto her mouth without a variation in speed.

Jack managed to excuse himself, pointing out the bathroom door to Sarah which was in her line of sight, and swallowed 300mgs of capsules before going back to the table and his congealing lunch. The burger's taste was lost in the dressing and toppings, but Jack had forgotten the simple balance of grease and salt crisped in a fast-food French fry.

"See." Tony leaned across like he'd pat Jack's hand but then sat back before he touched him. "Heavily processed food is not all evil." He made a cross with his fingers and aimed it at the food, rearing back in mock horror.

Sarah stopped in her repetitive reaching and chewing to look at him. She took a drink of milk, then set it down before reaching over to tap the wrapper serving as Tony's plate.

He grinned and did the campy horror routine again, this time using two of his fries as the cross before stuffing one in his mouth and offering one to Sarah. Tony had put the fry close to her lips, and for a second Jack wondered if Sarah would take the bait and bite it. But she took it in her hand and placed it off to the side on her own plate made out of a napkin before returning to her mechanical eating.

Brandon and Tony went through their burgers and mounds of fries with a sloppy enthusiasm that made Jack wonder if that was the same Tony who purred in rapture over stuffed quail. Then he remembered the bags of Doritos in the cabinet and knew Brandon would always find an eating companion at home.

When Tony drove them back to campus in time for Brandon's review class, Jack invited Sarah to give him a tour. She took his hand and led him around to her teachers who expressed some surprise in meeting him, but praised Sarah's schoolwork "in spite of everything"—the last offered in a confidential whisper. Jack wondered exactly what *everything* the teachers were aware of. They certainly wouldn't have learned it from the Howards.

When Sarah led him to her dance instructor, the woman was far more austere in her praise, though delivered it in such a way Jack knew was more meaningful. "Too soon to tell, of course, but she shows promise. You should find someone to work with her over the summer so she maintains. I can give you a list."

Jack explained that they were moving to Ohio. The woman's drawn-on brows shot toward her tightly bound hair. She suggested he find a city with a ballet company and ask there. "There are cities there?"

He assured her there were and thought that Ohio State in Columbus would be a place to start.

Through it all, Sarah clung tightly to his hand, face almost inexpressive as the adults talked over her. They headed back toward the administration building.

"Wow, Peanut, your teachers sure do like you. I never got reports like that." Tony flicked one end of her ponytail.

Sarah looked up at Jack.

"I can't remember what my teachers said. I wasn't allowed to go when they met with my parents," Jack explained. Sarah gave him a quick, solemn nod. He wondered if she remembered anything about her paternal grandparents, whether either of them remembered that Jack's mother was dead. Had he told them? He couldn't remember either of them asking. The Howards had been such a huge presence in their lives he would have been surprised if they ever wondered about another set of grandparents.

The secretary looked up from behind the counter.

"Could you tell me where Sarah should be at this time? I'm going to walk her to her class before we go."

At his words, Sarah's grip on his hand became an insistent tug and then a clawing grip, dragging him down. He knelt in front of her.

She shook her head, the violence of it sending her ponytail flying to whip his cheek.

“I’m not leaving for good, Sarah. We have to talk to the judge before you can come live with me.”

She shook her head harder, eyes shining as they filled with tears.

“It’s going to be okay, Sarah. You’ll just be at school like usual, and when school is over, you’ll live with me.”

The shaking started again.

“You’re safe here.” But it was a lie, wasn’t it? If he and Tony could roam about the halls, if one phone call from Barbara Howard could open any door, how could he guarantee Sarah’s safety anywhere? “It’s just for a little while.”

He pulled his hand free and the shrieking started. The sound hit bone then went deeper, a slice along the marrow, just as he remembered. Piercing, throbbing, shrill, it paralyzed him as it always had, left him helpless. She didn’t move, didn’t cry. Her eyes were open, but she didn’t seem to be aware of anything around her.

Jack swallowed back the paralysis and reached for her, certain she would turn and run as Brandon had, as she had when he’d tried to take her home after the accident. Instead she collapsed against him, still shrieking, but her fingers twisted into an unbreakable grip on his sleeves.

There were still no words to the scream, but Jack knew she was calling him, and that first ground-shifting certainty led to another. He wasn’t leaving her. Whether the courts took weeks or months, he was not abandoning his child again. Russ Brown could fire him. Ted could reign triumphant over the kitchen at The Royal Mile.

Jack wasn’t going anywhere without his daughter.

Chapter Twenty-One

Every time Tony looked over at Jack sitting with Sarah on the hotel bed, a smile hit and warmth burst in his chest. Tony knew he was screwed when all it took was Jack asking for help to have Tony running back after Jack had tossed him out. But now watching him sit next to his daughter, hanging on every deep, even breath of her sleep, Tony knew he was as gone as Sean and Kyle at their most disgusting.

He loved that man.

As Sarah turned and took a shaky breath, Jack brushed his hand across her forehead. Tony wanted to kiss him, hug him, blow him, fuck him and have five kids with him all at the same time.

In the middle of all the chaos this afternoon, Jack had been that strong quiet guy Tony had jumped to move in with in the first place.

Tony gave the secretary credit for not seeing just a tantrum when Sarah started that horrible screaming. Thinking about it now put a chill down Tony's spine the way no horror movie could match. The secretary called the school psychologist who got there at the same time as Brandon, proving that no matter what year it was, nothing could spread bad news faster than a bunch of teenagers in high school.

Despite the fact that Sarah barely paused for breath in her

shrieks, Jack laid it all out for Dr. Gates: divorce, gay, near-drowning in icy water, Patrice getting out of the hospital. In a strong, calm voice, Jack said, "I walked away from them once, but I'm not leaving them this time."

They carried Sarah to the nurse's office, shutting out the Head who'd been dancing nervously around them. The guy was probably torn between visions of bad press and being cut off from the Howards' cash flow. With Sarah on an exam table but still clinging to her dad, Dr. Gates took charge.

Man, was Dr. Gates pissed when she couldn't find anything about the accident or psychological care in Sarah's records. Tony would be willing to bet she hadn't been told about the not-talking thing. The doctor didn't raise her voice, but Tony could tell someone was in for an ass-kicking with the doc's Birkenstocked feet.

Turned out to be Jack's shitty in-laws, because the doc had a friend who was a child advocate or some kind of ad-litem thing for the courts, and after she showed up, a bunch of papers got faxed from Jack's lawyer, words like *founded abuse* and *medical neglect* got tossed about, and Jack had legal permission to take his kids with him all without ever letting go of his daughter's hand.

Tony knew if he ever needed anything done again, he was calling on the Lesbian Network of Massachusetts. Those girls worked fast. And they *were* everywhere.

Of course, the Mass judge's order wasn't binding in Ohio, but the whole founded-abuse thing sounded like it would get some mileage when they had to talk to the Ohio court. Maybe Jack wouldn't need the big fake stable-relationship thing and tell Tony his services were no longer required. Hell, maybe Jack was moving to Massachusetts with his kids, so they could stay at this school. It wasn't like Jack was going to tell him. He hadn't told him about Sarah not talking or her severe PTSD, something Jack promised the doctor to have addressed immediately. Dr. Gates had written out a prescription for something to help Sarah calm down, but from what Tony could see, getting to leave with her dad did the trick just fine.

Brandon said he was going to stay at school, that he wasn't going to mess up his grades because his dad picked now to remember he had kids, but Tony thought there was something else going on besides being pissed at Jack. The kid had looked torn when he made his decision.

Jack glanced up from Sarah and caught Tony in a smile.

"What?" he whispered.

It was sappy as hell, but Tony couldn't help it. "You."

Jack's brows came together like he couldn't figure out what Tony had said, and yeah, they didn't talk like that a lot, but Jack wasn't stupid.

"Looks good," Tony clarified.

Jack put a finger to his lips and nodded at the door. The little Peanut was exhausted, out cold and, given the dose of Valium from the doctor, likely to remain like that long into tomorrow, but Tony followed Jack out onto the motel balcony.

It was college graduation week or something like that and the best room they could find at seven that night had been a third-floor walkup in a chain motel in desperate need of some paint with exterior stairs and entrances.

Jack used the security latch to prop the door open an inch.

Tony dug at the chipping black paint on the rail, his nail sending flakes spiraling down to the parking lot like a sooty snow flurry, barely visible in the light from a couple spots on the building. "How romantic. You and me on a balcony."

Jack smiled as he stared down the length of gray-painted cement with the rusty railing. "Not what I would have planned."

"It's good though." Tony turned and leaned against the rail.

"I'm proud of you."

"What's that mean?" Jack didn't sound very happy to hear it.

"You, stepping in, taking care of your kid like that."

"Finally, you mean. And I don't need you to patronize me."

"It was a compliment. Asshole. See if I blow you in the bathroom now."

"Tony..."

Yeah, Jack was one to talk about patronizing, and yes, Tony knew what it meant.

"I was kidding." Half-kidding. It wasn't like the kid was going to wake up, but Tony wasn't exactly keen on doing it with a twelve-year-old in the same room.

Tony turned back to finish scraping down to the rust.

"I know this is a lot more than you expected." Jack put his hand near Tony's on the rail, but didn't touch him.

"Yeah, and a lot more than you told me about." A big hunk of paint snapped off.

"I didn't know she still wasn't speaking."

"Well, I didn't know it had ever been a problem. Like up till a few weeks ago I didn't know you had kids, or a psycho Barbie as your ex-wife."

"You want out?" Jack didn't turn, kept staring out at the dark trees at the edge of the parking lot.

A paint chip stabbed under Tony's thumbnail. "No. I'm not saying that." He sucked the chip out and spit it away, not sure if the metallic taste was from the paint and rust or blood. "Today, seeing you with them, both of them, kinda makes me wish I'd met you back then, like I wished they could be ours."

"I don't think they've invented a way for that to happen yet."

Tony looked at the black under his thumb. "Now who's making a joke?"

Jack's hands tightened around the rail, sending a few more crumbling bits to sift down through a halo of light. "I don't get what you want out of this."

A door opened under their feet and after a flick and a crackle, a plume of cigarette smoke floated up. Tony put his hand over Jack's.

"I've never wanted anything out of this but you, you stupid bastard." He leaned in to put his words right into Jack's ear so that they wouldn't be wasted on whoever was underneath them. "But that means everything. I'm not saying the kids should call me Dad, but if I'm around, I want to help raise them."

Jack's nod sent stubble rubbing across Tony's lips. Jesus he wanted to kiss him. Because that part of them had never gotten screwed up by words—at least not until Jack brought up skipping condoms.

"Going raw, trusting in us, that means you can't keep shit from me because you don't think I'll like it. I'm giving this grown-up thing my best shot." Tony looked down at his clothes, clothes he was stuck in for another day. "So I'm saying, I can't take any more lying."

The smoke drifted away, the door below opening and shutting softly. A quick smoker or someone trying to give them privacy?

Jack turned. "All right."

"All right?"

Jack put his hand on Tony's neck, thumb drifting over the tattoo and then moving back to the base of his skull. "What, you want it signed in blood?"

Unwilling to give into the smile or the touch, Tony met Jack's gaze steadily. "Maybe. Is there anything you're not telling me? Anything else?"

"Like what?"

"I don't know. Any other ex-wives, children, psychological conditions, medical problems?"

"Brandon's allergic to penicillin."

"Anything else?"

"Not that I can remember. I don't want the kids watching *South Park*."

"*The Simpsons* okay?"

"*The Simpsons*, but no *Family Guy*."

"Deal. You're going to have to give up *Bridezillas* though. Don't want your daughter becoming a diva."

"Okay." Jack stuck out his hand, and Tony grabbed it, pulling him in for a quick kiss.

"I'm holding you to that, you know."

"*Bridezillas*?"

Tony made a face. "That too."

Chapter Twenty-Two

Brandon decided to stay at school to finish his exams which meant Sarah got first dibs on bedroom choices. Jack's house had four, and Tony would handle being called selfish if he wanted to pump his fist in triumph when, after asking Jack with a head tilt which bedroom was his, Sarah selected the bedroom across the hall and not the larger guestroom with an adjoining wall. Tony wanted Jack to be a dad to his kids, he really did, and he was already fond of the little Peanut and the in-your-face brat, but hell if Tony was giving up sex for three months until the kids were back in school—here in Ohio or back in Massachusetts.

The bedroom Sarah had picked held a single bed and dresser that Jack had bought after hearing about Patrice on the loose, but the room was plain. Light gray carpet and white walls, nothing on the bed.

Sarah went in and sat on the bed, her feet dangling above it. Jack brought in the two suitcases the school had sent. Before all of them got freaked out with the whole *now what* Tony could feel creeping up on them, he said, "This room is pretty boring. I think we need a trip to the three B's."

For a kid who didn't talk, Sarah had no trouble making her wishes known. When they found their way back to the bedding, Sarah released Jack's hand long enough to grab at a set in raspberry pink and neon green. Apparently, it was the in combination for girls' rooms because you couldn't swing a dead cat without hitting some kind of accessory in the same color scheme. Tony grabbed one of those super fuzzy pillows and tossed it to Sarah.

She caught it and made a breathy sound, whether it was a laugh or a grunt from the weight of the pillow against her tiny frame, Tony couldn't tell.

He found a matching desk lamp, two more pillows and a blanket that was too soft and fluffy to leave on the shelf.

As Tony straightened from the cart, Jack murmured in his ear, "I've got money put away, but we don't have an unlimited budget with the kids around."

Sarah was a few feet away looking at some of the knickknacks kids put on their dressers. The earring trees didn't look that different from what Darlene had had.

"Okay. But feel this." He pulled a bit of the blanket out of the plastic cover and held it up against Jack's grin. As Jack rolled his eyes and nodded, Tony caught a movement behind him. "Shit."

"Language. What?"

"I think it's stalker Barbie."

Jack's brow wrinkled.

"Your ex-wife. I think she's in here. Like she followed us or something." They both looked at Sarah.

"Get her out of here." Jack grabbed the cart.

Tony didn't look back as he hurried forward. "Hey, Peanut, there's some more cool stuff around here."

Tony hoped that she'd gotten enough of Jack's interior-decorating genes to just follow him without trying to find her father. Since they'd arrived this morning, she'd actually let Jack drive without making him sit in the back with her. She seemed to trust that Jack wasn't leaving her behind now that he'd taken her out of school.

Sarah looked up at him with an almost smile on her face and put her hand near Tony's as he steered her into an aisle and toward the front of the store. She found a notebook covered in fabric and feathers and held it up. Tony nodded. Half the time he was with her, he forgot she wasn't deaf too.

"That's nice." He took the notebook from her before he realized that if Patrice caught them in the checkout, they'd be sitting ducks. Well, if it came to that, Tony was pretty sure he could pull off the old five-finger discount.

They wove around the back of the candle section and Sarah sneezed. Other than her screams and the hiccupping cry she made when the screams eased, it was the first loud sound Tony had heard from her.

"Bless you," Tony offered.

He got his first of Sarah's smiles in return. It was a hell of a thing to get hit with. That tiny pale face lighting up with a big grin under Jack's green eyes. Tony was a goner again. From one heartbeat to the next he knew he'd die for that kid.

"C'mon, Peanut. We've got to meet your dad outside."

First on the list was making sure she never had to come face-to-face with a mom who'd tried to kill her.

Tony scanned the front of the store, feeling enough like a secret agent to start the TV-show tune rolling through his head. He hid Sarah between his body and a tall display of chip clips and prayed the cashier could handle an exact-change cash transaction in something less than ten minutes.

Mission accomplished with zero casualties or enemy sightings, and Tony took Sarah safely out of the store and into the bright sunlight. Jack never handed over the keys to the X3, so Tony took Sarah down the strip mall to a pizza place.

Her smile had faded when they didn't find her father

outside.

"Dad's meeting us for dinner over here. What kind of pizza do you like?" Tony put her on the bench seat on the inside at the least sticky booth he could find and showed her a menu while tapping out a text to Jack. He figured that he might be able to head off a breakdown for ten minutes, but after that, all bets were off.

He showed Sarah a list of toppings and she pointed to ham, pepperoni and sausage while making a face and shaking her head. Tony was totally going to kick ass if he ever had to play charades.

"Anything you like?"

Her face lit up, but it wasn't over pizza toppings. Jack slid into the booth across from them, and Sarah ducked under the table and came back up on Jack's side.

Jack lifted her into his arms for a quick hug and settled her on the inside. "Next time go around, though. I don't want you to get hurt."

She nodded and looked back down at the menu Tony had open.

Tony raised his brows at Jack, who shook his head and shrugged.

"Maybe I was wrong." Tony shoved Sarah's notebook into one of the bags Jack had stuffed under the table.

"Better safe," Jack said, then peeled his arm off the sticky red-and-white-checkered plastic tablecloth, a look of horror on his face.

"Get used to eating at places besides The Mile and the Pinnacle."

Jack shuddered.

Chapter Twenty-Three

The next morning Tony's dick woke up before he did. As he dragged himself to consciousness and opened his eyes to Jack's smiling face, he realized that wasn't all that was up. With a slow stroke of Tony's cock, Jack moved on top, rubbing his own dick against Tony's.

Tony had something to say, but his lips were kind of stuck together and his brain wasn't getting much blood, so it came out, "Uhn."

Jack smiled again and slid his hips and that was—

"Uhn," Tony said again.

"Yeah?"

Tony nodded. Because it was. Silky-hot and hard-slick. Yeah. Letting his legs drop open, he put his hands on Jack's ass and added a little upward thrust to the friction.

"Did I wake you up too early?"

Tony realized his eyes had drifted closed. "No." Though a glance at the clock told him it was five-fucking-thirty in the morning.

His lips unstuck, but his brain was still half asleep and blood deprived. "What happened to no sex with the kids in the house?"

"Yeah. Well, you smell really good." Jack burrowed his face

in Tony's neck and huffed.

"I'll try to remember to wear hot chocolate to bed more often." Tony grinned against Jack's hair. The executive chef had made it from scratch for the Peanut last night, and she'd gotten startled by a shadow across the plate-glass window and sent it flying over Tony. He'd been left more sticky than burned.

Jack's deep chuckle on thin neck skin didn't do much to get any more blood in Tony's brain. He worked his hips in a grind as need burned in his balls.

Digging his hands harder into Jack's ass, Tony said, "Ready for a ride?"

Jack lifted himself off and let his cock slip down to rub along the crack of Tony's ass. "Are you?"

Jack was in a toppy mood, which was fine, because Tony was all for lying back and getting done. Until Jack reached for the lube and nothing else.

Tony hooked his ankles around Jack's hips and arms around his shoulders and pulled him back down. "This is nice too."

The tension in Jack's back said he wasn't buying it. "Because you're not in the mood to get fucked or you don't want to do it bare?"

"Why do you want to so much?"

"You said you were fine with it. I thought you wanted it too."

Jack in him, around him, nothing but skin. Yeah, Tony wanted it. And not just because it would feel good. But Jack had lied—maybe lying wasn't quite it, but he sure as hell hadn't been stinking with truth for the past year.

Jack sat up. "You don't trust me." His face was blank.

"I do."

Jack trusted him. Hadn't Jack handed off his kid to Tony yesterday? What else was Tony looking for? He wished he knew.

"Then what? Do you want specifics?" The matter-of-factness in Jack's voice only made Tony feel more like a freaked-out virgin.

Well, some facts wouldn't hurt. Except maybe their hard-ons.

Tony didn't ask out loud, and Jack didn't say anything else. A lighter blue shone in the windows, a crack of light slipped under the door from the hall, more than enough to see each other, read each other. For all that the sappy stuff drove Tony nuts when he watched it with Sean and Kyle, Jack did have a look. For him.

Whether Jack said it or not, he loved him.

Time to fish or cut bait, dude.

Screw it. Whatever had happened before, this was his Jack.

He put his thumb in his mouth and got it good and wet before he rubbed it over the head of Jack's dick. "Want you to fuck me, tiger." Tony smoothed the spit down the long shaft. "Just skin."

Jack drove Tony back onto the mattress, kissing a groan into his mouth. Tony's stomach got tight with nerves like it hadn't since the first time he'd been fucked. Want and fear twisted around inside like on his first trip up the two-hundred-foot-tall roller coaster at Cedar Point. Looking out at Lake Erie and the tiny track dropping away below, he'd suddenly wondered if it had been such a great idea and was it too late to take it back.

Jack's kiss had the same stomach-dropping effect as that shot down the first hill. It was too late now and no matter what happened it was a hell of a rush.

Jack's finger fucked inside while his tongue fucked Tony's

mouth. Tony couldn't breathe anymore and he moved his head on the pillow. Jack's mouth ended up next to Tony's ear.

"Last August. Physical. Full blood workup." Jack's words came out in grunts to match the thrust of his finger. At first Tony couldn't understand what Jack was talking about, and then he got it. Specifics.

Two fingers now. Curling up. Rubbing with every stroke. "HIV. Syphilis. Gonorrhea. Negative."

It shouldn't have been this sexy to hear about things that could kill you or make your dick rot off. But Jack had a hell of a nice touch working for him there. Tony's head flopped back as Jack drove his fingers in deeper with a longer pause to twist and press each time.

"Guys fucked since. Anthony."

The way Jack's voice made Tony's real name sound like something magic never failed to rev Tony's engines—even without the thrust inside him.

"Thomas." Jack had better be reciting Tony's middle name.

"Gemetti." Jack scissored his fingers as he got to Tony's last name, sending him up off the mattress to lick and suck on whatever skin he could reach.

He was surprised to find the sound that came out of him had words. "Do it. C'mon."

Tony didn't expect it to feel different, and at first he was too busy concentrating on the sting and cramp of Jack losing it and going way too fast, too deep with that long dick of his.

"Sorry," Jack breathed out.

No, Tony hadn't expected to be able to feel the difference, but damn, he could see it. See it in Jack's face, the way he was fighting for control right away. Then Tony did feel it. In the shudders running through Jack's muscles, and then in the power of his strokes as he started to move.

No starting slow. Hard solid thrusts right away. All the way out and then slamming deep until Tony swore Jack would hit the back of his throat.

Tony arched his hips and grabbed the edge of the mattress over his head. If Jack was losing it this fast, Tony couldn't wait for his turn.

"Sorry," Jack said again.

"Does my dick look like I mind?"

They both looked down and Jack smiled. "Nope. But, Tony—"

"Got it." Tony reached for his dick and started pulling.

"You feel so fucking good." Jack shuddered against him. "Hot and wet and Jesus."

Jack wasn't big with talking during sex and Tony loved it.

"Yeah." Tony jerked faster on his cock. "Tell me what it feels like."

Jack's face had that absolute gone expression he got when he was eating seventy-percent cocoa chocolate, tasting a perfect new wine or coming down Tony's throat.

"It's smooth but it's—oh fuck." Jack's hips bucked faster. He cradled Tony's head in his hands and kissed him. "Last chance." Jack breathed it against Tony's mouth. "Can pull out."

Tony shook his head in Jack's grip, catching a thumb with his mouth and sucking on it. Knew it was right when he looked at Jack's face and saw everything he needed. Hiking his legs up higher, letting Jack in deeper, Tony tightened his ass against Jack's thrusts.

Jack's forehead dropped against Tony's for a second. Then with a sloppy kiss and a love-you grunt, Jack arched over him and Tony felt him go, the quick jerks and the shock of wet warmth inside. Jack slammed into him again, and Tony's balls let go in a sweet rush, more heat splashing between them as they panted together.

Jack looked down at him, lips bitten to dark red, and Tony knew that look too. “Do not say thank you, or I swear to God I will punch you in the nose.”

Tony flopped forward, driving them both down onto the bed. Yeah, he could pass out right here. Since last week when they started doing it raw, they’d pretty much given up sleep for sex. And as much as Tony loved his sleep, it was a damned good trade. Despite his overactive imagination, nothing had prepared him for what it was like to feel Jack so hot and wet and God, moving on bare cock skin. He’d had no idea he’d be able to feel a change in texture, the way Jack’s muscles gripped when he breathed or tell exactly when he rubbed the head across Jack’s gland. And that first time, he almost came without moving.

Jack shifted under him and Tony squinted at the clock. Six fifteen. They could definitely get in another round before the Peanut woke up. Sitting on the edge of the bed, Jack rubbed his belly with a towel and tossed it back at Tony.

“Where’re you going?” Tony tried to hook Jack with an ankle and pull him back into bed without having to get up, but there was a reason ankle drags weren’t getting anyone in the Wrestling Hall of Fame.

“Sarah’s got an appointment. The doctor said after this third visit she’d want to talk to me.”

“Right.” Tony remembered. He even remembered the eight forty-five appointment time.

“So, you coming with me?”

“To the shower?”

“To the appointment.”

Tony thought jumping into Jack's arms would probably land them both on the floor with someone needing X-rays, so he settled for kissing Jack's shoulder and snapping his ass with a towel.

Their communication skills were improving all the time.

Chapter Twenty-Four

Sarah's doctor in Ohio didn't have that same granola vibe Tony had gotten from Dr. Gates in Massachusetts. She was a petite polished blonde who looked like she'd fit in at a law firm—not at all a Barbie. The office was a maze of rooms. There was pre-reception, reception and the waiting area where he and Jack sat while Sarah was in with the doctor. Tony supposed all the separate little cubicles were a nice way of making sure you didn't run into anyone you knew, patient confidentiality and all that. He wondered what it would be like if you had to see a psychologist and your dad didn't have lots of money.

"Tony," Jack said with a patient sigh.

Tony followed Jack's gaze to where Tony's knee was bouncing as he tapped his heel lightly. "Sorry."

The doctor stepped through the far door of the waiting cubicle and greeted them. "Mr. Noble."

Jack stood and offered his hand. "Jack, please. And this is Tony. My partner."

Partner. They'd never used that word before. Maybe boyfriend, yeah, like when Sean said "At least your boyfriend shows some taste", but half the time that was a joke. Like to say it out loud was going to curse it. Certainly not partner. Tony had never been anyone's choice of partner. Not for so much as a Spades game.

The doctor's smile didn't fade, but Tony knew she'd assessed his clothes, hair, ink and piercings in one glance and labeled him a kept boy. He'd done his best with his least-distressed jeans and a T-shirt from Metallica's Black Album tour, which was as close to plain black as he had. Blurting out that he meant to get some more grownup friendly clothes after he picked up his last paycheck from the bar wouldn't help his cause.

Jack hadn't asked, but as soon as they got home from Boston with the Peanut, Tony said he'd tell Ricky to take him off the bar's work schedule for awhile. Ricky didn't care. The rest of the guys were always looking for more hours. It made a lot more sense for Tony to stay home at night and watch Sarah than it did to have Jack out of work. But looking at it like that, Tony kind of was...kept.

The doctor shook Tony's hand. "It's good to see you have some support, Jack. It would be difficult to manage the transition even under optimal conditions as a single parent. Do you have children also, Tony?"

"No." He tried to keep the relief out of his voice. "Two nephews, though. My sister's kids."

"How old are they?"

"Five and six."

She nodded and led the way into her office. Visible through a window, Sarah sat in a larger area at a table, intent on a design she was coloring with markers.

"I've scheduled some time for us to talk today. I'm sure you're both eager to hear an assessment and I can reassure you that Sarah shows no cognitive impairment with language." She handed Jack a file folder with papers in it. "In fact, in written language and auditory comprehension, she is in the ninety-sixth percentile for her age. She also has above-average scores in spatial relationships."

Tony looked over Jack's shoulder at a bunch of test scores.

"She is aware of why she has been brought to counseling and does not demonstrate resentment or unwillingness to answer questions, although I have not discussed the accident with her yet. I did ask her today about her speech." The doctor pulled out another paper from a different file and read, "I used to be afraid to talk because I might scream again. Then when I tried, it chokes me and I can't breathe. I don't like it."

Tony had something choking in his throat too as he looked through the window at the kid focused on her drawing.

"You don't recall any speech problems from before the trauma, is that right, Jack?"

He'd been staring at the paper with his daughter's handwriting, rubbing his chest. "No."

"And the screaming produces sounds, correct?"

"Yes." Jack looked up.

"So I believe we can rule out an organic speech obstruction, though you may want her to see an ENT to rule out anything physiological."

Tony was glad the doctor wasn't talking down to them—or him in particular—but he was starting to wonder if she got paid by the syllable.

"Has she laughed?"

"A little, I think," Tony said when Jack was silent. "It's kind of a huff, like a breath, but she smiles sometimes."

Jack nodded.

"And what is her play like at home?"

"She draws." Jack turned to watch his daughter. "She stays close to us or in her room." His voice trailed away at the end of the sentence as if he felt guilty about that.

"We took her to a toy store and she picked out mostly art

stuff, those thread bracelets and marker sets," Tony explained. "She has a scarf thing half started with some yarn, and she wanted me to pick out colors for a bracelet. She doesn't watch much TV, didn't want any videos from the store, though she sits and colors with me if I'm watching something. She writes a lot in that notebook I bought her."

"What notebook?" Jack asked. "Where is it?"

"It matches her room, and I don't know where she keeps it. You don't mess with a girl's diary, right?" Tony smiled at the doctor. "My sister had one. One time I tried to take it and she broke two of my fingers." He held up the first two fingers of his left hand where the knuckles were thicker before he realized that family violence probably wasn't a great selling point for him in terms of childcare. "She got in trouble for that, though," he added quickly.

The doctor almost smiled. "Eschewing violence as a means of maintaining privacy, it is often helpful for preteens and adolescents to record their feelings, though I'm sure we would all like to encourage Sarah to do so aloud as well. Ask her if she wants to bring her notebook to our next session, but don't force it. What sort of things does Sarah draw or choose for her coloring?"

Tony looked through the window. On Sarah's paper, diamonds radiated out from a center star in alternating bands of color. "Designs, like that. Shapes in different colors."

Jack shifted in his chair. "We eat lunch in the yard every day when it's not raining. She didn't want a bike and when we took her to the park, she wouldn't take more than a few steps away from us. She wouldn't get on the swings." He sounded like he was apologizing.

The doctor's voice was soothing. "Of course it will take her time to feel at ease in a new environment, and you are right to continue to offer activities without forcing them."

"She was taking dance at school. I've been trying to find the right class for her here," Jack said.

"I think that will be good for her, but don't be surprised if she refuses to go at first."

The doctor took a breath and Tony could tell that they'd finished the good news part of the conversation.

"Her selective muteness isn't the only concern here. It's a symptom of her larger detachment. In order to reduce her exposure to fear, Sarah has withdrawn from any representation of feelings. Most children engage in representational play whether through video games or toys, that is, make-believe, even through their adolescence. Sarah is choosing to live at a distance."

"So what do we do?"

"Offer her opportunities to engage. She appears to be free of the worst of her anxieties in your presence, Jack, and her willingness to extend the same trust to you, Tony, is reassuring. But she needs to see other children at play, whether or not she's ready to join them."

"Her brother will be out of school in another week," Jack said.

"I'd like her to have more contact than just an older sibling."

"We'll work on it," Jack assured her.

"Sarah's reconnection with the world may be gradual or it may be sudden, but it's going to be a difficult readjustment. It might not be a bad idea for the whole family to engage in some counseling."

Jack nodded, but the lines around his eyes were tight. Tony wasn't sure whether Jack or Brandon would be the toughest to get through that door.

"And in the event that Tony brings her to any appointments

without you, we should have his permission to authorize treatment on file. Just in case."

Just in case Sarah had another screaming fit and they had to medicate her. Christ, this kid stuff was complicated. Even if Tony had been there from the minute the kids were born, legally he'd still be a stranger to them. Tony wanted to crack away the tension in his neck and back, just one good roll of his shoulders, but he was sure the doctor would take that as a sign of some kind of psychological whatever.

"If you leave me the information, I'll have a report sent to the law guardian and the attorney regarding Sarah's previous level of care and recommendations."

The recommendation that she stay with Jack and her mom be kept on another continent, right? Tony wanted to ask, but they were being led into the room to meet Sarah.

She flung herself at Jack as she always did, like she was afraid he'd disappear if she didn't hold on to him right away. Tony supposed from Sarah's experience, Jack just might.

Tony thought the custody thing would be a lot more like the stuff on TV. Not *Judge Judy*, but more like something on a soap—with a better set. Mostly it was papers. Jack kept having to go sign papers or call somewhere to get papers. That fucker Brandt was still waiting in the wings with his threat to go public with the Howard empire's crazy murdering daughter, but Jack's lawyer said there wasn't a lot of push back, and that the Howards' lawyer was drafting up something new. As sucky as it was for the poor little Peanut, medical neglect was on their side. No one battered down the door to yank Sarah out of the house. Apparently when it came to kids, possession was nine-tenths of the law.

On the Thursday before the week they were supposed to meet with the judge, Jack and Sarah went to pick Brandon up at the airport. Tony didn't know what had gone down on the ride home, but Brandon came into the house with his face twisted in a sneer, weighed down by his backpack and dragging two more suitcases behind him.

As soon as Jack shut the door, Brandon faced his father. "I'm here because the only person I hate more than you is her. I sure as hell don't need a dad anymore, so you and your boy-toy can just keep playing house without me."

Chapter Twenty-Five

Brandon's exit would have been more impressive if he hadn't been slowed down by the luggage he'd refused to let Jack carry. His son's departure still left Jack paralyzed with the same sense of helplessness he felt every time he tried to interact with his children. Everything he said seemed to make it worse. What was he supposed to do, beat the kid?

Sarah slipped her hand free of Jack's and took her seat on the floor next to the coffee table. She picked up her markers and went back to work on the edges of the large geometric design she was coloring.

Tony was leveling a look at him that Jack couldn't return. "Jack, you've got to say something to him."

He'd love to. He just wished he knew what he could say. "I tried that in the car. You can see how well that went." He hadn't tried to lay down any rules, just broke the silence when they turned into the development with a simple *I'm glad to have you home.*

"For f-crying out loud." Tony turned and stomped off in Brandon's direction.

Jack followed more quietly, though he took the stairs two at a time and hit the hall in time to hear Tony open the guestroom door and walk in on Brandon.

"What the fuck do you want?"

Brandon's snarl was about what Jack had been expecting. Moving closer to the door, he waited for Tony's response.

Tony's voice was even. "For starters, I'd like not to be treated like sh—crap in my house."

"It's not your house, it's my dad's."

"Maybe, but like it or not, dude, we're all living here now."

"Don't call me dude."

"Don't call me boy-toy."

That shut Brandon up for a second.

"So listen," Tony said. "Nobody expects you to be happy. But you're not the only person life ever bitch-slapped."

Jack winced.

"It doesn't give you the right to treat other people like crap. And even if you don't respect me or your dad, you should respect your sister enough not to talk like that in front of her."

"What are you going to do if I say tough shit to that?"

"To you? Nothing. But I don't think it would be much fun hiding up here in your room if all your stuff was downstairs in the dining room."

There was a thump that sounded like furniture hitting the wall. Jack stepped forward, but all he saw was Brandon sprawled on the bed, kicking his foot against the headboard. Tony was in the center of the room. The only sign of his emotions was that his hands were talking almost as much as his mouth.

"But if you think you can not act like a jerk for a couple days, I was thinking we could all go to Cedar Point and hit the rides. Have you ever been there?"

"No. My friends get to go to Universal."

"Well, I've never been there, but from pictures, the coasters at Universal look like pu—kiddie rides compared to Cedar Point.

Why don't you check it out online?"

Brandon sat up. "You guys got wireless? What's the password?"

"Just log on."

"You guys should really have a password. Anybody could be using your IP address."

"Talk to your father about it."

"Right. And then we'll have a great bonding moment because he listened to me for five seconds."

The burn in Jack's chest was fairly constant now, but at Brandon's words, an extra spurt of acid got things roaring. He never thought it would be easy, but he wasn't sure he was cut out for this.

Tony just laughed. "Have fun being pissed off, kid. There's lots of food in the fridge. Your dad's going to work, and I'm having dinner with Sarah at five thirty."

Jack ducked into their bedroom, fumbling for his antacids, but Tony followed him.

"You gonna hide from him forever?"

"How about the next four years?" Jack tucked the roll of chewables back in his pocket. "Cedar Point, huh?"

Tony's mouth twisted in a half smile. "Too big a bribe?"

Jack shrugged. "It's cheaper than a Lexus."

"And he's only fourteen."

"That too." Jack put his hand on the back of Tony's neck and pulled him close. "You know, I must have been out of my mind when I asked you to leave. I'd be screwed without you here."

Tony didn't pull away, but his body was rigid. "You didn't ask. You threw my ass the hell out. Twice." He locked his eyes on Jack's.

Jack wasn't sure which burned more, the guilty pressure in his chest or the weight of the hidden antacids in his pocket. He knew damned well Tony would be pissed, but more, Tony would make him go to the doctor and he couldn't. Not with court next week. Jack didn't have time to be sick. He moved his thumb along the top of Tony's spine and got an answer in a blue-eyed wink.

"You know, I kind of like the way you're screwed with me here too." Tony gave him a quick kiss.

The joke felt good, normal. Like there weren't two kids Jack didn't know how to deal with in the house. Like he wasn't responsible for fixing everything he'd left so broken.

He pulled away, headed into their bathroom.

"My breath that bad?" Tony asked.

"I need to piss if that's all right with you."

Jack managed his cover and a one-handed pop of a few tablets. He'd need to stop for more of the capsules before work or he'd never make it through the night. At least he'd stopped throwing up blood. The capsules were helping.

As he shut off the water and shook his hands, he looked up at Tony in the mirror. "You need me to pick up anything while I'm out?"

"I bought out the Giant Eagle this morning. They're probably still restocking the shelves."

"Maybe we can wean Sarah off the boxed mac and cheese, then. I'd like to see her eat something in a color other than Day-Glo orange."

Tony came up behind him and tucked his chin on Jack's shoulder. "She's your daughter. Tell her that on the way out."

Jack left Tony rinsing with mouthwash and stopped in front of the closed door of Brandon's room. He probably couldn't make it better today, but he could damn sure make it worse. He slunk downstairs to Sarah.

She smiled when he sat next to her on the floor.

"I have to go to work."

The smile faded and she nodded.

"But Tony's going to be here. What do you want for dinner?"

She pointed at a swirl on the paper that was orange.

"How about a hamburger?"

She shook her head.

"Some green beans? Tony will make them in the steamer and they won't be mushy."

She shook her head again.

Jack picked up a piece of paper and drew a circle on it. With the black marker, he divided it into four pie pieces.

Sarah watched him closely.

Jack picked up a green marker and colored in one of the pieces. "This is your plate, okay? And I want you to try to put this much stuff that's green on it." He picked up a red marker and scribbled. "This part is for some chicken. You like chicken." Trying not to sigh, he picked up the orange marker. "This is for Sarah's mac and cheese." He colored in the third space.

She pointed at the fourth space.

Jack passed the paper back to her. "That's for dessert. Can you show it to Tony?"

She nodded, blue marker busy in that last space. He started to get up but she grabbed his hand. She traded the blue for a brown and then for the red and then shoved the paper back.

It wasn't going to get her into art school, but it was a clear image of a fudge sundae. Jack remembered what the psychologist had said about representational drawings. She'd never shown him anything but shapes.

He gave her a hug. “I think a sundae would be great. Who’s going to eat it?”

She looked at him for a second and then drew a spoon, but when she started to add something to the handle, her hand shook and she put the marker down.

Had he pushed too hard? “Do you want me to show you what I’m going to serve for dessert at the restaurant?”

She nodded and pushed a fresh piece of paper his way.

Chapter Twenty-Six

A large party came in at ten, and despite the best efforts of politely hovering servers, showed no signs of getting their butts out of The Mile before midnight. The X3's clock read 1:27 when Jack tapped the garage door opener. In the upstairs hall, the soft green of Sarah's nightlight shown from her slightly opened door, and light came from the tightly shut door of Brandon's room.

Jack took a deep breath and knocked. If he could handle snotty Cordon-Bleu-trained sous chefs, he could handle his teenage son.

"What?" was Brandon's response.

Jack opened the door. At least Brandon hadn't locked it. His son was on the bed, laptop on his stomach and bent knees, clicking away at the keys.

"It's one thirty."

"And? It's not like I have school."

Jack tried another tack. "Did you look up Cedar Point?"

"He told you?"

"We live in the same house. We're bound to run into each other."

"Yeah." Brandon looked away, tapping at the keys again.

Whether it was an acknowledgment about the living

arrangements or the amusement park, Jack couldn't say.

"They've got seventeen roller coasters. Have you been on them all?"

Jack shook his head. "I've never been. But from what I understand, the lines for the biggest rides can be really long. We'll have to go early in the morning."

The emphasis wasn't lost on Brandon. "Yeah, but that's not tomorrow."

"No. But if you get in the habit of staying up late and sleeping late, it will be hard to get up when you want to do something."

"I'll manage it."

Maybe Jack should just let Brandon talk to the judge, except what would Brandon argue for? *The only person I hate more than you is her.* It wasn't a great recommendation of Jack's qualifications as a father.

He fell back on Tony's tactic. "You don't have to like it, but I think midnight is a reasonable bedtime for a fourteen-year-old."

"I'm in bed."

Frustration, not anger, had Jack biting his tongue. Should he make a threat? Could the kid hate him more? Probably not. "You can shut off the computer or I can take it with me."

A few more taps on the keys, then just when Jack thought he'd have to get into a wrestling match, Brandon flipped closed the lid and shoved the computer under the bed. "I'll be fifteen in October."

"We can renegotiate then." Jack was turning to leave when he heard a quick breath, as if Brandon had started to say something then stopped. Jack turned back.

"When we see the judge, will she be there?"

The burn in Jack's chest had nothing to do with his ulcer.

All he wanted was to keep them safe and he couldn't even promise them that. "I don't know, s—Brandon."

Brandon turned to face the wall, and Jack shut off the light behind him.

His own bedroom was chaos. Tony had moved the bed to the opposite wall, away from the side that adjoined Brandon's.

"Cleaning or did you have other plans?"

Tony flung all of his one hundred seventy-five pounds onto the mattress, and neither the frame nor the headboard made a sound.

Jack arched his brows. "You have been busy."

"I'm too old to keep doing it standing up, and my knees can't take the floor."

"Your knees?"

Tony winked. "Bought a few cheap quilts for some cheap thrills. Padded the mattress and the headboard into absolute silence. Wanna try it out?"

"Oh yeah."

Jack peeled off his shirt and lowered himself to the bed with less enthusiasm and more care. After he shifted with more force, he could tell the familiar squeak was gone. Tony grabbed Jack's ass and hauled him up till they faced each other.

"It won't make a sound. The Peanut and I jumped on it."

Jack tried to imagine his too-quiet daughter bouncing around on a bed and failed.

"Nice job with the kid in there."

Jack pressed himself up with straightened arms.

"Hey, if you can listen in the hall, I can too."

Jack looked down. "I told you not to—"

"It's not patronizing. We're both trying to figure shit out. I need to hear it, and so do you."

He did, wanted to sink into the warmth of Tony's approval until he was drowning in it. His career hadn't come easy, but every level had a reward, a way you knew you'd made it. This—how did you know you were doing it right? If the kids weren't screaming through the night, was that success?

Jack shoved Tony's T-shirt up and kissed and licked down his chest, fingers playing in the soft blond whorls around his nipples, rasping a stubbled cheek through the darker hair arrowing down to his navel and the cock bugling in his boxers. Jack cupped Tony's balls through the cotton and teased him with licks at his hips, always threatening to dip lower.

When he did, he yanked the boxers down and ignored the temptation to swallow the thickening head, ducking instead to tongue the sac, outlining each ball with the pointed tip before sucking one then the other into his mouth.

Tony was panting, his dick full and hard against his stomach when Jack finally lapped his way up the shaft.

"God, I've been missing this."

Jack raised his head and smiled. "You were the one who said 'I want to keep my bare dick in your ass forever.'"

"Oh yeah. I remember that."

The last word cut off as Jack closed his mouth around the head and Tony snapped his teeth together.

They both froze at the knock on the door.

Jack lifted his head and rolled off.

"It's for you, Dad," Tony said with a resigned sigh, tugging his boxers back up and wiggling under the covers.

On the days Sarah went to the psychologist, she usually tapped on their door around two. Today wasn't a visit day, and Jack wasn't sure if that was a good sign or a bad sign. He pulled a T-shirt over his head and opened the door to find her in a long pink nightgown that made her look half her age. She took his hand and they walked back to her room.

They all assumed she had nightmares, though Sarah just shrugged when they asked her. She usually fell back asleep fairly quickly, but tonight her eyes glittered long after he'd tucked her into bed and sat on the edge.

"Is the nightlight too bright?"

She shook her head.

"Do you want another light on?"

Another shake.

"Can you write for me about it?"

A harder shake.

Jack sat with that helpless ache in his chest until her eyes finally closed. He waited, and after about fifteen minutes she started to squirm. Her arms flew out and he caught them, tucking them back on her chest, smoothing her hair from her face.

When she rolled on her side away from him, he waited another fifteen minutes to be sure she was really out and slipped back across the hall. When he saw Tony still awake with his laptop open on the bed, Jack regretted not slipping down to sleep on the couch. After watching his daughter fight whatever horror chased her into sleep, he couldn't summon the energy to deal with Tony's expectation of them picking up where they'd left off.

Tony looked up. "How's she doing?"

"I think she's out for the night. I thought you'd be asleep."

"Nope. Just keeping things warm." Tony shoved back the covers and turned the screen so Jack could see it.

Despite the glare on the screen and the blur of a home video, it was easy to see what had been keeping Tony up. Two guys were enthusiastically sixty-nining, the one on the bottom moving his head to shift to rimming. It was hot.

Jack slid under the duvet, and Tony put the computer away, rolling back to press against Jack before he'd stretched out.

"Need me to turn things back on? How 'bout I blow you till you forget your name?"

Normally, Tony's dirty whispers sent a spark right to Jack's cock, but not tonight. At least not now.

Tony rolled away, onto his back. "Oh."

"Tony, I—"

"No, it's okay. Long day. Lots going on."

It would have been easier if Jack was so exhausted he dropped right to sleep, but the weight on his chest made it hard to breathe. He was still awake when he heard Tony get up and turn on the shower, awake when he came back damp and smelling good. And when the birds started talking about what a nice day they thought it was, Jack was down half a roll of antacids and really tired of staring at the ceiling.

Chapter Twenty-Seven

Brandon woke up and made breakfast out of the peanut butter and bread he'd smuggled up to his room last night. It wasn't really smuggling, because at least neither Dad or his weird boyfriend had gone all dictator about food rules. It was his food anyway, since his dad bought it, so there was no reason he couldn't eat it in the shower if he wanted to.

His legs ached from sitting around so much yesterday, first in the airport and on the plane, then trapped up here. He did some stretches as he ate, wondering if maybe Dad and the freak would go somewhere with Sarah and he could check out the rest of the house. Maybe go for a run.

He did his quad stretches while he looked out the window. The backyard was big and neat, like the one he remembered from the old house before. Everything in a row, in boxes, straight lines and one circle around the tree. Except in one corner by the back fence, where there was fresh dirt.

Brandon had always loved the smell of dirt. It was one of the reasons he ran outside, made Varsity Cross Country before he was in high school. Dirt smelled different with the weather, but it always smelled clean. Especially at the end of winter when it was fighting the dirty smell of snow with that scent of something starting to wake up under the ground.

As he watched, Dad and Sarah came out from around a shed and started putting in a row of tiny plants. The sight slammed into Brandon's gut like a punch, driving the air from his lungs.

Last fall he'd turned his head during a run, answering someone, and smashed into an iron gate, belly first. That still didn't feel as bad as this.

Is that what his father thought? He'd just start doing stuff like he'd done when Brandon was a baby and act like that made it okay? Maybe he thought he'd get Sarah more attached to him with his stupid garden, so she'd be more scared of everything when Dad dumped them somewhere else.

Brandon put his forehead on the cold glass, a lot more than dry bread and peanut butter stuck in his throat. Maybe this was worse. At least Grandma and Gramps hadn't pretended to get too involved. He'd known what he could expect from them.

"Hey." There was a knock at his door.

"Yeah?"

Tony walked in. "I heard you bouncing around in here. I'm going to run out for some things. Maybe you want to pick out some stuff for your room so it doesn't look like an old folks' home."

Brandon folded his arms. "I don't care about that fairy decorating stuff. It's just a room." Under his arms, his heart pounded a little faster. Would Tony take his computer away now? It was his only link to all his friends at school.

"Okay by me." Tony shrugged. "You want clowns or cowboys?"

Brandon felt his mouth hang open. "Jesus. Okay. I'm coming."

"Fine. Take a shower first, kid."

When Brandon got downstairs, Tony still had on an Ozzy T-shirt and ripped jeans. His blond hair stuck up in the middle like a short fake Mohawk.

Brandon stared. "That's what you're wearing?"

"Yep. At least my pants won't fall off if I decide to break into a jog." Tony nodded at Brandon's cargo shorts.

Brandon hitched them up. "They won't fall off."

Tony drove them to a mall. He let Brandon get some cool stuff at Spencer's, only vetoing a Budweiser banner and a mirror with a chick's tits etched into it. Brandon had known they were probably off-limits, but he wanted to see.

Then they got the boring stuff at a department store. The place didn't have any black or red bed stuff, but he found a dark gray. Tony gave him a twenty and turned him loose in the food court, saying he needed to go pick something up.

Boston had way better pizza, but a soda and a couple slices beat breakfast this morning. Brandon handed Tony the five and the change as they walked out to the piece-of-shit car Tony drove.

"It's not like nobody's ever bought us stuff, you know. Grandma and Gramps are rich. We can have whatever we want."

"I know."

"And I know it's my dad's money, not yours."

"You got a point, kid?"

Brandon got in the car and slammed the door. Even though the thing looked like it was held together with duct tape, it didn't fall apart.

As they drove by a park, Tony pulled the car off in a little patch of dirt.

Brandon's heart started pounding again. What the fuck was going on?

Tony pointed out a path through the trees. "Want to go for

a run?"

Brandon looked down at his shorts and untied sneakers. "Like this?"

"What, will the running police arrest us?"

"You too?"

"You know that trail?"

Brandon shook his head. "How did you know about me running?"

"Besides you taking off like you had a chili pepper up—uh, like you had wings, your dad got a bunch of stuff from your school: transcript, activities, sports."

Brandon's legs were pulling him out of the car. He hitched up his shorts and tied his sneakers. Tony threw something that landed at Brandon's feet. It looked like a snake.

"It's a belt. Told you your pants would fall off."

With the trail next to him, sun splashing through the leaves to make the dirt spotted with light and dark, Brandon wanted to run more than he wanted to throw the belt back in Tony's face.

He tucked it through the loops on his pants and took off. Tony stayed behind him for the most part, and that wasn't weird. He was used to running with the cross-country team. If he didn't think too hard, he could imagine he was back at school, and things hadn't changed, and he and Sarah would be going to camp in Pennsylvania, not moving in with their useless father and his tattooed boyfriend.

They came out of the woods onto a ridge of a hill that ran above some school's playing fields, passing soccer, baseball and football. The long squat school building looked kind of familiar as they looped around the front of it.

Tony jogged up next to him. "That's McKinley High."

The name made the memory clear. "That's where the shooting was, last fall." Brandon's legs didn't feel too sure about the return trip right then. "Would I have to go there?"

"Your dad's house might be in a different school district. I'm not sure. I know this place better because I have a friend who teaches there."

They ran side by side as they passed the fields again.

"Is he gay too?"

"Is that a problem?"

"It's not some kind of big deal. Some of my friends at school have gay parents."

"Okay."

Brandon had never known an adult who could piss him off so much from agreeing with him, or who would run through the woods with a chain slapping off the hip of his ripped jeans.

"You know, kid, if I found out my mom was gay, I'd be freaked out for awhile."

"But I've known forever."

"But you didn't have to live in the same house with it."

They were almost to the trees again and it would be hard to run side by side, too hard to hear each other. He wasn't sure why it was easy to talk to Tony. The guy might be trying to buy him stuff or fake being nice so Dad would keep him around, but at least right now, things didn't suck.

Brandon squeezed out one last question, something that had been bothering him since he and Jenny had started making out.

"Did you always know about you? Liking guys, I mean."

"Pretty much."

"Did Dad?"

"Sorry. Gonna have to ask him that." Tony accelerated, disappearing into the trees. Brandon ran after him.

Chapter Twenty-Eight

Jack had planned on getting up at five and waking Tony up with a tongue in his ass, but the insomnia from the night before caught up with a vengeance. When Jack woke up at eight thirty, Tony was gone, his side of the sheets cold.

Time for Plan B.

The small white box was heavier than Jack remembered. It probably would have been better if he could have made Tony dinner and then given it to him, but Jack didn't see many dinners, breakfasts in bed or picnic lunches in their future. He hoped Tony still wanted to stick around for it.

Hell, Jack had gone the orchestrated-presentation route with Patrice, right down to presenting a glass slipper on a satin pillow along with the ring. But that had been for show. He meant it this time. With everything he had, he meant it.

He found Tony in the kitchen, making French toast and shaking his ass and nodding his head, keeping time with the bass line thumping from his classic rock station on the Bose. Jack slipped up behind him.

"Hey, you were out cold when I came back from the restaurant last night."

Tony flipped the bread in the pan and looked over his shoulder. "I was beat to hell. You know, it's not enough you've got one kid who's a cock-blocker, the other one runs like a fucking deer." Tony shook out one of his legs like it was stiff.

Jack stepped back. "Wow. Change your mind already?"

"No. It's just a big switch in my to-do list, going from *wash jeans* to *take care of two kids*. I don't know how Darlene does it, but I get why she's got a short fuse most of the time."

The edges of the box cut into Jack's hand. "If you're going to change your mind, it would be great if you could hold off until after Tuesday."

Tony turned his head to give Jack a confused look, like Tony hadn't just said he hated what their life had turned into.

Jack explained, "Because my lawyer called yesterday and we see the family court judge on Tuesday at eight."

"I told you. I haven't changed my mind."

"Okay." This was going just great. Well, at least court gave him an excuse for the box he dropped on the counter. "I got you something to wear on Tuesday."

"I've already got a suit. And a tie." Tony eyed the box warily, like there were a million possibilities in what was obviously a ring box from a jeweler.

"It's not a tie. They don't come in boxes this small." Jack grabbed the pan. "You're burning the toast."

Tony stepped away.

Jack dumped the blackened bread in the trash. "Open it. I'll take care of breakfast."

From the way Tony took his time, pouring himself coffee and juice before touching the box, Jack knew Tony had figured it out. He was probably stalling to decide what to say.

Jack had already added vanilla and cinnamon to the batter and folded the bread over banana slices by the time Tony got around to taking off the lid.

Since Jack already knew what was in the brown velvet, he

watched Tony's face instead. It went blank as he took out the thick, solid band of brushed platinum inset with a thinner strip of yellow gold in the middle. The one that matched the ring in Jack's pocket.

Jack turned his attention back to the pan, readying another slice.

"Is this for real?" Tony asked.

Jack didn't look up. "At that price it had better be."

"You know that's not what I meant. Is it just for show? Like my suit."

"You really think I'd buy solid platinum bands for decoration?"

Tony made a pointed glance at the custom lighting, the Bose and the Jenn-Air range.

"Okay. Don't answer that." Jack swallowed back the weight in his throat as he put the toast in the oven to keep it warm before taking his own band from his pocket. Holding Tony's hand in his, Jack closed it around the ring. "It's not just for looks. I bought them for us." Jack pulled the band on the ring finger of his left hand, the metal cold and heavy. He hadn't worn a ring during his marriage, claiming it wasn't a good idea to have it on in the kitchen.

Tony still hadn't said anything.

"Try it on. I judged based on my size." Jack turned away and put two more slices in the pan.

"It fits."

When Jack turned to look, Tony was holding up his left hand, waggling his fingers.

"Gee, Jack, you didn't give me time to send out any wedding invitations."

Great. Another joke. "Does that mean you like it or not?"

"I like it." Tony leaned out to scan the hallway and then gave Jack a quick kiss. "I like it a lot. Thanks."

Jack put his hand around Tony's neck. His skin heated the metal of the ring. "Thanks?"

Tony kissed him again. "I don't know any movie lines like Sean and Kyle do." He grinned. "I already gave you my ass. I guess you can have my hand too."

With their foreheads pressed together, Jack shook his head, but he chuckled. The sound of bare feet on the stone tiles had them jumping apart.

Sarah climbed up on one of the barstools. As Jack put on some bacon to fry, Tony poured her a glass of milk and some orange juice. He made a production of putting them in front of her, switching them back and forth like some kind of shell game, and she huffed out one of her laughs.

Jack wished being with the kids came as easily to him as it did to Tony. No matter how hard Jack tried, it seemed to come out wrong.

As Sarah picked up the juice, she tapped Tony's ring, a big smile on her face.

"Did you help your dad pick that out?"

Jack had taken her to the store while Tony was out with Brandon. With sober attention, she had examined each of the rings the jeweler took out of the case. He thought for sure she'd have been drawn to something diamond encrusted, but she'd pointed to the one he'd liked from the first.

Tony put his hand on her head and she didn't shrink away. "Nice job, kid."

Jack heard the tap of the ring as Tony drummed it against every available surface on his way to the stairs to yell for Brandon.

Chapter Twenty-Nine

Tony turned away from the courthouse window. There wasn't much to see through the bars anyway. Jack was pacing, and the kids were perched on a wooden bench. The way Sarah swung her feet made her look much younger than her age until she reached into her purse then handed her fidgeting brother his PSP along with a look of superior patience. Brandon glanced around and then shook his head.

Jack's lawyer had been in a conference room with the Howards' lawyer since they got here. Tony dug at his collar, trying to find some breathing room between the noose made out of silk and his windpipe. Jack looked up at the top of one of his laps and caught Tony at it. Making a desperate I'm-choking face got him one of Jack's smiles in return.

It was only the second time in Tony's life he'd worn a tie, and he'd been too numb at his mom's funeral to really notice it. Tony smiled back and ran his fingers through what was left of his hair. The longer spikes he liked to gel up in the center were gone, courtesy of a haircut to make him look a little less punk gay bartender and a little more upstanding-gay-parent material.

As he pulled his hand down even the dim light through the barred window was enough to flash on the thick band on his left hand. That was worth the tie and the haircut. Tony got why people wore wedding bands now. It wasn't to remind you not to lie and fuck around. If you couldn't remember what the rules were, you probably shouldn't be in a relationship in the first place. Nope. The ring was there to say they were a team, a reminder that they were in this together, almost like a private joke only the two of them got.

Jack saw Tony look at his ring and gave him a wink.

Tony smiled back.

When the lawyer popped out from behind the closed door down at the other end of the hall, his smile made Tony's bigger.

The lawyer shook Jack's hand. "They aren't going to contest your permanent guardianship. They're ready to sign off on custody."

"What's the catch?" Tony asked.

"No financial claims, Jack signs non-disclosure with respect to the incident."

"And the order of protection?" Jack had wanted to make sure Patrice got nowhere near the kids.

"We got that too. I put in a request for a lump-sum settlement regarding Sarah's future medical care. We're getting it drafted right now."

"I don't want anything from them. I'll handle her care." Jack might be pissed now, but that psychologist couldn't be cheap and Tony didn't know how much insurance would pay. Hell, he'd never even asked Jack if he had insurance through the restaurant. Tony didn't have any.

"I think you should reconsider." The lawyer tried to steer Jack down the hall and into his way of thinking. Tony wished him luck with that.

Their voices trailed off as the lawyer got Jack around the corner.

Tony looked at the kids on the bench. Nice system when the kids never got to get a word in, though he hoped they would have wanted things to turn out like this. "What do you guys think?"

"About the money?" Brandon asked.

"About any of it."

"Someone's actually going to ask what we want?"

"Sarah already said what she wanted. Did you want to stay with your grandparents?" *And your mother?* Tony didn't say out loud, but he knew Brandon understood him.

"No."

"So, this is how you guys are when you're happy?" Tony asked.

Brandon made a sarcastic stadium wave from the bench.

Tony tried again. "I'm just glad it's all over and you guys get to stay with your dad, but I got to say coming here was a complete waste of a shower." Tony ran his hand over his hair again. "So when your dad gets back, what do you say we blow this joint, make like the commercial and go to Disney World—or at least Ohio's version of it."

Sarah looked up.

"Today?" Brandon asked.

"Why not?"

Chapter Thirty

Jack wished Tony had asked him before telling the kids they'd go to Cedar Point right after the paperwork was signed. When they went home to get changed into shorts and T-shirts, Jack already felt like he'd put in an eighteen-hour shift as a line chef. The park was only a hundred miles away, but Jack still had to go in to the restaurant later. He couldn't take back Tony's offer without making things worse.

Brandon seemed more nervous than excited, though Sarah bounced around in the car as they drove out along the causeway to the amusement park that was practically in Lake Erie.

How did they have room to keep putting in more roller coasters? According to Brandon and Tony, there were seventeen, one topping four hundred feet in height. As they got close enough to see some of the man-made mountains, Sarah tapped his shoulder and pointed. From this angle, the drop looked like it was eighty-five degrees. The kids had been in his custody for less than three hours, and now Tony wanted Jack to fling them off a skyscraper.

"Is that the big one?" Brandon asked.

"It was for awhile," Tony said.

As they came around a curve, a taller structure loomed over the horizon. According to the odometer, they were still two miles away.

"We should probably go on some that Sarah can ride too." Brandon's normally dismissive tone held a wobble of uncertainty.

"She's tall enough for most of them, if she wants to ride." Tony looked over his shoulder into the backseat.

Jack would have sworn Tony was baiting Brandon.

For his own piece of mind, Jack made an executive decision about riding one of the smaller, older coasters close to the entrance. What he didn't take into consideration was that it was made of wood.

As they waited in line, Brandon muttered, "Is wood really strong enough for this?"

Jack pointed out the redundancies in the framework, the multiple support beams. That the blue paint on the wood showed signs of a losing battle with Lake Erie weather he kept to himself.

"Hey, kid," Tony said. "How many people you know who've been hurt on an amusement-park ride?"

"None," Brandon admitted.

"How many people do you know who've been in a car accident?"

"Tony." Jack glared at him, hands spread to ask him what the fuck he thought he was doing.

Tony winced. "Okay. Bad comparison. But really, what are the odds? A park can't stay in business if people get hurt."

Jack tried for an angle and a tone low enough to get through Tony's thick skull, but not loud enough for the kids to hear him. "Are you trying to freak them out?"

"The Peanut's not freaked, right?"

Sarah nodded, swinging Jack's hand while she looked

around.

"Tony," Jack warned again, but it was a lost cause.

"I just want them to have some fun."

"Or you do. If you wanted to come up here yourself, you could have done it anytime."

Tony's look of hurt disbelief was almost comical. Oddly, the more conservative haircut made him look younger, playing up the inherent innocence in blond, blue-eyed and freckled.

As Jack settled Sarah in the seat, he was relieved to see that there was a separate lap bar for each passenger as well as a seat belt. He pressed Sarah's bar down until it locked against her hips, and then checked it. Three times. He looked around the headrest at Tony and Brandon behind them.

"Check his lap bar."

Tony gave Jack an exasperated look before turning to Brandon. "Lift up on that to see if it's locked, man."

Jack watched as Brandon checked, and checked Sarah's one more time before the train rolled out of the station. Tucking an arm under and over Sarah's to act as a final human restraint system, he slid back against the seat as the chain dragged the cars up to the top of the wooden hill.

He glanced over at Sarah and found her grinning. As they were flung down the first hill, she laughed. An actual laugh, not just one of the huffs she made sometimes, but a spurt of laughter each time they crested a hill and popped out of their seats.

From Tony, Jack caught an occasional *woo*.

From Brandon, silence.

Jack imagined his son enduring the experience with the same stoic expression he knew was on his own face.

Sarah skipped down the exit ramp, dragging Jack and

pointing to the station again.

With something like a growl, Brandon yanked the park map out of Tony's back pocket.

"Let's go on this one next. I'll ride with Tony, and Dad can take Sarah on this kiddie coaster."

The stare Sarah leveled at her brother couldn't have been more targeted if it were a heat-seeking missile, but she didn't try to stop them as they walked along a midway toward the middle of the park.

Jack asked for the map and studied it. The coaster Brandon had pointed out wasn't either of the two super coasters, but it was still over two hundred feet tall. Searching for an alternative selection proved time-consuming. The coasters that weren't suicidal in height made up for it in contorted loops and riding positions: standing up, swinging from an overhead track. It was a bizarre form of entertainment. He'd found something that looked like a good compromise when he realized Brandon wasn't with them.

After a moment of frantic crowd searching, he demanded, "Where's Brandon?"

Tony pointed.

Brandon had been suckered in by one of the games along the midway, something involving a crossbow shoot and stuffed lions and tigers. Jack went over to collect him, Sarah still clinging to his hand. At least he didn't have to worry about her wandering off.

Brandon saw him coming and after a belligerent assertion that he had his own money, kept playing. After at least twenty dollars had disappeared into the attendant's apron, Tony leaned on the counter.

"Dude, you could buy it for half that. C'mon."

Sarah took Brandon's hand and he allowed himself to be

led away.

When they arrived at the entrance for the roller coaster Brandon had selected, the boy pointed across the paved path to where some cartoon characters decorated the entrance to the Woodstock Express. "The kids' coaster is over there." He pointed for Sarah.

"I remember when they opened this. Best ride ever," Tony said looking at the entrance to the larger ride. "I waited four and a half hours to get on back then."

With them standing at the base, the track was hidden behind trees and the boarding station.

Sarah dragged Jack behind Brandon and Tony.

Tony turned around. "Hey, Peanut, this is a really big roller coaster, are you sure?" He took the map from Jack and showed it to her, his finger tracing the track.

She nodded, her eyes gleaming. As he watched, Jack would have sworn she was about to say something. Her throat bobbed, but her lips pursed tight together and she nodded again before marching up to the height measure at the entrance.

An attendant measured her against his stick. She had inches to spare.

"I know you're tall enough, but are you sure you want to ride?" Jack asked. He'd be happy to skip it in favor of Woodstock or SpongeBob or whatever bright yellow animal was used to attract the children.

She pointed at all of them.

Tony crouched down next to her. "I've already been on it, honey. Your dad can go with Brandon, and you and I can go on a different one."

Brandon gave a long, drawn-out sigh. "C'mon, Sarah. The kids' coaster has Snoopy, and there's one that's like a mine train we can all go on."

She stomped back into the line. Jack looked at Tony who shrugged.

Despite the screams and the way the station shook when the trains went by, Sarah looked excited. She clung to Jack's hand and grinned, sometimes jumping up and down. Jack remembered Tony's words about the park not being able to stay in business if it wasn't safe. Exactly what would the insurance run on a place like this? It had to be substantial, which would explain the ticket price for an overgrown carnival.

"Does this go upside down?" Brandon asked.

"Nope," Tony said. "Some of the other ones do. The last new one I went on you stand up and go upside down. I think your sister's too short for that one though." He patted her head, and she smiled up at him.

Jack had been studying the way the riders dispersed on the loading platform with people flocking to the first car, the middle section and the very end. "If we head for the second car in the train, we'll be able to get on much faster." He'd rather get this over with.

"They take your picture on one of the bunny-hop hills at the end," Tony said. "Everybody smile and put your hands in the air."

"Everybody keep your hands in the car and on the safety bar, thank you very much," Jack corrected.

As they moved into the corrals for their seats, he and Sarah together with Tony and Brandon behind him, Tony said, "Brandon, if you want to ride next to your dad, I'm sure he'll take you again."

Jack was going to kill him.

He controlled a sigh of relief at Brandon's answer. "Doesn't matter. Sarah's happy with it like this."

Despite the obviously conscientious workers checking the

lap bars and seat belts, Jack couldn't resist multiple checks as well. He wished he could turn around and give Tony a look that told him he was responsible for anything that happened and to keep a tight grip on Brandon. He tucked his arm under and through Sarah's again as the attendants ran one final check and held their thumbs up.

The brakes hissed loose and they rolled out of the station amid claps and laughter from the riders in front of him.

Sarah kept turning her head as they slowly ticked up the lift hill. It wasn't the up part that worried Jack. He pointed out the tiny people below in the water park and the campground, and she gave another one of those quick bursts of laughter as she waved. He pulled her hand back into the car.

For the last twenty feet, all they could see below was the lake.

"If it was clear today, you could probably see Canada." Tony's arm came between the seats, pointing.

On a clear day, they could probably see the house in Marblehead. It was less than four miles by boat.

Despite the thick clouds, patches of sun bounced off the waves, and the wind that made whitecaps on the lake also made the track sway. Jack couldn't have been imagining it. The track was swaying.

"Does this go into the lake?" Brandon asked, the fear in his voice making him sound like a child again.

"No. It looks like it will, but it turns away. You won't get wet or anything," Tony answered, barely audible above the tick of the chain and the wind.

The clicking slowed and they seemed to hang at the top for a long time. Long enough for Jack to hear the fear in his son's voice.

"The water. It looks... It's hard. Cold."

The scene clicked together in an instant for Jack. Strapped tightly in a car, the water waiting for them under a gray sky.

He knew how bad a mistake this had been long before Sarah started to scream.

Chapter Thirty-One

It wasn't the ride.

Jack had had that same nightmare too many times, and just like then, there was nothing he could do to help her.

The water rushed toward them as they slid down the hill, swerved and then popped out of their seats at the top of the next. Jack held her, but he knew all she saw was the water of the lake waiting for them.

Her body tightened into another prolonged scream. The track veered away from the water and into a turn so tight the track doubled back on itself, but even the squeal of the brakes couldn't cover the sound from his daughter. As the train turned back toward the station, Sarah's wail cut off so suddenly he thought she'd fainted.

When they bounced over the hills Tony had called bunny hops, rising and slamming back onto the seat, Sarah made a sound like a hiccup and started to cry. It wasn't anything like her screaming—this was new, soft, a little girl's cry.

In the station, Jack scooped her up and carried her down the stairs through the exit, while she clung to his neck and sobbed.

Behind the hut that sold pictures of screaming riders, he stroked her back and whispered her name.

"Da—ad—dy."

Jack froze. Hell, he almost dropped her.

"Da—addy." Less of a break and louder this time. Jack wanted to fall to his knees and thank God right then.

"You're okay, honey. You're okay. We'll go home now. I'm sorry the ride was scary."

"No." That word came out with such force he felt it leave her body.

Brandon and Tony ran over, Brandon practically crawling up Jack's leg to get a look at Sarah.

"She's all right. Can you stand for me, honey?" Jack put her on her feet and knelt next to her.

She nodded. Jack used his polo shirt to wipe her face.

"Bran—don."

"I'm sorry about the ride, Sarah. I didn't—" Her brother broke off and then smiled.

She nodded again, breath coming in quick pants.

Her throat worked, and Jack felt her shoulders tense, like she was trying to push something out of her.

"Still chokes." Her voice. God, he never thought he'd hear his daughter's voice. Harsh and choppy, it was the sweetest thing he'd heard.

She grabbed Brandon's hand. "Water."

"I know. I remember it too." He hugged her.

Jack glanced at Tony, who rubbed his cheek against the shoulder of his Led Zeppelin T-shirt.

Almost had a fuckin' heart attack, Tony mouthed at him.

Jack looked away. He had more to deal with than Tony right now. "We'll go home now, Sarah," Jack said.

"No." She pushed the word out, but still shook her head like she was relying on that for communication. Jack remembered a tiny spoonful of squash flying over his head, an imperious "No" ringing after it.

"We can come back another time, Peanut. It's not far away."

Her shoulders tensed again and she put her hand on her throat as if she could clear it of whatever held her words in. "To—ny."

"Yeah." Tony nodded, the awe in his voice sounding like she'd just handed him a pile of diamonds. Jack wanted to hand him his ass in a sling.

"More rides." She grabbed the map from his pocket. "Not with..." she took a few deep breaths, "...water." She pointed at a flume ride illustrated with splashes.

"Yup. No water rides. Got it."

Brandon shifted from foot to foot. "Shouldn't she go to her doctor or something?"

Jack looked down at Sarah and cleaned her face again. She took a deep breath. "I'm. Okay. Doctor said."

"The doctor said she might start slowly or all at once," Jack explained.

"Sarah?" Brandon asked.

"More rides."

"Brandon, stay here with your sister for a second and don't move."

Too angry to put a hand on him, Jack steered Tony down the path with his body.

"Pretty awesome, huh? I think she's getting better by the second." Tony looked around Jack at the kids.

"Jesus, Tony, I know you're not that fucking stupid. How could you let my kids get on that ride?"

"What the hell are you talking about?"

Jack had Tony's attention now.

"You knew about the accident, and you'd been on that ride before. How could you not think?" Jack dragged a breath past the tightness in his chest. God, please let that just be an ulcer.

"How can you even think I'd let anything happen to them?"

"I didn't say you did it on purpose, but you've got to use your head. It's not just about us anymore."

"Believe me I know."

Tony's rueful laugh made Jack's stomach churn worse than the thought of more of these damned rides. Jack started to walk away.

"Jack, they're your kids. I'd never let anything hurt them. I just wanted them to have some fun doing things that kids do with a dad. Not courthouses and custody and psychologists. But fun."

"You mean you wanted some fun, and they were a convenient excuse."

"I'm not the one who passed off a fucking wedding band as *something to wear to court.*"

"So why are you still wearing it?"

"Why are you?"

Now Jack needed to touch him. But that wasn't happening in the middle of a crowded amusement park. "I told you."

"No, actually, you didn't."

Jack couldn't believe they were having this conversation, here. Now.

Life was spinning out of control in so many directions sometimes he couldn't breathe, but when he looked into the eyes of the man in front of him everything was worth it. He just wished he knew what Tony saw in him that put that look in his eyes.

Jack forced another breath around the rock on his rib cage.

"Because I'm standing in the middle of a crowded amusement park and my daughter just said her first words in four and half years and even though I could strangle you, all I want to do is kiss you."

"Okay then." Tony turned and walked back toward the kids.

They ended up staying another hour. Jack had to take over on the spinning rides when Tony came off the Matterhorn looking green. Sarah loved everything that took her up high, and they avoided anything near water. Her favorite was the twin racing coaster, and she insisted on doing both the blue and the red trains. She rode the second time with Tony, sending Jack and Brandon on the blue train.

They found a table near a food stand, and Sarah inhaled some fried cheese on a stick, something Jack refused to believe existed until Tony came away from the window with two artery-clogging chunks skewered like popsicles.

Jack turned down Tony's offer to share. Brandon was on his way through his third taco. Jack rubbed his chest and drank bottled water.

"You okay?" Tony asked.

"I think I hit it on one of the rides. It's fine."

After lunch, Tony went off to the bathroom. Brandon tossed his trash and said he was going too, but when Tony came back, Brandon wasn't with him.

"Did you see him? He followed you," Jack asked.

"Yeah. He went into the bathroom."

"And you left him?"

"I can't stalk a fourteen-year-old in the men's room, Jack. I'll get arrested. Besides it's right over there." Tony jerked his thumb at a building on a little grass hill.

“I’ll go. Stay with Sarah.”

Brandon wasn’t in the restroom or getting more tacos or cotton candy or another pop.

“He’s lost.” Jack came back to the table, both the acid and adrenaline pumps kicking into overdrive. The ink wasn’t dry on the custody papers. If he made it through the day without his chest bursting like he was giving birth to an alien, it would be a fucking miracle. “You lost him.”

“I didn’t lose him.”

Between a seventy percent chance of rain and the fact that it wasn’t a weekend, the park wasn’t overly packed, but there were still thousands of people around. Brandon didn’t seem to be likely to head off to one of the rides alone, and he’d already checked the food vendors in the area.

“Tiger.” Sarah’s voice was still so surprising, it was as if the metal bench had begun talking to them.

“Sh—crap.” Tony slapped his head. “The tiger, that shooting game on the midway. I bet he went back. I’ll go get him.”

“No. I’ll go. Meet us at that hat shop near the entrance. Don’t lose Sarah.”

“I didn’t lose—fine.”

Brandon was exactly where Sarah had said he would be. When he saw Jack, he stepped away from the game, and then back a couple of steps, like he was thinking about running. Finally, he just waited with his hands in his pockets.

Jack knew how his father would have handled this. He could guess what a parenting book would say. But his father’s methods were out of the question, and judging from the look on Brandon’s face, he had to have known how scared they’d be when they couldn’t find him.

"I would have been back in another minute," Brandon said.

When Jack looked at the school pictures of Brandon, he'd never been able to see himself. His son had Patrice's coloring, her fine bones on a boy's face. Now Jack could see the jut of his own chin as his son stood up to him.

"I just want you to tell me why you had to do this today. After what just happened with Sarah, why you had to take off like that."

"It was for Sarah. She wanted the tiger. And she would never have gone on the ride if I—if I didn't make such a big deal of her going on the other one."

"Brandon, I don't know what happened to her on the ride, but she's talking. If you got her to go on that roller coaster, I'd say it was a good thing." *But don't repeat that to Tony.* Jack would have preferred a less dramatic return to vocalizations, and he had a feeling there'd be a couple taps on his door tonight.

"She always used to listen to me."

Jack swallowed. "Oh." He hadn't just yanked his son out of the only world he knew, he'd come between Brandon and his sister. "You and I both know that the only reason your sister made it that day was because of you. I owe you for that."

Brandon wouldn't meet his eyes.

Jack sighed. "How much have you lost on the game?"

"Fifty. The sights are all off."

"I know. It's how they make money. So you use that. If the sight is off, gauge by how much. And try shooting at the target one over."

"How do you know?"

"My mom's brother worked a carnival for a few years."

"Really? Where—is he dead, like Grandma Noble?"

"I don't know," Jack admitted. He'd never bothered to keep in touch with any of his family after he left. Didn't have anything to say to them. "Let's do this. But if you don't get it in twenty bucks, we're still leaving."

Jack didn't know if it was luck or Brandon relying on strategy instead of frustration to guide the dart, but after ten dollars worth, he had a white tiger to give to his sister, and Jack had made it through his first official day as the sole guardian of his son and daughter.

Chapter Thirty-Two

Jack leaned against the kitchen counter and watched Tony twist the band around his finger. In just a week the gesture had become familiar. Tony didn't do that with his skull ring, and Jack wondered again if Tony was comfortable with wearing a wedding band.

"So I thought we'd have a party. You know, to celebrate the kids moving in and it being official," Tony said.

"It can't be like one of your Super Bowl parties."

"Wow. Then I'd better take the giant sub sandwich shaped like a penis back to the store of Duh-I-Know-That-Jack."

Jack folded his arms.

Tony waved through the sliding glass doors. "We'll have a barbeque kind of thing in the backyard."

"Who's coming?"

"Just Sean and Kyle and Darlene and the kids, and some-people-from-Canton-Akron-Gay-Parents-Association." Tony ran that last bit by really fast as if Jack wasn't going to understand him.

"People we've never met?"

"How can we meet them if we don't invite them over? The doctor said Sarah should interact with kids more. And these people have kids. It might be good for Brandon too," Tony added.

"And you think the kids will get along because they all happen to have gay parents?"

"They've gotta start somewhere."

Sometimes Tony's logic made sense, if Jack didn't spend too much time thinking about it. "I reserve the right to leave early 'for work' if it all goes south."

"It will be fine," Tony reassured him.

Jack had to admit that the prep went well. Tony didn't overdo the decorations, sticking to a beach theme, and Sarah seemed to enjoy helping him prepare, decorating bikini-and-swimsuit-clad sugar cookies cut like gingerbread men. The doctor was teaching her relaxation techniques to help with the spasms she got when she tried to talk. Her speech had more of a flow now, though it sometimes took her a minute to get started.

On the morning of the party, Jack made them a late breakfast. Brandon still hadn't come out of his room by the time Tony and Sarah were leaving to pick up the balloons.

"Tony." Jack threw him the keys to the X3, and Tony's eyes widened in surprise. "I feel better about you driving the kids in something with a little more protection," Jack said. "I'll get something else to drive to work."

After Tony and Sarah left, Jack took his coffee out onto the deck. He sent an over-the-counter heartburn pill down with a swig of coffee and managed a good deep breath. The meds weren't working much anymore and Jack was starting to wonder if it was his heart instead. What the hell was going to happen to the kids if it was his heart? They'd never let them stay with Tony. Tony had said he'd been arrested for possession when he was eighteen.

Jack put his hand over his chest wishing he could use it

like an X-ray to find out what was going on under the skin. The first thump sounded at the same time as his heartbeat, and he thought it was in his head until the next thump had him looking at the shed.

Dirt flew as a clump of soil hit the roof and slid down. Jack stepped off the deck.

Brandon ripped another seedling out of the herb garden and threw it over the fence.

Jack threw the coffee mug aside and ran toward him. Brandon looked up, and the next clod of dirt hit Jack square in the chest.

"Nobody asked me about a fucking queer party," Brandon screamed as he wrenched the sage free from the soil and whipped it against the fence. "Or if I wanted to go to a school where people get shot. And nobody gives a shit as long as Sarah's all right and it was just us and she never said a word to me."

Jack stood frozen. He could grab him, stop him, but it hardly seemed worth a wrestling match over dirt and herbs. Maybe Brandon needed this. Jack should have that child psychologist on speed dial.

Brandon picked up the bubble machine Tony had placed in the corner and flung it against the fence, spraying chunks of plastic over the torn earth.

"Brandon."

"Shut up. Don't fucking talk to me." His voice broke, grew more shrill with every word. He yanked one of the tiki torches out of the ground and smashed the torch against the side of the shed. The basket at the top slipped off easily, leaving Brandon with a four-foot wooden spear to brandish. "I don't know anyone here and you're a fucking jerk and I hate you."

Brandon flung the spear, and Jack ducked. The wood

whistled over his head to land embedded in the ring of hostas around the tree. Brandon ran for it, and Jack took off after him.

He got to his son just as Brandon's hand closed on the stick. Brandon's rage gave him a surprising strength, but Jack pried the stick free and flung it away, wrapping himself around Brandon and dragging him onto the ground.

The boy wasn't crying, just making ragged gasps that tore through his lean frame. After a few breaths, he struggled to get free, reaching out and yanking at the hostas for leverage. Jack caught his arms and tucked them into the embrace. The first time he'd touched his son in five years, and he was restraining him in the backyard to avoid being skewered by a party torch.

"Let me go."

"When you calm down."

"I can't. I'm never going to calm down. Fuck you."

Jack held on tighter, and Brandon's elbow caught him under the eye.

"Brandon, I'm not letting go and I'm not leaving you."

"It doesn't matter. You can't fix it. I hate you." Brandon kicked back, heel slamming into Jack's shin right below his knee.

Brandon stopped moving, but Jack was pretty sure he was just gathering strength for another attempt at freedom. Brandon went into full rebellion, kicking back and pinching with his fingers.

Jack rolled him underneath and kept his arms tight. "It's all right. You're all right."

"I'm not. I'm not." Brandon's voice broke again and the fight drained out of him. He slumped in Jack's arms, sobbing.

Jack sat up, still holding tight. "You're okay. I've got you."

"I hate you." But Brandon leaned against him, body

shaking with every breath.

"I know. I don't blame you. Most days I hate myself."

"Good." Brandon made a raspy sniff and started crying again.

They sat on the grass for a long time while Brandon's sobs slowed and stopped.

"I'm okay," Brandon said at last.

Jack loosened his hold, but Brandon didn't get up right away.

"I'll pay for your stupid plants." Brandon's voice shook a little.

"It's all right. They're just plants."

"Are you going to take my computer away?"

"I think we'll give this one a pass. But if you're angry like that again, tell me first. It's okay to be angry but it's not okay to—"

"I got it." Brandon sounded more like himself.

Jack wished he could carry him in the house like this, like he would have that little boy he'd left behind, but the garage door rattled open. As soon as Tony's voice floated back, telling Sarah to bring the balloons into the yard, Brandon scrambled up and ran into the house through the kitchen.

Jack climbed to his feet more slowly. Sarah came around through the gate, a big smile behind her huge handful of balloons, Tony trailing after with a bag of tablecloths. He turned from putting the bag on the table and looked around the yard.

"What the hell happened?"

Jack tipped his head in Sarah's direction and shook his head.

"Hey, Peanut, do you think you could help me out with a pitcher of lemonade before we put these balloons out?"

Tony tied the balloons to a chair and set her up at the counter with mix, measuring cup and pitcher before following Jack into the living room. "What the hell happened?" Tony reached for the throbbing spot on Jack's cheek, and Jack ducked away.

"I saw the kid go tearing into the house. Did he hit you?"

"Not on purpose." Jack avoided mention of the more purposeful attempt at impaling.

"What's going on?"

Jack managed to condense it to "He was ripping up the garden and hit me by accident."

"And the other stuff, the torch and the bubble machine."

"He was upset."

"What about now?"

"The fact that I fucked up his life."

Tony ran his hand through his hair. "What do you want to do?"

"Not having this party would be a good start."

"C'mon. I can't do anything about it now."

"Did it occur to you that maybe we should have let things settle for awhile? That we shouldn't have forced this on him?"

"Did it occur to you that maybe you should have said something about that last week when I suggested it? Or are you going back to not telling me things?"

Jack could take it from Brandon, but he was sick to death of Tony's one-note concert. "It has nothing to do with telling you things. Moving here is hard enough on—"

"The doctor thinks Sarah needs to interact with people. I sure as hell think Brandon does. Or are you going to leave him in his room forever?"

"And you became an expert on adolescent psychology

during which repeat of twelfth grade?"

Tony's cheeks flushed, but it was too late for Jack to take it back.

Tony recovered quickly. "It's better than just sitting around with my thumb up my ass. You told me I couldn't understand what you'd been through because I lived with zero expectations. You're so damned afraid of the kids you run to work rather than deal with them. I said I wanted to do this with you, not for you. So don't think you can turn me into a fucking wife you can leave sitting at home."

"So what do you expect me to do? Quit my job?"

"You could start by talking to your son."

"He needs time—"

"To what? See even less of you?"

"If you don't want to be a wife, you could skip the nagging. Brandon needs some time right now to cool the hell off. I sure do." Jack turned around and walked out.

Chapter Thirty-Three

Tony stared so hard at the place where Jack had been standing that the sound of the doorbell made him jump out of his skin. The doorbell rang again, and he stomped into the hall and yanked the door open.

Sean stood on the step, juggling his cane, a bowl holding enough potato salad for an army battalion and a grocery bag full of chips. "Kyle brought the extra table around back."

Tony took the bag of chips, and Sean followed him into the kitchen. Jack wasn't in there bitching because they were using a mix instead of lemons and syrup and water, and this time Tony didn't give a rat's ass where Jack had disappeared to.

Sean left his cane propped up against the house as he helped set up the extra table to put the food on. Kyle watched carefully for a minute and murmured to Tony before going into the house, "At least he let me carry the table. Baby steps."

"I'm not deaf, babe," Sean said, but his voice didn't have the exasperation Tony had heard so often last year.

Kyle turned back at the door to offer Sean a grin and a wink. "I know, *papi*. I love your teacher hearing." He shifted his hips away from the swat Sean aimed at his ass.

Sean's laugh and threat of "Later, babe" chased Kyle into the house.

Tony waggled his eyebrows at Sean, who gave him a look of

utterly fake innocence as they weighted the tablecloth against the spring breeze. Tony didn't know why, but at least if things were going to hell with him and Jack, knowing that Sean and Kyle had managed to put it back together gave Tony a little hope.

Sean nodded at Sarah who was carefully choosing locations to tie off the balloons she'd been put in charge of. "Aren't you afraid she'll blow away?"

"She's stronger than she looks," Tony said.

Kyle came through the sliding glass doors with extra napkins and plates. "Hey, look at that. Child labor. Now that's a reason to breed. What happened to the yard?"

"Jack's son decided to take up landscaping this morning. He's not really good at it." Tony filled one of the drink cups with the bundled silverware and napkins. Sarah had tied each bundle with red and yellow ribbons.

"Maybe the kids would be happier with a wicked stepmother who didn't make them work." Sean grinned.

Stretching his leg out under the table, Tony aimed for his good leg and kicked him. Hard.

"Ow." Kyle stepped back.

"Sorry." Tony winced. Who could have thought a party would be such a bad idea?

Sean grabbed his cane and hobbled off the deck. "Replacing the hostas is going to be pricey."

Kyle rolled his eyes. "He's really starting to act like an old man."

"Maybe he's going to take up subcontracting."

As they watched, Sean walked around, checking out the damage. Unless you knew what it had looked like before, it wasn't too bad. Or unless you knew how much Jack liked everything to look perfect.

“What are you going to do with him?” Kyle asked.

“Who, Sean?”

“The kid. Braden.”

“Brandon. I decided putting his head on a pike was a little excessive, so I told Jack he needed to talk to him.”

“Hey.” Sean held up one of the stakes from the tiki torches. “You guys playing Mastodon Hunter or is the piñata game a fight to the death?”

Tony hadn’t seen that. He was starting to think a lot more had gone down than some torn up plants. *Damn it, Jack.*

“This is new.” Kyle flicked at the ring on Tony’s hand.

“Yeah.” Tony looked at Kyle’s hand. Sean and Kyle didn’t wear rings. Tony had never asked them why. God knew the rings weren’t doing much for him and Jack.

“So you’re sticking around, not just to help Jack with the custody.”

“You know that. I’m not saying this wasn’t a hell of a curve ball, but I love the guy, Kyle.”

“So, then maybe you should both talk to Brandon.”

“I’ve tried. Did everything but take him out and buy him a beer.”

“You can’t be his big brother, Tony. If you’re staying, he’s your kid too. Talk to him together. I always knew I was in serious shit when Dad and Mami teamed up on me.”

The bang of the gate and the sounds of a rhinoceros charge warned Tony his nephews had arrived. He grinned. “I think I’ll send Eric and Damien up to see if Brandon wants to play.” Even if Brandon was holding back-up weapons, Tony would bet on his nephews in any hand-to-hand.

Sean took over the grill and sent Tony into the kitchen for the dark mustard Sean insisted they had to have because he’d seen it here before. Tony was leaning on the fridge door, shoving stuff around, when his sister grabbed his wrist.

"Fancy. I didn't know it was a wedding reception."

"Huh?" The mustard was behind a jar of wheat germ. What did you do with wheat germ?

Darlene tapped his ring.

Despite what Tony had managed to drag out of Jack that day at Cedar Point, he still looked at it and wondered what the fuck it was doing on his hand. Sean and Kyle didn't wear them, and they were still together. A ring hadn't kept Darlene's husband around. Hadn't stopped Mom from dying alone.

Tony slapped the mustard bottle on the counter. "We just got the rings to wear to court, for the judge."

She picked up his hand again. "And you couldn't find something at the dollar store."

Tony pulled his hand free. "Eh, weddings are bullshit anyway."

"Works for me." Darlene reached around him and grabbed the relish. "This way I don't have to buy you a present."

Tony hadn't just invited random people from the Parents' Association to the party. The woman at the contact number had been really helpful, and though Tony didn't go into specifics about the reasons behind how hard things were on the kids, she knew right away what he was asking. Two other couples came, two guys with a baby girl and a twelve-year-old boy, and two women with two girls, fifteen and twelve. If the leggy blonde fifteen-year-old didn't get Brandon out of his room, Tony didn't know what would, and from the way Sean oohed over the baby, it looked like Kyle would be having some interesting discussions in his future.

Tony had suggested that Sarah stand behind the table and serve, rather than turn her loose with a bunch of strangers, and at least that part of his plan went well. At first, Brandon slunk around the edges while the two girls played with the baby, but when Sarah hung up the piñata, he took a turn. Tony suspected that had more to do with the fact that the teenaged girls were doing the blindfolding and the spinning.

Even after it cracked though, Brandon helped keep the three other boys from coming to blows over the candy that spilled out. Tony watched from the deck as one of the dads offered to let Sarah hold the baby. She was attentive and cautious, but once she was seated with the baby in her lap she looked happy.

"Okay." Jack came up behind him. "It was a good idea."

"Not bad for someone who repeated twelfth grade English and Social Studies?"

"C'mon, Tony." Jack ran his hand up from the top of Tony's ass to his neck, a hard deep rub that did a hell of a lot more than his half-assed apology to take the ache of tension out of Tony's back.

Tony leaned back. "I'll let you make it up to me later." Another stroke on his spine, the heel of Jack's hand going all the way up to the base of the skull, where his fingers played in what was left of Tony's hair. "You going to tell me the rest of what happened this morning?"

"Later. I think blowing off steam did him some good, though."

Tony did a quick sweep, checking for the presence of boyfriend offspring and other assorted G-rated viewers. Getting a negative reading, he cupped Jack's ass and squeezed. "Whatever happens, you know I've got your back, Dad."

Chapter Thirty-Four

That night, Jack came in through the kitchen. There were no traces left of the party. When he'd gone into work, Sean and Kyle had been helping him clean up while Darlene kept an eye on things in the yard. The bruise on Jack's cheek had earned him some comments at work, and Russ had thrown a rib-eye sirloin at him to the amusement of the kitchen.

In spite of the rib-eye, it throbbed. The murmur from the TV clicked off, and Tony came out in bare feet, sweats and a rag that passed for a T-shirt. He looked at Jack's face under the track lights and winced.

Jack knew better than to mix antacids and ibuprofen, but he downed a couple anyway, hoping it would cut back on the bruising. Mostly he didn't want Brandon to see the damage and feel guilty. Jack had it coming.

Tony wrapped a bag of frozen snap peas in a kitchen towel and handed it over. "Was it really an accident?"

"Yeah. I was holding him and he was trying to get away."

"This parenting stuff is pretty dangerous, huh?"

"It's not for sissies," Jack said dryly.

"I can see where Brandon gets his wit from. And the whole bottling shit up until he detonates."

Jack held up a hand in surrender while keeping the ice on his cheek. "Detonation free. I'm too tired to fight."

"Is that what it feels like? I want to fight?" Tony moved behind him and pulled Jack in tight.

"I don't want you to feel trapped. I did that to myself for ten years."

"I'm not trapped. I want to be here."

Jack let some of his weight rest on Tony. "I want you here. I wish I knew a better way to make things work."

"We'll figure it out." Tony's palms stroked down his chest.

"Are you sure you want to?"

"Hell yeah." Tony turned Jack to face him. "Where's that coming from?"

"I don't want to make you..."

"Your wife? Yeah, well I was kind of pissed too. How about we call me your devoted sex-slave houseboy?"

"*Pas devant les enfants.*" Jack summoned the proper horrified inflection.

"That doesn't sound like swearing, sex or food."

"It means *not in front of the children.*"

"Yeah, we should skip the sex-slave part there. But speaking of that, exactly how tired are you?"

Jack had been looking forward to crawling into bed, but the smell and feel of Tony in his arms was offering a nice incentive for consciousness. "Depends on whether I can sleep in tomorrow."

"Sounds doable. No parties, no appointments."

"Then I think I can make good on my promise to make it up to you."

Jack tossed the peas back into the freezer and flipped off the lights. On his way to the stairs he found Tony staring at the couch.

"What's wrong?"

"I was just thinking. We'll never have sex on this couch again."

Jack had been thinking about replacing it anyway, and they'd never managed to work out a position they could hold for long so why was Tony looking like he'd lost his best friend?

"I suppose we could put something like it in our room."

Tony looked up and grinned. "All this time and you don't know when I'm yanking your chain?"

Jack slapped Tony's ass softly. "Asshole."

They stripped and moved around each other in a smooth bathroom routine. Tony stopped brushing his teeth for a second and stared.

"What's that?" His finger traced a spot on Jack's hip, just above his ass.

"My ass. Feel free to kiss it."

Tony dropped a kiss on the spot. Jack hadn't really looked at it for ages, since it took a lot of neck twisting and an extra mirror, but he knew what Tony was talking about. A thin white scar. There was another one on his shoulder.

Tony met Jack's eyes in the mirror, thumb rubbing the spot. After rinsing his mouth he said, "It's from your dad, isn't it?"

"I've always had it. What's the difference now?"

"I didn't look before."

Jack felt Tony's gaze like heat on his back.

"This one too." Tony found the spot on Jack's shoulder.

"Yes."

Tony put a deliberate line of kisses on that skin, mouth cool and tingling.

"Do you want to see the chicken-pox scar on my jaw? I've got one on my temple from falling when I was three, and my hands are covered with knife scars."

"Shut up." Tony backed him into their bedroom, pushing Jack right to the edge of the bed. He held Jack's head in his hands and kissed him, hard. "I love you."

Jack let Tony's weight carry them both onto the mattress. Tony kissed him again, kissed him until Jack felt like he'd drown in it, in Tony's intensity. His love.

Jack flipped them over, pinning Tony's hands next to his head on the mattress, and licked across his chest and neck. Tony's dick slid along the crease of Jack's ass, and Tony moaned under him.

A kiss and a rub and they were good to go, bodies working better without the interference of words. Jack slid down until he could get his mouth on Tony's cock and tell him the best way Jack knew that he was sorry for what he'd said, sorry for dragging Tony into his mess of a life.

Wrapping his arms around Tony's hips, Jack relaxed his throat and took the thick length as deep as he could and urged Tony up to make Jack take the rest. Tony made a fist-stifled moan as his hips jerked, cutting off Jack's air with every thrust.

When he felt dizzy, Jack lifted his head, panting.

"Christ, look at your mouth. Sorry, sweetheart." Tony pulled Jack up until they were face-to-face and brushed Jack's lips with a gentle thumb. "Now you really look like you were in a fight."

"Sure felt like it."

"C'mere and let me kiss you all better." Tony flashed his grin.

"Uhn-uh." Jack straddled Tony's hips. Wetting two fingers in his own mouth, Jack coated his hole with spit and reached behind him for Tony's cock.

Tony's hands tightened on his ass, eyes gone dark blue.

Jack pressed up for a better angle, and Tony sucked in a sharp breath.

"What are you doing?" Tony's fingers dug in, keeping Jack still.

Jack's own breath was a little tricky as he tried to line them up. Tony wasn't inside yet, but the pressure was still raw and aching. Exactly what he needed. "Last time I checked this was called fucking." Jack shut his eyes and gritted his teeth.

"Was there a recall on our lube?"

Jack managed to move in Tony's hold enough to feel the full stretch of that soft silky head against his hole. He looked down and forced a smile. "Thought we'd switch things up."

With one knee and one foot on the mattress as he crouched over Tony, Jack was already off balance. Tony hooked the ankle bearing most of Jack's weight and easily rolled him onto his back.

"Bullshit." Tony kept him pinned down, but Jack didn't want to wrestle.

"What is?"

"I'm not fucking you without lube when we've got a drawerful three inches away."

"It's my ass."

"It's my dick." Tony brushed a hand across Jack's throbbing cheek, his swollen lips, and down his chest before reaching around to find the scar on Jack's hip and stroking it with a thumb. "I'm not going to hurt you because for some fucked-up reason you think you deserve it."

"What the fuck does that mean?"

"It means I know you, Jack. Hell, for the first time, maybe I even get you."

There was nowhere to go. Nothing to hide behind. Jack

couldn't look away from that steady gaze.

"You don't deserve it. And it won't fix anything." Tony rubbed his body on Jack's, a slow easy grind of chest and hips and thighs.

Their dicks came back to life against each other, soft-slick first, then velvet-hard as the friction increased.

"I want you in me," Jack breathed against Tony's mouth.

"I want to be there." Tony kissed him and then arched up, looking down at Jack's face and smiling.

Jack wrapped his hand around Tony's neck as they moved together. Tony kept smiling. Tony saw all those failures and the ugliness inside Jack and wanted him anyway. If there was ever going to be a time to tell Tony about the ulcer, about the fear that it wasn't something that could be fixed with a prescription-strength version of what he'd been downing, it was now.

But what if that was the last straw for Tony? What if one more failing was too much and Jack lost him?

He brought his legs high so Tony's cock slid along the crack of his ass, a sweet drag on the sensitive skin, good pressure that had him moaning as Tony's mouth came down on his.

"In me, c'mon."

"Feel good right here."

Jack lifted his hips higher and the thick head slipped into the right space.

Tony laughed. "Easy. Okay. I get the message."

But after Tony had made them both slick and ready, he still made Jack wait, curled up behind him while they lay on their sides, cock nudging under Jack's balls, gliding on the thin skin, tugging pressure on his hole.

Jack squeezed Tony's arm just under the tattoo on his biceps. "Thought you weren't punishing me."

"Just tryin' to make it last. Feels so good bare I get a little crazy."

"Want it like that."

Tony's thumb rubbed over Jack's nipple until his head fell back on Tony's shoulder. Everything was so primed Jack was sure he'd go off like a rocket if a breeze hit his dick. Tony's hand moved down over Jack's stomach, fingers playing in the hair right in the center, following the trail. One tug on Jack's cock, almost a warning the way the fingers closed tight under the head, and then Tony pushed inside.

It was just the head, the first tearing stretch that Jack loved, a burn no matter how slick, how ready. Tony let Jack ride it out, until Jack told him with a squeeze of Tony's wrist to go deeper.

Each short thrust of Tony's hips set off a burst of pleasure behind Jack's cock, flooding over his skin until he felt like he'd turned to liquid. Tony breathed a gasp into Jack's neck as he worked deeper, shifting and finding room inside Jack's body.

Jack wanted all of him, wanted the hot flood to pull Tony inside him, to absorb all of the fun and love and faith that was Tony until it burned away those times Jack had failed him, failed himself.

Tony was looking down at him as he moved them, and Jack had to shut his eyes.

"Feels so good in you. C'mon, Jack. Look at me."

Jack opened his eyes.

Tony licked Jack's neck, put a whisper of a kiss on the bruise on his cheek. "Yeah, sweetheart. Don't close 'em. Want all of you." Tony reached between them and lifted Jack's thigh up, driving into him with long hard strokes that made them both gasp.

There wasn't anything Jack wouldn't have given him, but

when he tried to tell him that, all he could do was groan. Tony was going faster now, quick jabs that lined up to make Jack's cock and ass pound with a constant throb of pleasure. The trigger inside coiled, tightened, as his balls drew up close, hard and ready.

Tony put his hand over Jack's and brought it to his dick, the metal of their rings clicking against each other as they stroked his cock. So good, so perfect it was hard to breathe, too good to want to let go, too good to stay on that edge. Tony's hips worked faster, balls slapping Jack's ass. No matter how much they kept their moans behind their lips, the sound of their skin filled the room. The smell of them together left a sharp tang on Jack's tongue.

The metal bands slid over the head of his dick, and the switch flipped inside. Spasm after spasm of orgasm sent him pumping over his thigh and belly. It rolled through him until he thought he'd die from it, and right then it seemed like the best idea he'd ever had.

The moan Tony kept behind his lips vibrated against Jack's back, and their hands pulled one last jet from Jack's cock. Tony eased out and planted sloppy kisses over his neck and face, while his hand stroked through the come on Jack's stomach, made a soothing press just above his dick as the shocks eased into bone-deep relaxation.

"I keep thinking it can't get hotter, then it does." Tony put an open-mouth kiss on Jack's shoulder.

"Everything improves with practice."

Tony's teeth sank in a fraction before he lifted his head. "I need improving?"

"I know what you need." Jack rolled onto his stomach and looked at Tony over his shoulder.

"Yeah?" Tony stroked more lube over his cock. "Think you've got it all figured out?"

"Yup." Jack tilted his ass up off the bed.

Tony loved to fuck like a jackhammer just before he came.

"We'll see." Tony straddled him.

The first thrust burned again, more of an ache with his body already spent, but the moan Tony couldn't completely swallow made Jack glad he could give him this, and as Tony started moving, it felt good.

Tony arched up, hands flat against the mattress, and Jack covered them with his own, tangling their fingers together as Tony's hips worked faster, slamming him hard and deep.

It still took him by surprise when Tony jerked and spurted inside. He'd gotten so used to judging by the snap of Tony's hips, the shift in his moans, the way his fingers clenched so hard their knuckles went white. Jack couldn't feel it after the first shot, but he loved the way Tony collapsed on him, stayed in him, rather than dealing with the condom. And tonight, he loved the way they fell asleep, just like that.

Chapter Thirty-Five

Now Tony knew why soccer moms drove such big-ass cars: they spent most of their day in them. He'd have been claustrophobic if he had to haul the kids all over in his Rabbit. Especially now that he drove Sarah almost to Cleveland twice a week for her dance lesson from a lady whose accent made Tony think she was going to warn him of a dark presence in the woods outside the village.

The Peanut liked her, though, and Jack's X3 had a kick-ass sound system. It was easier for Sarah to sing than to talk, and Tony had her working through Aerosmith—figuring Jack would lose his shit if the Peanut burst into some AC/DC lyrics while helping load the dishwasher.

It turned out that Haley and Samantha Baker-Sawicki, the teenage girls who'd come to the party, only lived a mile away in one of the neighboring developments, and they had kids hanging out at their house all the time. Brandon had become a regular. With a good memory about what he'd been up to at fourteen, Tony still checked out any invitation with one of the girls' moms every time Brandon went over, and insisted on dropping him off. Over the two weeks since the party, Brandon hadn't exactly turned into a charmer at home, but he showed up for meals and spoke in complete sentences most of the time. Which, given his age, Tony thought was pretty reasonable.

Tony swung into the Baker-Sawicki driveway, popping the

CD out before Steven Tyler could start wailing about his "Big Ten Inch". A splash rose over the fence from the backyard pool. He didn't know if Brandon liked swimming or if the accident had put him off it. He was always dry when Tony picked him up. As a topic of conversation, the accident fell squarely into the Demilitarized Zone of the Noble-Gemetti household.

Paula Sawicki came out through the back fence and waved as Brandon hopped out of the car.

"Should be about three hours. Is that okay?" Tony stuck his head out of the window.

"It's no trouble. Someone can always run him home," Paula said.

"I can run there myself," Brandon huffed.

He was right by the driver's window, so Tony leaned out. "Yeah, but there aren't any blonde chicks at our house."

Brandon shot him a glare, but Tony thought the kid was almost smiling. Jack didn't mind Brandon staying in the house alone, but both of them were glad when he didn't have to spend the three hours either stuck at the house or stuck in the car.

Brandon and Paula disappeared through the fence, and Tony looked at Sarah in the rearview mirror. "So, Peanut, what's the plan?"

She did a few of her relaxation breaths and then sang, "Dude looks like a lady."

Maybe he should have started with Journey.

Chapter Thirty-Six

Brandon didn't think Jenny had anything to worry about from Hayley since she didn't seem to like him that way. But Hayley was nice and funny, and she and her sister had lots of friends at their house. Maybe because of the pool, but Brandon bet it was the same thing in the winter.

A deep boom of thunder had Hayley and Sam's mom calling them all out of the pool at four. Brandon got bored when everyone started talking about people they knew at school, so when the girls' other mom came in, Brandon accepted the offer of a ride back to Dad's house. Tony and Sarah would be back soon anyway. The rain still hadn't started when Ms. Baker dropped him off, and Brandon wished he'd just run home.

It was kind of cool to have the house to himself. Being at the Academy didn't give you much privacy. He flopped on the couch and clicked on the TV. Someone—Dad probably—had locked the pay-per-view since the last time Brandon had the TV to himself. Whatever. It wasn't like he couldn't find a movie online.

Without any housemates or a sister to tell him to stop, he flicked through the channels again and again. The weirdest thing about living with Dad was not having everything scheduled all the time. He missed the guys at camp this summer, but it was kind of nice to just chill. As long as he went to bed around midnight and put his clothes in the laundry room, Dad and Tony didn't try to make him do anything. He guessed it would be different when school started, but maybe by then he could get Dad to buy him a phone. He'd have to start a conversation with him first, and although Dad hung around the house until two or three every day, Brandon didn't know what to say to him.

The doorbell rang and Brandon tossed the remote on the couch as he went out into the hall. He opened the door, and she was there.

His heart kicked hard and fast against his ribs and his ears buzzed so loud he almost couldn't hear her say, "Brandon, honey, it's Mommy."

He slammed the door. His head felt like he'd tried to swim all the way around Haley's pool on one breath. She couldn't be here. Dad had said she wasn't allowed to be here. They had something from the court so she couldn't be here.

The doorbell rang again, the deep chime right in his ear. He jumped.

"Brandon?" She pounded on the door.

He stood there frozen, but when she turned the knob his fingers found the lock and he twisted it.

"Brandon. It's Mommy. I just want to see you, honey. Please let me see you."

Brandon ran for the phone. His fingers felt cold, like they were fumbling for his seat belt—for Sarah's seat belt as the icy water climbed over them. He managed to stab the right number for Dad's work.

The phone rang and rang, and over that thin whine he heard her still knocking and calling him, pressing the doorbell until it was a constant chime to pierce his head. She wouldn't break the window, would she? The doctors let her out. She wouldn't try to hurt him anymore.

Finally someone answered and Brandon swallowed quick, asking for Jack Noble.

"Just a minute" was the answer.

Not *just a minute* Brandon wanted to scream, but he heard the phone get put down.

Dad never picked it up. Of course not. He was at work.

Brandon swallowed tears and slammed the phone back into its cradle. The pounding and the calling and that stupid chime buzzing finally stopped. He turned and she was at the living room window, waving at him. He grabbed the phone and ran into the hall, pushing the number for Tony's cell.

When Tony answered, Brandon blurted, "She's here. Tony, she's here. At the house."

"Hang on a second."

There was a click and Tony was back. "Took you off Bluetooth."

"My mother. She came to the house, and I can't get Dad at work and she kept knocking and now she's at the window."

"Fuck." Tony's breath sounded loud. "Did you lock the door?"

"Yeah."

"The garage door? The sliding glass door?"

"I just got home."

"Listen carefully. Hang up. Call 911. Tell them someone's trying to break into the house, and you do not hang up until the cops get there. Double check the other doors. Don't go outside."

It sounded good. Like Tony knew what to do, but why couldn't he or Dad just be here? How far away was he? "Tony—"

"You're going to be fine, kid. Call 911, right now. Your dad and I will be there as fast as we can."

Still crouching in the hall, Brandon tapped the emergency number. Would they tell him *just a minute* too? As soon as Brandon told the operator the nature of his emergency, she asked him his name and age and address and if there were any adults with him and told him to stay on the line. She went through the same thing Tony had, asking him about the doors. He checked the garage door first, not opening it, just making sure the deadbolt was turned. She hadn't started knocking again. The TV was still on, but that only creeped him out more.

He went to check that the safety bar was in the sliding glass door, and jumped back. She was on the deck. Waving at him. Smiling.

He must have gasped or something because the operator asked him what had happened.

"She's at the back door."

The blinds were open. They worked on some stupid switch and he couldn't figure out how to shut them, and she just kept calling him. She looked the same. She'd never stopped smiling that day either. She'd said it was good for them. For all of them.

He couldn't even shut his eyes to that smile, so he ran for the windowless hall again, put his back against the hall wall and crouched against the floor.

"The police will be there any minute, Brandon. I want you to wait until they identify themselves and I confirm it for you. Can you still see her?"

"No."

There weren't any sirens, but the flash of lights cut across the front window.

"Brandon, the police are there."

A hard knock on the door. "Police."

"It's okay, Brandon. You can let them in now."

They were two guys in uniforms, names and smiles that

came and went too fast for Brandon to catch them. Somehow Brandon didn't feel much better. He wanted Dad, or Tony. How could the cops understand why she couldn't be here?

He repeated what Tony had told him to say. "Someone tried to break into the house."

The cops looked at the undamaged door, the unbroken plate-glass windows and then back at him. "Where?"

She walked up the driveway with her smile firmly in place and greeted the police like she hadn't just been chasing him around the windows downstairs.

"Who are you, ma'am?"

She held out a hand, but neither of the cops shook it. "I'm Patrice Howard Noble. I'm so sorry you came out here for nothing. My son and I had a disagreement and he locked me out of the house." She waved a cell phone. "I was just going to call my husband."

"Is that your car, ma'am?"

A Mercedes was in the driveway. "Yes, of course."

One of the cops wrote the license number down. "Do you have ID, ma'am?"

"Certainly." She dug a license out of the small purse tucked under her arm.

The police passed it back to her, and then they turned to look at Brandon.

"It's not true. She's not allowed to be here. My dad has custody."

"Oh, Brandon, another one of your stories? Stop it now, honey. The policemen are very busy."

"Is she your mother?"

"Yes. But she's not supposed to be here. There's—"

"There's going to be a big fine for this, isn't there?" she

said, her smile never wavering.

The cops turned to Brandon. "This isn't a joke. You put people's lives in danger."

Were they just going to listen to her and leave him? Let her—

"She tried to kill me," he blurted out.

One of the cops glared at him. "You want to be arrested, kid? This isn't funny."

"He hates going to summer school. Come on, Brandon. Get in the car now, honey."

Tony's beat-up white car came flying down the street and swerved off onto the lawn in front of the house. Brandon's heart sank. They'd never believe Tony over her.

Dad jumped out of the car. Relief hit like a hot blast from a shower. Brandon would have run to meet him, but he wasn't sure his legs would work. Brandon had forgotten Tony was driving Dad's car.

Dad was here. She couldn't take him because Dad was here. He came. Brandon called and he came.

"Brandon, stay in the house," Dad ordered.

"Who are you?"

Dad handed his license over to the cops. "This is my son. This woman is my ex-wife. She's violating an order of protection from Judge Murphy of Stark County Family Court." Dad's voice was calm and cold.

"Now, Jack, I just wanted to talk to them, see them. It's not fair, is it?" She turned to the policemen. "A mother should at least be able to see her children."

"Do you have this order of protection, sir?"

"I do."

"Can we see it?"

"Certainly." One of the cops went with Dad and the other one stayed with her on the step. She tried to go into the house, but the cop put his arm out to stop her.

Dad came back into the hall with the cop and the blue-backed legal papers.

"Mrs. Noble, I'm sorry, but you're going to have to leave," the cop with Dad said. "You're not allowed contact."

"Can't they arrest her?" Brandon asked.

His dad gave a tight shake of his head. His lips were pale and he was breathing like he'd run to the house from downtown.

"Let's go, Mrs. Noble."

"Brandon—" she said.

"If you don't comply with the court order, we can arrest you."

Still with that smile, she walked to the car. The cops waited until she drove away.

The one who'd waited outside looked at Brandon and then at Dad. "He said she tried to kill him."

Brandon could feel that anger coming up from his toes. If the cops had listened to him— "She did."

The cop glanced at Dad who nodded.

The cop shook his head and walked away.

Brandon slammed the door shut. "They almost let her take me. They would have let her take me. What if Sarah was here?"

"She wasn't," Dad said softly.

Dad came. Brandon repeated that to himself, hardly able to believe it.

"Are you all right, son?" Dad's voice sounded funny.

Brandon looked over at his father. His mouth was tight, and he looked kind of sick. He was holding on to the wall.

"Dad?"

He slid down the wall and pitched forward.

"Dad?"

Chapter Thirty-Seven

Jack knew exactly where he was when he woke up. He'd woken up a couple of times in between. Once in the ambulance, spitting up blood, once in the ER, dizzy and nauseous with pain as they asked him when he'd last eaten and what he'd had. The room was empty.

Patrice. Brandon. He pushed to sit up, found the call button. Brandon was okay, wasn't he? The cops had made Patrice leave before Jack had passed out.

It seemed like an hour before a nurse came in. "How is your pain?"

It had subsided to something like a smaller piranha-toothed alien baby chewing its way out, instead of something more like the great white that had torn at him as he raced home from the restaurant.

"My son. My children."

"Children aren't allowed except in maternity."

After checking all of his vitals and making him point to a number on a pain chart, she said, "You do have someone waiting to see you. A friend. Would you like to approve a visitor?"

Family only. Hospital policy. Christ, had Kyle had to put up with this shit with Sean? Tony, downgraded to just a friend.

"Yeah, send him in. Send anyone in."

It wasn't Tony. It was Kyle.

"How are you doing?"

"Where's Tony?"

"Watching bad TV with two freaked-out kids in the lounge."

"I need to see them." Why hadn't Tony left the kids with Kyle? Tony couldn't know already about the ulcer. Not that there was any hope of him not finding out. Why hadn't Jack just told him?

"Probably not tonight, but in the morning." Kyle lowered his voice. "The nurses and I go way back. They're more reasonable in the morning. Especially if you bring donuts."

Jack pressed his fist against his chest.

Kyle winced. "Bad?"

"No. I need to talk to Tony and a doctor. Find out what's going on."

"I'll tell him. Though he did tell me that you'd better hope you died because he was going to kill you."

Jack wanted to laugh, but Kyle looked pretty serious. Tony knew. Somehow he knew.

"He's pretty pissed off?"

Kyle tilted his head. "On a scale of one-to-ten, he's at I've-never-seen-him-this-mad."

Jack winced.

"Speaking as someone who's been on his side of things, it's not easy. He's scared and angry, and throw two kids into it..." Kyle spread his hands.

"But you'll tell him I want to see him. I need to see him."

"Yeah. Sean's with him. I think the two of us can keep an eye on the kids for a few minutes."

Kyle went out and Jack waited.

Tony would be pissed, he had a right to be, but he never stayed angry for long. They'd barely argued until all this happened.

I can't take any more lying. Jack hadn't lied. Not about his negative tests, not about who he'd been with, not about anything that mattered like that. All those reasonable excuses evaporated when he looked up and saw Tony standing in the doorway, hands in his pockets like he wasn't sure he'd be invited in.

"Hey. C'mere. I'd get up, but..." Jack shrugged.

Tony came in.

"The kids okay?"

"Yeah, they're fine. Or as fine as they can be after seeing you unconscious on the floor. What happened?"

Kyle had stood next to the bed; Tony stood three feet away.

"After you called me at work I went to the house. Patrice was there. You know the cops would have let her take him? Jesus." Jack rubbed his chest again.

Tony's eyes narrowed. "I got all that from Brandon. What happened to you?"

"I felt dizzy and my chest hurt and I couldn't breathe. Felt like a heart attack."

"Well, from what little we've managed to get out of them, you didn't. They'd only answer Brandon's questions. I was afraid to push because I didn't know what would happen if Child Protective Services got involved. They might put them in foster care with you in here." Tony snapped that like Jack had planned to be in the hospital.

Instead of pissing him off more, Jack said, "Thanks. I don't know what I'd do without you."

Tony snorted. "So what happened?" he asked again.

"I'm waiting for the doctor to tell me." Jack didn't know why he tried that last line of defense, but if he could convince Tony that he hadn't been hiding it, maybe he could still get out of this with everything he wanted.

"Tell me now, Jack. Because you're not stupid and you know what it is."

Jack looked away and licked his lips. It was dry in here and they wouldn't give him anything to drink. "An ulcer."

"An ulcer? An ulcer made you pass out in the hall?"

"A bleeding ulcer."

He looked at the red-tainted bag running into one of his IVs. "I'm guessing I was down some."

"How long?"

He wanted to lie. Lie to Tony, lie to the doctor, protect everything that had started to work. He surrendered and told Tony everything.

"It started last month or so."

Tony looked away.

"I've had one before—the last year I was married to Patrice. They just check it out, put you on antibiotics and medication."

"And why weren't you on antibiotics and medication now?"

"I didn't get to the doctor."

Tony threw his hands up in the air and walked away to smack the wall.

"The last time, the doctor said if it came back, I might need surgery. How could I have surgery and get custody straightened out? I was waiting until things were settled."

"The papers were signed almost a month ago. How much longer before it's settled, Jack? When your stomach liquefies? Would that be settled?"

"It was better."

"Oh, better. Better for me to come home with Sarah and have Brandon come running out in front of the car so I almost fucking hit him. Better so I could see you looking like a fucking dead man in our house. I thought you were dead, Jack." Tony's voice broke and he walked away, past the empty bed to the dark window and stared out of it. "And Sarah. Jesus."

"Did she—?"

"No, but she broke my heart anyway. Both of them, all three of us calling you. Shaking you and you didn't move."

"Mr. Noble? I'm Dr. Ryerson." The doctor looked about as exhausted as Jack felt. He tapped on a portable computer screen. "Let's see—oh." He looked at Tony.

"It's okay. You can say anything in front of him. In fact, make sure you tell him everything. He's my partner."

"I see." The doctor slipped glasses up on his nose. "Very well, when you were admitted this evening, we ran a series of tests on your blood. Everything appears to be fine though you showed blood loss and an elevated white count and a fever. We've given you two units of blood and started you on an antibiotic. I understand there was some dark emesis in the ambulance."

Jack looked at the doctor for clarification.

"Did you vomit? Perhaps something looking like coffee grounds?"

"Yes."

"I see. Is this the first time that has happened?"

Jack shot a glance at Tony. "No."

Tony turned back to the window.

"Well, the symptoms are very consistent with a gastric ulcer with significant damage to the lining of the stomach. One of our gastro-intestinal specialists will do an endoscopy on you tomorrow to confirm it. Nothing by mouth until after the test."

Jack nodded. He remembered that. It wasn't much of a procedure. It had just left him a little loopy from the drugs.

"Unless you have your own GI?"

"No."

"In the meantime, the IV will keep you hydrated and the nurse can administer pain medication as needed." Dr. Ryerson pocketed his glasses and tapped the screen again. "You're scheduled for endoscopy at six a.m."

"Thank you, Doctor."

"Ah. Would you like me to put your partner's name in the records as a contact? Do you have some sort of health-care proxy?"

Jack remembered Kyle saying something about that when Sean was in the hospital. "No."

"It would be a good idea for the future." Dr. Ryerson left.

Tony came away from the window and stood next to the bed. Jack couldn't meet his eyes.

"So now what?" Jack said.

"Now I take your kids home. I'll explain what's going on as best I can. I'll sit in Sarah's room in case she has a nightmare. I'll feed them. If I can, I'll drop by for whatever piece of information about your fucking life you care to share with me, like whether or not I might find you passed out again somewhere."

"Tony. C'mon. You heard what I said to the doctor."

"Right. You can tell my partner everything, now that he's already found out that it's impossible for me to tell the fucking truth about anything."

They must have overdone it on restocking Jack's blood, because his head was pounding with it, his pulse loud in his ears and throat. "I didn't lie to you."

"You did. I asked you. I gave you every chance to say something. I trusted you. With everything."

"This doesn't have anything to do with you or being safe. I didn't lie about those other tests. You can't catch an ulcer, Tony."

Tony took a deep breath. "Sure feels like it." He twisted the ring off his finger and held it out.

"You want me to put this with your stuff in the closet or put it in your safe in your house?"

"I want you to put it back on."

Tony opened up the closet and dropped the ring inside.

"It might not have been something like your big fake vows in a church, but it meant something to me. Doing it raw, it meant something to me."

Yanking out the IVs to crawl after him probably wouldn't help Jack's cause. "Of course it did. I love you. I don't want to do this without you."

"You're going to have to." Tony started to walk out.

"So that's it. You're going to be the dad who leaves, right?"

At some point they'd shut down the bright lights in the hall. In the shadow, Tony's eyes were black and empty. "I'm not leaving the kids, Jack. As long as they want anything from me, they've got it. I'm just leaving you." Tony stopped at the door. "Oh. Tomorrow's Sunday, did you know that? Happy Father's Day, Jack."

Chapter Thirty-Eight

Jack had to be the only person glad to get a roommate who moaned and coughed like he was hacking up a lung. It saved him from hearing Tony's voice all night listing all the ways Jack had fucked up the best thing that ever happened to him.

Being awake saved him from other problems too. Like having to wake up to piss, or to have the nurse check on his vitals, or from forgetting that he needed to go home and beg Tony to listen to him, remind him how much they'd been through this month, find a way to prove that Tony could trust him.

But Jack had already thrown away any chance of that. When he came back from pissing out the gallons of fluid they were pouring into his veins, he stopped and opened the closet. His tubes got caught on the clothes as he dug around in the bottom, his skin tore around the needle, making him lose some of the blood they'd put back in, but he got his hand on Tony's ring.

The nurse found him out of bed and bleeding and retaped his hand and wrist, scolding him with a warning to ask for help if he couldn't get out of bed without pulling on the IV.

"I came in an ambulance. Do you know what happened to my wallet and watch?"

"They're probably in a locker or at the station. You don't

need anything right now."

"Can you make sure this gets in with them? I'm afraid of losing it." He handed her Tony's ring.

"Now that's funny. I don't know why they didn't put this with the other stuff when you were admitted." She closed her hand around it.

The man in the other bed moaned.

"I'll be with you in a minute, Mr. Petersen."

"Is Dad going to be all right?" Brandon dipped one of his French fries in ketchup and put it back on the paper plate.

Tony looked up from where he was drawing a design with the ketchup and mustard on his wrapper. "Yeah, he'll be fine." After a midnight trip to McDonald's, they were eating at the kitchen counter. Brandon had managed a few bites of his cheeseburger, but Sarah had barely nibbled at one of her chicken tenders.

Tony forced a smile for the kids. "They're going to do another test tomorrow to make sure they're giving him the right medicine. As soon as his stomach's better, like so he can eat without throwing up, they're going to send him home."

"Like the flu?" It was the first thing Sarah had said in four hours, and Tony couldn't help hugging her.

"It's a little like that, Peanut. His stomach's sore from throwing up a lot."

"And we can stay here with you?" Brandon asked.

"Yeah. I guess. I'd be like a babysitter."

Brandon picked up his burger and then put it down without biting it. "Was it the thing this afternoon?" He glanced at his sister and then back at Tony. "You know?"

The stress had probably tipped the scales, but Brandon

didn't need to know that. "No. It could have happened even if he'd just been at work."

Brandon didn't look like he believed Tony.

"Your dad had this before, so he knows he's going to be fine."

"Why didn't he go to the doctor?"

Jack, you are so screwed. This kid is way too smart for you. But Tony wouldn't be around to see it. The thought made his own stomach try to toss back the two bites of food he'd managed to swallow.

"Well your dad got busy, and he wanted to make sure you guys were safe, right? So he put it off, but he didn't get better. Which is why if something's wrong, you need to tell someone. It doesn't get better on its own."

Sarah nodded emphatically.

"You, Peanut, need to eat something. Five French fries or one tender."

She held up four fries.

"It's a deal."

Jack was back in his room by six thirty the next morning. He finally managed to doze when Mr. Petersen and his phlegm machine left for his round of testing. The doctor came in around eleven, listing the results. Nothing unexpected from the endoscopy, discharge from the hospital when he could tolerate solid food, prescriptions for when he left.

"What's your stress level, Jack?"

Astronomical. And it just got worse. "Pretty high. I've just taken sole custody of my children and—it's been challenging."

"I'm going to add in a prescription for Xanax too. But if the stress remains the same, you should think about taking some classes on stress management or consider seeing a therapist."

Jack tried not to think about anything but getting discharged with the doctor's blessing so that he could start fixing the mess he'd made with Tony. Despite the foulness of the broth and gelatinous mass on his lunch tray, Jack obediently downed every bit of the food, hoping they'd move him to solids by dinner. He'd called the house and Tony's cell a bunch of times but got no answer.

Around two, Sean came in with the kids. Jack wasn't sure if the relaxation in policy was due to the fact that he wasn't spreading Ebola or because Sean still enjoyed a lot of leeway in town as the hero of the McKinley High shooting.

"Where's Tony?" he asked around Sarah's careful hug.

Sean's lip twisted. "He said to tell you he's doing the laundry."

"We went shopping," Sarah said. "Tony likes to shop."

"Yes, he does," Jack agreed. Tony had never had much, and Jack loved to spoil him. Now Tony was doing that for the kids, though Jack was sure that at least his children hadn't lacked financial resources.

"I got a new purse and a dress, and Tony said to ask you if I can get my ears pierced."

"Mine too," Brandon added.

"He did not," Sarah snapped over her shoulder.

Jack wondered if Brandon regretted Sarah regaining her power of speech. The slight hesitation, the forced emphasis as she grasped for some words, it was only apparent if the listener knew to look for it.

As Jack offered approval for Sarah's new purse, he wondered how Tony had managed to pay for shopping. Jack's wallet was in hospital custody, stores didn't take checks without ID, and Tony hadn't worked in a month.

"I made this for you." Sarah reached into her new purse. He opened the envelope and the generic commercial Happy Father's Day card made his eyes sting. A condition made worse by the folded drawing accompanying it. Sarah still didn't draw people, but she had started drawing trees and flowers, and she was surprisingly good at that. He recognized the backyard instantly.

"It's beautiful, honey." The word slipped out with ease now. He even called her Peanut sometimes, eliciting giggles and a that's-only-for-Tony rebuke.

"The other one's from me." Brandon had taken Tony's post by the window.

The other paper was a computer-printed picture of the backyard. The herb garden. With a fresh row of seedlings in dark rich soil.

"I asked Tony to take me to get the stuff," Brandon said, mostly to the window.

"And I helped plant them." Sarah leaned down close to his ear. "Tony stayed with me last night just in case, but I want you to come home soon."

"I will."

She hopped off the bed.

Sean did something Jack couldn't figure, some mystical teacher thing, because the kids looked up at him before he spoke. "Okay, guys. I've got to take you home and your dad needs to sleep. He looks like sh—he's tired."

Brandon rolled his eyes, but he stopped by the bed to whisper, "It's not because of yesterday, right?"

"Right. And I'm going to make sure it can't happen again."

"Thanks, Dad."

Jack swallowed. "You're welcome."

"Wait in the lounge for a couple of seconds, okay, guys?" Sean said.

Jack waited for whatever Tony's best friend was going to unload on him. It wouldn't be anything less than he deserved.

"What happened? You kick him out again? Now?" Sean's arms were folded across his chest.

"No. He says he's leaving."

"What did you do?"

The fact that Sean was right didn't make the accusation easier to take, but it was time to start admitting it to everyone.

"I screwed up."

"No shit. What are you going to do about it?"

It was a hell of a question, one Jack had been trying to answer since Tony walked out last night. But at least Sean sounded as if he thought there was some hope for them.

"You know, you asked him for a hell of a lot with this." Sean jerked his thumb toward the door the kids had left through.

"Don't you think I know that?"

"And for what?"

Two months ago Jack could have answered that. A computer, a car, a nice house, anything Tony wanted.

He remembered asking Tony what he wanted out of this. *I've never wanted anything out of this but you, you stupid bastard.*

He looked up at Sean. "For everything."

Chapter Thirty-Nine

"He's in the hospital and you're not going to go see him?" The magic of a teacher's summer off put Sean in their—Jack's kitchen at an ungodly early hour.

Tony moved around him as he cleaned up from breakfast. "I can't."

"And when he comes home?"

"Is that today?" Tony's skin prickled. He hadn't packed. Hadn't shown the kids some of the places he'd meant to. He wasn't ready.

"It could be."

"I guess I'll see him then." Tony slammed the dishwasher shut.

"But you're still leaving." Sean leaned against the counter. "Going where?"

"I can't stay here, Sean. He'll just—I can't say no to him. And I can't trust him." Jack would come home. He'd make promises, and it was so easy to want to believe everything he said. Until Tony thought about waking up and finding out that everything he thought he knew was a lie. Again.

"Trust him? With what? When does he have time to f—mess around?" Sean was being determinedly stupid. Like that was a surprise.

"It's not about that. Just because Brandt was all about talking your dick out of your pants—"

"So what, then?" Sean asked, like cheating was the only way to fuck up when Sean damned well knew better.

"I can't explain it." Because even in Tony's head it sounded stupid. But until that kid took his mental-health issues and a gun to school last fall, Sean hadn't seen any of the serious shit life could dish out. Didn't know the way you could wake up and find that the guy you'd gotten used to having around wasn't there anymore.

"You know what's in the living room?" Sean's tone was edging close to deserving an ass-kicking, and Tony would love to have someone to unload his frustration on.

"Besides a flat screen that makes you piss yourself with envy?"

"His kids. He trusts you with his kids, Tony. What the hell else do you expect?"

"Everything."

Brandon picked up the phone before Tony could stop him. They'd kept Jack another day, something about his blood work.

"Tony, it's Dad. Maybe they changed their mind at the hospital."

Tony took the phone from Brandon and walked out of the living room. "I told you to call Sean for a ride. I'm busy."

"They're still keeping me tonight."

"So?" Tony had made it to the kitchen where he might be able to yell at Jack without the kids hearing.

"I could have signed myself out, you know."

"So why didn't you?"

"I've got people counting on me."

This was why Tony couldn't talk to him. Jack made everything seem like a good idea. He didn't even have to do that rubbing-Tony's-neck trick. Jack could do it with his voice.

"Will you come see me?" Yeah, that voice right there.

Tony shut his eyes, as if Jack was standing there and he could block out that pleading voice. "No."

"Please. Give me one shot. One."

"Jack."

"Do you know why I love you, Tony? Because you're the kind of man I always wanted to be. The kind of man I want Brandon to grow up to be."

Tony walked out onto the deck, but all the fresh air in the world wasn't helping him breathe any easier. "You fucking bastard."

"One shot."

"One."

Tony took a deep breath before he walked into Jack's room. He wasn't changing his mind. He wasn't giving in. There was nothing left for Jack to say. *I love you* didn't cut it when Jack couldn't stop lying to cover up whatever it was he thought Tony shouldn't see.

He walked into the room to find Jack's lawyer Steve sitting in the chair, a thick folder on the table next to a half-eaten tray.

Steve stood up when Tony came in. "Hi, Tony."

"What's going on?" Tony should have known there would be some sneaky shit involved, but he couldn't figure how a lawyer could be added into it.

"Steve brought some paperwork I needed," Jack said. Like he always conducted legal business from his hospital bed.

"Now?"

"Yes. Right the hell now. Unless it's already too late."

"Jack, I am already so pissed off you do not want to play games with me."

"Okay. Steve, you're on."

Steve pulled a long form out of the legal file. "This is a health-care proxy. It basically says that in case Jack is unable to make medical—"

"I know what it is," Tony interrupted.

"I want to assign you as my proxy," Jack said.

"Pick someone else."

"Steve?"

The lawyer picked up a more substantial-looking form. "Against my better judgment and legal advice, this is a Durable Power of Attorney agreement. This means that you have the right to act as Jack's attorney and conduct business for him as if you were Jack. You can make him liable for debt or contracts, you can even request his health-care records."

"You can look at anything, Tony. Everything. It's yours. No secrets."

Tony sat down in the chair. He hadn't seen this coming.

"This is an agreement of Joint Tenancy with Rights of Survivorship. Also not recommended by Jack's attorney. What it means is that if Jack dies, you get the house."

"I don't want it."

Steve looked at Jack. "It also means that he's going to get nailed in taxes because that counts as a gift."

"Maybe we won't need it." Jack pulled a paper out from underneath the stack. "This is my letter of resignation to Russ at The Mile."

"What?" Tony stared. Jack loved that job. Tony would have sworn he loved it more than anything in the world.

"And this is a contract for a real-estate broker."

"You're leaving?" That cut pretty damned deep. What the hell was all that legal stuff for if Jack was leaving?

"Nothing's signed yet," Jack said. "I wanted to talk to you first. I know your friends are here, and your sister and nephews, but, Tony, if anything happens to me, the kids would go back to the Howards."

Tony put his swimming—hell, back-flipping with a double twist—head on the stack of papers.

"I want you to adopt my kids. And we can't do that in Ohio, right?"

"Well, it's not Florida, but it would be highly problematic, even with the termination of the mother's parental rights," Steve explained with an apologetic shrug.

"So I want us to live where we can get married," Jack said.

Tony lifted his head and stared at the man in the hospital bed, the words rattling around as he tried to make sense of them.

Jack put Tony's ring on top of the file. "You don't have to decide about us moving right away. But I want you to sign the power-of-attorney stuff while Steve's here to notarize it."

Tony looked down at the ring and the pile of papers.

"I know it doesn't look like much, but it's everything I have, Tony. If you can't trust my words, can you trust that?"

Tony picked up the ring. "Why didn't you just tell me when I asked you?" His heart was pounding so hard he felt it in his fingers where they touched the metal.

"I didn't want you to see that I was as much of a fuckup on the inside as I was on the outside."

"And which of us repeated twelfth grade?"

"That's the whole me. Everything. No lies. No secrets. Do

you still want it?"

Tony took a long look at Jack. He wasn't cajoling or patronizing or pleading. He was waiting, his eyes soft and full of the same thing that made Tony grab the ring and climb onto the bed. "Hey, Steve." Tony didn't look over his shoulder. "Can you lock the door on the way out?"

Chapter Forty

Tony had been damned sure that beach house of Kyle's was never going to be anything but a big blue piece of paper on his draft board, but they broke ground on it in February and by June, Tony and Jack had been invited for the first guest weekend at the house.

The water off Delaware was still icy, but Brandon went in for a few minutes and even Sarah, clinging tightly to Jack and Tony, braved the huge threat of open water to go in up to her waist.

At seven-thirty in the morning, the inside of the house was freezing. Tony came back from the bathroom and climbed into bed.

Jack jerked away. "Your feet are fucking ice blocks."

"No shit. Did Kyle forget to put heating vents on this side of the house? I knew he'd think of a way to keep from having company."

Jack kept jerking his legs away as Tony tried to warm his feet.

"C'mon. What happened to the man I married, the one who said I could have every bit of him?" Tony tried to snuggle close again.

"He's home in Massachusetts, working. I'm your piece of ass for the weekend, and I don't have to put up with cold feet.

Or your morning breath." Jack rolled to the edge of the bed.

"Well, there's something that would keep us warm and keep my breath out of your face. At least like this." Tony curled up against Jack's warm back, wrapping the fingers of their left hands around each other. It would take a serious act of torture to get Tony to admit it out loud, but he got a little goofy when he looked at their hands like that. When he was on top of Jack—or Jack was on top of him—and their hands with their wedding bands, their real wedding bands, tangled together just like their bodies were. Since Jack's head always turned that way now too, Tony thought maybe he wasn't the only one who got off on looking at it.

"You know what would keep me warm and your feet and your breath away from me?" Jack squeezed their fingers together. "A bl—"

A knock on the door made Tony roll away. "C'mon in." How did people with kids ever have more than one?

Sarah had a tray in her hands with some donuts on it. Brandon stood behind her.

"Uncle Sean took me to the donut place and said I should bring them up before they get stale."

"He's a peach, that Uncle Sean," Tony said. Payback would be sweet. Just wait until Tony proclaimed it Uncles' Day when Sean and Kyle tried to find some time alone.

Sarah brought the tray over, climbed onto the bed and helped herself to an éclair. Tony swore she'd grown six inches this year. Little pink butterflies sparkled on her earlobes.

"Sarah," Brandon urged.

"Oh. Happy Father's Day." She gave Jack's and Tony's cheeks each a sticky kiss.

"Thank you." Jack grabbed the one plain donut and Tony picked up one that was stuffed.

"Lemon, custard or jelly, what do you think, Brandon?"

"One way to find out," Brandon mumbled through a chocolate glazed.

"I cannot believe you taught them this." Jack sighed.

Tony held it up, ready to stab it and make it reveal the truth. "Call it."

"Jelly," Sarah said with a giggle.

"Lemon. I'm in." Jack yanked the donut away and stuck it to his open mouth.

Tony popped his finger through the center, hiding the result quickly in his own mouth as Jack sucked in the rest of the donut.

"So what was it?" Brandon asked.

"Ask Tony." Jack's voice was muffled by a mouth full of filling and dough. "Was it what you wanted?"

"Better." Tony gave Jack a wink just for him. "I think it was a bit of everything."

About the Author

K.A. Mitchell discovered the magic of writing at an early age when she learned that a carefully crayoned note of apology sent to the kitchen in a toy truck would earn her a reprieve from banishment to her room. Her career as a spin control artist was cut short when her family moved to a two-story house, and her trucks would not roll safely down the stairs. Around the same time, she decided that Chip and Ken made a much cuter couple than Ken and Barbie and was perplexed when invitations to play Barbie dropped off. An unnamed number of years later, she's happy to find other readers and writers who like to play in her world.

To learn more about K.A. Mitchell, please visit www.kamitchell.com. Send an email to K.A. Mitchell at authorKAMitchell@gmail.com.

CPSIA information can be obtained at www.ICGtesting.com
Printed in the USA
LVOW110502041111

253497LV00002B/1/P

9 781609 283131